BOOKS BY MICHAEL MEWSHAW

NONFICTION

Short Circuit   (1983)
Life for Death   (1980)

FICTION

Year of the Gun   (1984)
Land Without Shadow   (1979)
Earthly Bread   (1976)
The Toll   (1974)
Waking Slow   (1972)
Man in Motion   (1970)

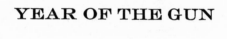

YEAR OF THE GUN

YEAR OF THE GUN

MICHAEL MEWSHAW

New York   ATHENEUM   1984

*I would like to thank the John Simon Guggenheim Foun-
dation for its support, the American Academy in Rome for
its hospitality, and Robert Katz for sharing his wealth of
information about Aldo Moro's kidnapping.*

Library of Congress Cataloging in Publication Data

Mewshaw, Michael, ———
  Year of the gun.

  I. Title.
PS3563.E87Y4   1984   813'.54   83–45511
ISBN 0–689–11433–8

For my sons,
Sean and Marc

"*Invention is the finest thing but you cannot invent anything that could not actually happen. That is what we are supposed to do when we are at our best—make it all up—but make it up so truly that later it will happen that way.*"

ERNEST HEMINGWAY *in a letter to*
F. SCOTT FITZGERALD

BOOK ONE

CHAPTER I

WHAT BROUGHT DAVID RAYBORNE TO ROME nobody ever learned. The best he offered by way of explanation was one of his whimsical, self-deprecating stories.

Before Italy, he said, he had worked somewhere in the South for a slick city magazine, one of those clones of *New York* which have cropped up in towns all across the country and which specialize in short peppy articles and long earnest shopping guides. When he refused to do another piece on "The Scandal of Public School Lunches" or "Ten Summer Tips About Attic Fans," the editor informed him he would have to let him go; he and the magazine were no longer growing in the same direction. Then his girl friend dropped him because she too said they were no longer growing together. As David laughingly told it, he felt like an obstinate shrub, uprooted because it refused to be espaliered.

Whatever his reasons, he wound up in Europe and eventually

3

arrived in Rome along with the rest of the young people who pitched up in the offices of the *American News,* eager to become international correspondents. David, however, harbored few illusions. At least he professed no great disappointment when the job proved to be little more than cutting and pasting pieces from the wire services. He put in an honest day's work—rare in that time and place—then after hours set about enjoying himself with a verve that rivaled any Roman's.

David Rayborne seemed content. That was what distinguished him from so many homesick foreigners in the city. He was cheerful and exuberant and, unlike his fellow workers at the *American News,* he stayed on. Having taken time to learn the language, he discovered he admired Italians as much as he did their country.

Afterward, as they attempted to reconstruct events and comprehend his motives, people remarked that there had always been something bizarre about the intensity of his attachment to Italy. To them it was especially illogical that he had abandoned the South, the glittering gold buckle of the Sun Belt, and had settled in Rome where crime, inflation, and violence were said to have wrecked *la dolce vita.* Since they couldn't imagine a good reason for his hanging on there, they speculated that there must have been a bad one.

David would have been amused by their bewilderment. An avid reader of books about Italy, he recognized that for most foreign writers the country served as little more than a backdrop against which philosophical and political allegories were played out in bold relief. Newcomers were depicted as pilgrims searching for beauty, knowledge, and salvation. With startling frequency they wound up disillusioned or dead. That was the moral of much of the fiction and the bottom line in most of the journalism. Yet behind the ornate brocade of this backdrop, Italian life went on, equally indifferent to the shape people tried to impose on it and to the lessons they drew from it. It was in that hidden space that David believed he lived.

Eventually, he inhabited a city that bore no resemblance to

the one tourists love. His eyes slid over the landscape in a slow
ellipsis that eliminated stock footage. St. Peter's, the Forum,
the Colosseum, the Spanish Steps exerted little claim on his
attention.

Not that he had grown oblivious to the place. He had simply
readjusted his sights. He liked seeing courtyards with cats sleeping in the sun; white marble slabs veined with green moss; the
rugged Aurelian wall tufted with delicate purple flowers;
anonymous statues, their uplifted hands gloved in grey moss,
their toeless feet shod in dead leaves.

Just as he believed he lived in a country that bore little relation to its postcard image, he objected to journalistic clichés
about the times. The calendar read 1977, and after hundreds of
riots, bombings, kidnappings, kneecappings, and killings, newspapers had taken to calling it the Year of the Gun. But David
maintained it was ridiculous to make Rome sound like Beirut or
Belfast. As he pointed out to Pierre de la Chasse, editor of the
American News, more people died every weekend of random
violence in Houston and Detroit than the Red Brigades had
killed in a decade.

"You know who invented this 'Year of the Gun' business?"

"Who cares?" said de la Chasse, blotting the moist crown of
his bald head.

"Nanni Balestrini."

"Who the hell's that?"

"A leftist poet. That's the giveaway. Any time a poet starts
prattling about guns and revolution, you can be sure you're safe.
The only real danger is to art."

Whether David believed Italy was safe or just wished it
were, he called 1977 the Year of the Fun, or, when the weather
was good, the Year of the Sun, and each day as he laid out the
paper, he inserted filler items at the bottom of the page that
tended to disprove the frightening alarms at the top. De la
Chasse told him to knock it off. But David asked what he was
supposed to do with the contradictory facts and figures that
came off the wire.

"For all I care, you can stuff them."

"Wait," David said, persisting in part because he liked to rile his boss. "Take a look at these two stories from AP. One says the economy is about to crater. Inflation over twenty percent, unemployment eight percent, the lira down thirty percent. But this other piece says Italy is still Europe's largest importer of Scotch whisky, champagne, Rolls-Royces, diamonds, and furs."

"So what are you driving at?" de la Chasse demanded. "Nobody ever claimed the news or anything else in Italy is consistent."

Abruptly, in mid-August, when all but the most benighted Romans had decamped for the beach and the sunbaked ruins were abandoned to cats and lizards, David flew to the United States. He had to resolve some personal problems, he explained to de la Chasse, who was more than willing to grant him leave without pay.

Employees at the *American News* were always flying off to the States to resolve personal problems. Most never returned. They wrote and sheepishly asked David to clear out their desks and ship home their belongings. Given the rich, vivid texture of their memories, given the melancholy longing they professed to feel for Rome, they must have imagined they had left a lot behind. But there was seldom anything except an English-Italian dictionary and an ashtray stolen from a famous restaurant or a towel from a deluxe hotel.

During his absence, Rayborne wrote no letters. In late September he showed up at the office unannounced, ready to get back to work.

At the *American News* the staff still moved with the dazed somnolence of summer. The news was slow, they said, and de la Chasse worked half a day. They clustered around David, excitedly asking about America, anxious for assurance that they were better off here.

They told him he looked terrific, looked as though his time off had been tonic. In truth, he looked unchanged. Spare and tall, with curly blond hair and a reddish beard, he had a youthful appearance which was due as much to his clothes as to his clear steady gaze and unlined face. On his salary he couldn't afford to wear anything except blue jeans and sport shirts. Although he mentioned nothing to friends at the *American News,* he had turned thirty-two while in the States.

He discussed his trip in an uncharacteristically reserved fashion—after an all-night flight he had some cause to sound laconic—and told them he had visited his family in Virginia for a few days, then had spent the balance of his vacation in New York City. He had never been tempted to remain there. He far preferred Rome.

When they invited him to lunch, he begged off, then, waiting until he was alone, leafed through the last month's issues of the paper, occasionally scribbling a comment in a thick spiral notebook.

On September 5, in Cologne, West Germany, the Red Army Fraction had abducted a wealthy Daimler-Benz executive named Hanns-Martin Schleyer. Attacking at an isolated intersection, moving with military precision and ruthlessness, the kidnappers had killed Schleyer's driver and three bodyguards. There was a photo of his car with the windows shattered. On the pavement lay four bodies slick with blood, spangled by slivers of glass. Police estimated the attack had involved twenty terrorists and half a dozen stolen automobiles. Now, three weeks later, the kidnappers were still at large, still threatening to execute Schleyer unless the government released eleven imprisoned members of the Baader-Meinhof gang, including Andreas Baader himself. David photocopied the original article and the follow-up stories.

By comparison, Italy seemed quiescent. Maybe the Red Brigades were still on vacation. But since Renato Curcio, one of the founders of the group, was in jail in Turin awaiting trial, journalists predicted a "hot autumn" of political violence.

Autumn heat had already infiltrated the newsroom, and David felt drugged by it. He poured himself a mug of coffee, dark, strong, and aromatic, then stood at an open window, staring out at the piazza which was paralyzed by dense light. Nothing moved except the gleaming shimmer of cobblestones, ingots of melting iron. There was no noise, or almost none. Rome at peace, all its people in cool shade, eating, sleeping, or making desultory love.

A shrill siren ripped a seam through the closely woven fabric of the city. Rising and falling and rising again, it wailed on and on until a fellow in an undershirt scurried out of a building and fiddled with something on the hood of his car. David smiled. A burglar alarm, the national anthem of Italy.

Back at his desk, he jotted a few more notes.

Covo—literally, a den or secret place. Refers to safe houses and apartments used by terrorists.

P trent'otto—the .38-caliber special is the weapon of choice of the Red Brigades. Those who carry it are commonly called P-38s or *P trent'ottos*.

When he heard people coming back from lunch, he quickly closed the notebook. Pierre de la Chasse was with them, smelling of cigar smoke and *pasta al pesto*, wearing a safari suit which, in his case, required as much material as a pup tent. Like everybody else, the boss asked about America. David told him it was a swell place to visit, but he intended to go on living in Italy.

"You going to get residence papers and a work permit?"

David didn't like to joke about this, not even in front of friends. When he first arrived in Rome he had tried for months to land a legal job. Finally he had had to accept an insulting arrangement with de la Chasse, who hired him on the strict understanding that he work off-the-books, without a permit, without residence papers. The advantage to de la Chasse was considerable. He didn't have to pay union wages, fringe benefits, or medical insurance and could fire David whenever he wanted. He could also keep him docile by reminding him of his vulnerability.

"Something I learned in the States," David said. "It's now very chic to be an illegal alien."

"Back there, maybe so. Not here. You get caught, they'll bounce you out on your ass."

"Still, I'd rather stay between the lines. You guys with your papers in order, the Red Brigades know all about you. You might as well kiss your kneecaps good-bye." He stood up and started for the door, carrying his spiral notebook. "I were you, I wouldn't leave the building. I read in the *New Yorker* that at night the streets of Rome are abandoned—I'm quoting now— 'except for muggers and nervous bachelors walking their new Dobermans.'"

"So where are you headed, sweetie? Out to walk your dog?"

"I'm still on vacation. Think I'll go window-shopping on Via Condotti. I've got nothing to worry about. Terrorists don't have a clue about me. Officially I don't exist."

He went to the central post office, not Via Condotti, and waited in line an hour to rent a box. Previously, he had received his mail care of the *American News*, but this fall he expected letters he didn't want anyone to see.

Afterward, he strolled out onto Piazza San Silvestro and into the jostling crowd that emerged as the shops reopened and the city drew its first cool breath of evening air. Backpackers came here to check for mail and money orders, or to use the international phones. With them were sad swarms from the Third World—shabby blacks selling cowrie bead necklaces and mahogany carvings, bedouin women with tattoos on their faces, Arabs reading newspapers with elegant blue and red lettering, dusky men who shook hands, kissed their fingers, then touched their hearts.

Cars sluiced out of Via della Mercede, making a terrific racket with their tiny tires and high-pitched horns. For David, after six weeks in the States, there was something comic about Italian traffic, something laughable in the manner of a Punch and Judy show or a maniacally cruel cartoon. He realized he would feel differently in a few days, but for now the cars were so small, so colorful, so loud as they stampeded through the piazza, they resembled schoolkids on holiday, shouldering and elbowing for room, racing to be first. They left behind a haze of exhaust fumes that stung his eyes and grated his throat. Even this didn't diminish his delight at being back. Everything he saw induced in him a deep sense of well-being.

He walked past buildings that displayed subtle variations of the city's earth tones—ocher, saffron, mustard, orange, terracotta, and burnt sienna. Above him, flocks of screeching swifts wheeled against the sky, circumflexes of black against a surface of blue. He crossed the Corso and, at every step, was more certain he was where he fit in, where he belonged.

In his reading about Italy he had underlined a passage in Eleanor Clark's *Rome and a Villa*, which remarked that the streets here constitute "a great rich withinness. . . . Even a tourist can tell in a Roman street that he is in something and not outside something as he would be in most cities. In Rome to go out is to go home."

Far past the point where he could regard Rome as temporary, as no more than a cheap, colorful pensione he could check into and out of whenever he wanted, he felt committed to the place. Toward the people he knew there, his emotions were more complicated. While the city might be his home, he wasn't convinced he could afford a family.

Yet he had one, ready-made, waiting for him, and he hurried toward it bearing gifts in a plastic bag emblazoned with a red heart which proclaimed that he loved New York. On Campo di Marzo, he stopped to buy a flower—a chrysanthemum as big as a cabbage, the kind he used to pin to girls on autumn afternoons at football games—and he thought of Stephane Von Essen, just as he had been thinking of her off and on all day. He had missed her, he was anxious to see her, he knew where she stood. Of these things he was sure. But there were others that filled him with uncertainty. It had cost him more than he could easily calculate to come this far, and ahead of him lay another long stretch, murky in its dimensions, leading toward a nameless destination. He wasn't convinced it made sense to carry someone with him.

As he turned down Via della Scrofa, he recalled an evening last winter, shortly after he met Stephane, when he had walked this way with a bottle of wine for her and a pastry for her son, Marc. The streets had been deserted then and slippery with rain, and as he entered Via Teatro Valle he smelled the varnished rattan furniture and wicker baskets sold in shops along the block. Diamond-shaped cobblestones, iridescent under the lights, rippled in front of him like a snakeskin.

Two burly men, bolting out of a doorway, had bumped David hard, knocking him to his knees. One man hauled him to his feet, leaned him against a parked car, and just when he expected them to apologize, they began pummeling him, digging their fists into his belly, walloping his head. The wine bottle exploded against the cobblestones.

Caught off guard, he didn't have a chance to cover up. He tried to drop to the ground and curl into a ball. But they dragged him up straight and kept slugging.

When, at last, they let him crumple to the wet cobblestones, they didn't rifle his pockets or swipe his wristwatch. They took turns dealing him half-hearted kicks until someone shouted, "*Basta!* Don't kill him. Just hurt him."

David recognized the voice. Before he blacked out he recognized the face too. In the doorway, watching impassively, was Stephane's estranged husband, Lucio Novelli.

He revived with rain needling his face, diluting the wine and blood that had pooled under his head. His eyes pulsed in their sockets; every breath was a stab at his chest. Staggering to Stephane's building, he sounded the buzzer until she rushed down to see what was wrong.

What was wrong was that David had a concussion, three broken ribs, and a deep gash on his forehead. For days he lay in Salvator Mundi Hospital, wondering how he would pay his bill and considering how neatly Lucio had arranged things. By not touching David, by gazing on from a distance as if at a mildly distasteful spectacle, he had made his point, exposed David's impotence, and still protected himself against legal action. It was not simply futile but dangerous to go to the police. They might demand his papers, and once they learned he didn't have a residence permit, they would deport him.

When he explained this to Stephane, she sat, head bowed, beside his hospital bed, whether deep in thought or in despair he couldn't tell. She had been separated from Lucio for three years. According to law, two more years had to pass before she filed for divorce. How long the divorce proceedings might last no one could predict. As the old joke ran, "For the average Roman how long is life?" Answer: "Three lawsuits."

Stephane said, "This country is impossible to live in. How can you be sure Lucio won't do this again?"

Since there was no way to be sure, David didn't respond.

"You should stay away from me," she said. "It's dangerous for you to be around me."

"He's not going to scare me off."

She raised her head and looked at him. "You really want to go on?"

The question, like her dark eyes, had depths he couldn't fathom. He kept to the surface, his voice buoyant, glib. "Of course. But maybe I better buy a helmet."

Although he never bought a helmet, he didn't care to be caught off guard again. Everywhere he went he watched for Lucio and his baboons. Next time there was trouble, he'd lunge straight at Lucio. The thugs would have to pry him off like a lamprey. He wanted to pay Lucio back, not just for the scar above his own eyebrow, but for the pain he had caused Stephane, for all the scars he had inflicted on her.

In her building, the elevator was a *belle époque* extravagance, with polished wood panels, filigree grillwork, and panes of glass etched with palm fronds and ferns. Against the back wall, a banquette of plush red velvet invited one to recline during the ten-second ascent to the top floor. David remained standing, debating how much to tell Stephane of what had happened in New York.

On her door, encased in clear plastic, was Lucio's last name, Novelli. Although it was a practical advantage for Stephane to continue using her husband's name, David always called her Von Essen. He told her he enjoyed the confusion. And what could be more confusing than a Frenchwoman with a German maiden name? Of course, this also eliminated Lucio.

Lena, the maid, answered the door, and if she experienced any emotion at his unexpected arrival, it didn't register on her face. An ageless Sicilian with an incipient mustache, she was an unrelenting worker and equally unrelenting in her dislike of David. In her world—he imagined it as a medieval passion play full of moral lessons—you remained with your husband regardless of how brutal he was. You remained with him until he died or until he killed you.

La signora was in the *salone*, Lena said and withdrew to the domain of her kitchen.

He heard music—a tape he had given Stephane as a joke. Something to remind her of him while he was in America, he had told her. As Willie Nelson crooned "Blue Eyes Crying in the Rain," Stephane hummed and danced with Marc in her arms. It was some kind of slow, swaying waltz wholly inappropriate to Willie's Texas twang, but perfectly in harmony with her physical grace and with the classical contours of the room— the high curved ceiling, the intricately carved cornices, the walls washed with the warm gold leaf of evening light.

As she swung around, she saw David and at first showed no more emotion than Lena had. She just stared.

He had never been able to make sense of her sharp, angular features. They demanded attention, they drew him in. Yet long after he had fallen in love with her, he couldn't decide whether she was more haunting than beautiful. With her black straight hair parted down the center and her mouth pressed shut, she could look very grave, even stern. But when she smiled, as she did now, the effect was not so much to soften her looks as to bring them into more acute focus and render David's previous notions of beauty irrelevant.

He crossed the room and hugged them both. Because of the

chrysanthemum and the plastic bag full of gifts, because Marc was squealing and squirming between them, he could do no more than peck Stephane on the cheek.

Then he noticed another person in the room. A short, stocky man strode toward them, a splash of color in a tight sport shirt. David pulled back, and the man embraced him just as he realized who it was—Italo Bianchi.

"Enough, enough!" he cried out, as Bianchi kissed him on both cheeks. "Stephane'll start to wonder about us."

"Always the same." Italo held him at arm's length and, smiling, gave him a rough shake. "Always the jokes. Always this self-doubt, this sexual insecurity."

"It's just that I haven't had any fat whiskery men nibbling at my ears for the last six weeks."

"Did you bring me something?" Marc broke free from his mother's arms. "Did you?"

"*Mais non.* That's not nice," Stephane said.

"Of course I brought you something." From the plastic bag David took a gold star and pinned it to the boy's polo shirt. "That's a real sheriff's badge. There's a cowboy hat too."

When Marc raced to the kitchen to show Lena, David said to Stephane, "I don't understand why I get two kisses from Bianchi and only one from you." He handed Italo the flower and the plastic bag.

She moved close, slender in his arms, and pressed her lips to his. When Bianchi laughed at them, she leaned back and David held her loosely around the waist. She was wearing white denim jeans and a white shirt with a red appliqué of a Marlboro cigarette pack on the breast pocket.

"You look like a billboard," he said.

"*Comment?*"

"You look wonderful. I got you something, too."

"What?" Bianchi demanded. "This dreadful flower? After all your years in Italy, don't you know what it is?"

"Sure. A chrysanthemum."

"You *cretino*, that's the flower for dead people. It's what you put on someone's grave. I'm not letting you give it to Stephane."

"Okay, okay. There's other stuff in the bag. Perfume and a sweater and—"

"I don't care about gifts," Stephane said. "Tell me about your trip. When did you get back?"

"This morning."

"And you didn't call or come by right away?" She pouted and made a show of pulling away. He wouldn't let go of her.

"I wanted to surprise you."

"Have you slept? You look tired." She touched her cool fingertips to his forehead.

"No, I had things to take care of at the office."

"How was it?"

"The office?"

"New York," she said, exasperated with his joking.

"Hot, crowded, noisy, more run down than I remembered. You know, every place in the world is becoming like Rome— only without palm trees and pasta. We're all better off here."

Marc burst back into the room, screeching an uncanny imitation of the burglar alarm David had heard earlier that day.

"Let me give him a bath and put him to bed," she said. "Then you tell me everything."

"Here, I'll do it," Italo volunteered. "You two sit and talk."

"No, I'll help." David swung the boy up into his arms. "You're getting heavy."

"I'm twenty-two kilos. I go to your kind of school now, you know."

Although there was a public school in the neighborhood, Stephane had enrolled Marc at an American kindergarten on Via Cassia for the express purpose of tormenting Lucio with the knowledge that she would not raise her son as an Italian. David didn't blame her. She had endured more than her share of torment from Lucio.

While Stephane was in the bedroom laying out Marc's pajamas, David and Italo crowded into the bathroom, filled the tub, wrestled the boy out of his clothes, and lifted him into the sudsy water. Then, lowering the lid on the john, David sat and watched Bianchi, who had an easy way with children, a knack David admired but feared he seldom succeeded in imitating. Italo impersonated a monster, a pirate, a robot, a policeman, and did a credible job with each. Marc was a demanding audience, as David knew well, and would not accept a slipshod performance.

In tan linen slacks and a sport shirt unbuttoned to the sternum, Bianchi didn't appear to be the type to bother about kids. He had the look of a dandy, a cartoon Latin lover, the Wop womanizer. Ringlets of black hair receded from his broad forehead; his nose had an imperious curve; his mouth, when he smiled, was swollen with insolence. Italo had the face of a corrupt emperor, the kind one saw stamped on ancient Roman coins.

But his decadent aristocrat's head was balanced on the broad shoulders of a peasant. Webbed with thick veins, covered in a shaggy rug of hair, his torso was apelike, his arms long, his legs short, his hands large and callused. As David had learned on clay courts throughout Rome, this stumpy, muscle-bound man was quick and tireless, and possessed the delicate touch of a surgeon. Bianchi had been nationally ranked as a junior, yet regarded tennis as a pleasant diversion from his true passion, which was mountain climbing. By profession he was a sociologist, a member of the faculty at the University of Rome, an author of articles often quoted on both sides of the Atlantic.

"Time to get clean," Italo said and, kneeling next to the tub, scrubbed Marc with a washcloth that was sewed in the shape of a mitten. After he had rinsed off the soap, he told David, "I'm going to let you dry him. I have to leave."

"A hot date?"

"Actually, I'm going to church."

"That'll be the day."

"And I'm taking that flower with me. It's bad luck to have it in the house."

"Why's a guy who believes in bad luck going to church?"

"To pray for good luck. To pray I beat you next time we play tennis. Call me when you've rested and are back on Italian time."

"Italian time? You mean late?"

"You hate us so much, why do you stay?"

"You know I love you. Every oily one of you."

Once Italo had gone, David said to Marc, "He's a nice man, isn't he?"

The boy nodded. He had his father's heavy bones and plump face, his mother's eyes and straight dark hair. David wondered whose disposition he would inherit. Did that depend on who raised him?

While David dried him with a towel which Lena had left penitentially stiff with starch, Marc asked, "Why didn't you stay at your home in America?"

"My home is here now."

"Right here?"

"No, in Trastevere. You've been to my apartment. Remember, we ate hamburgers on the roof?"

"Yes," he shouted, delighted by the memory.

"What did you do at school today?"

"Learned about fire."

"What about fire?"

"We learned how to spell it and how to draw pictures of it and how not to light a match."

David was puzzled. "How *not* to light a match?"

"Yes, because in kindergarten we're too little and fire is dangerous."

"I see."

"*Au lit,*" Stephane called. "*Vite! Vite!*"

"Bedtime." He kissed Marc good night. "Glad to see you again. You know, I missed you while I was away."

"Really?"

"Absolutely."

"Sometimes I missed you too," Marc admitted.

"I left food for you in the living room." Stephane had come

to the bathroom door. "I thought you might like something to bite."

David laughed.

"What's so amusing?" she asked.

"You are. You're something to bite."

"*Bon,*" she said. "I'll be right back. Get ready to tell me everything."

From where he sat on the sofa sipping a glass of white wine, he heard her reading Marc a story about Asterix, the Gaul. Although she had an accent, she was an experienced translator and seldom made a mistake in English, seldom misused a word. Or maybe he had grown deaf to her errors and didn't notice unless she came out with an uncommonly funny remark like "something to bite." Seeing Pierre de la Chasse for the first time, she had whispered, "But how can he be editor? He doesn't look like he has anything on the balls!"

The wine, which was very cold, had the curious effect of making David feel warm, then drowsy. After so many hectic nights in New York, he had begun to wonder whether he would ever sleep again. Now that he was back, he had no doubt. The cars, the racketing motor scooters, the shopkeepers shouting in the street as they rang down their shutters for the night, they soothed him as surely as a lullaby. He set his wine glass on the coffee table and listened to Stephane's voice grow fainter.

Then abruptly it was louder; somebody tugged at his beard. Fuddled with sleep, he thought Marc had sneaked out of bed to tease him. But it was Stephane.

"I'm sorry," she said. "I should have let you sleep. You must be exhausted."

"Just catnapping. Waiting for you." He pulled her onto his lap. "You don't weigh any more than Marc."

"I starved myself while you were gone. Now that summer's over, I almost look right in a bathing suit."

"You look terrific." At last he got a real kiss from her. Then she broke away.

"I don't know what I want more—to touch you or talk to you." She stood up. "I'd better hear your news first. Otherwise we'll never speak about your trip." Taking a chair opposite him, she poured herself some wine and topped off his glass.

Still undecided how much to tell her, David said, "What did you do while I was away? Other than go on a hunger strike, that is?"

"*La lotta continua.*"

That got a chuckle from him. *Lotta Continua* was the name of a radical leftist group and the strident newspaper it published as a mouthpiece for its revolutionary cant. Literally it meant "continuous struggle." Stephane maintained that that was the perfect description of daily life for everybody in Italy, an ongoing battle.

"Honestly," she said, "I was miserable without you."

"You had Italo to keep you company."

"*Pas du tout.* He called a couple of times, but tonight's the first he's come by."

"I still think he's crazy about you, just waiting for his chance."

"No, he likes blondes with big bosoms."

"And you, what do you like?"

"I'd like you to stop torturing me. Tell me, did you see your parents?"

"Yeah. I went home a few days. They want to know when I'm moving back. I think they're afraid I'll convert to Catholicism and become a priest. They don't have any idea what I'm doing here."

"How could they? Half the time I don't know. What happened in New York? Will you start doing articles on Italy?"

"Better than that." He leaned forward, taking his time, deliberating. He splashed more wine into her glass. "I got a contract to write a book. Something on the situation here."

"Which situation? Politics? Eurocommunism? Terrorism?"

"Depends what develops in my research. The publisher wants something different, off-beat, behind the scenes. Not the usual song and dance about Italy's charm and chaos."

Stephane pulled her legs up under her in the chair and pressed the base of the wine glass to her jeans, making circles of moisture on the white denim. "I must say you don't sound very excited or happy."

"Oh, I am. The advance'll keep me afloat for a long while. It's just I have a lot of work ahead of me. And there's another thing, another reason not to get carried away about this. I can't publish under my own name."

"Why?" She sounded indignant.

"A pseudonym'll give me the protection I need."

"I don't understand."

"What if I dig up a lot of dirt about the Christian Democrats? They might kick me out of the country. And say—I don't know —say I discover some inside dope on the Red Brigades. I'd catch it from both directions. The police would squeeze me to find out my sources, and the Red Brigades would come gunning for me. Believe me, it's better if I'm anonymous. Better for Marc and you, too. This way you won't get in trouble just for knowing me."

"You're becoming a true Italian. More secretive than a Sicilian. Lena will be proud of you."

"Jesus, don't mention the book to her! Or anybody else. Not even Bianchi. Especially not Bianchi. Can I count on you to keep this between us?"

"Of course." Frowning, she pressed the wine glass to her jeans again. This time there was no moisture to make a mark. "But I'm sad for you."

"Don't be."

"If you weren't worried about Marc and me and didn't have to stay in Rome . . ."

"I've told you, I like it here. I live here because I want to."

It was clear she didn't believe him. Moving from her chair to his, she curled into his lap and kissed him. His hands followed the frail articulation of her shoulders, her spine, her ribs. Her scent, the familiar texture of her hair—he had lain awake nights in New York remembering them. Yet when she touched him, David said, "Careful. Where's Lena?"

"In bed by now."

"Wouldn't it be safer at my place?"

"I want to stay here tonight. I want you next to me. I've been so lonely."

Still, he was reluctant. "Look, baby, let's—"

She touched him again, then took his hand and led him toward her room. She didn't bother switching on a lamp. The closed shutters let in bars of silver light that slanted across the bed and up the headboard. It occurred to David that anybody sleeping here would be striped like a convict.

Stephane unbuttoned her blouse and reached back to unfasten her brassiere. Falling to the floor, it looked insubstantial, a scrap of foam evaporating. He touched her small breasts, the hardening nipples; she pulled down her jeans and underpants together, stepped out of them, stepped close to him.

If he believed she wanted this, if he believed she wasn't doing it just because she thought he wanted to, he could have moved with more confidence. But she was tense—he felt the taut gatherings of muscle on her back—and that left him tense too, his every gesture hesitant.

Soon after they met she had admitted she didn't enjoy sex. Then she had explained why.

The spring of her twenty-first birthday, Stephane left her family's home in Alsace for a vacation in Italy, intending to return to France to finish at the university. But then she fell in love with Rome and with Lucio, and never returned. Like so many northern Europeans, she described herself as spellbound by the south, seduced by palm trees, the sun, and the meridional light. She compared herself to those Americans who gravitate to California, only her dreamy predisposition toward the place was based on literature, on Gide and Mann, not movies. Her mistake, she said, was allowing her feelings for the country to become confused with her emotions toward Lucio, so much so that she willfully ignored what was wrong with both.

Although he had sometimes hit her before they were married, she persuaded herself he would change. Instead, he got worse, and she welcomed those nights when he didn't come home, even though she suspected he spent them with other women. When he was near her, she froze, terrified at his touch, for she never knew what excuse he would use to beat her again.

It wasn't only when angry that Lucio battered her. Depending on his mood, he could be tender and loving. But in the next moment he might squeeze her breasts until she screamed, slap her face, or choke her as he came. He had bitten her and drawn blood, leaving the bruised print of his teeth on her shoulders and thighs. He had raked her back with his nails. Drunk, he had forced her over the side of the bed and buggered her. Nothing Stephane said could convince him that she didn't find pain as exciting as he did.

After Marc was born, she demanded a divorce. Although that put a stop to the worst battles—the ones that ended in bloodshed—it started a prolonged war of attrition during which Lucio, furious at not being near enough to strike out at her directly, inflicted his wounds long distance. He tortured her by telephone, he harassed her with legal injunctions, he wrangled with her about visitation rights and was cruelly late with his support payments.

When David first learned of her problems, the solution had seemed simple. Why didn't she leave Italy, escape her husband? But she explained that until the divorce was final and the question of custody resolved—and who knew when, in the future imperfect, that would be?—Lucio had a legal right to dictate where his son lived. Marc needed his father's permission and a judge's approval to obtain a passport and cross the border. Lucio swore that as long as he had the power to prevent it, he would never let the boy leave the country.

Once he realized what she had endured and what she faced for the next few years, David assured her they would do whatever she wanted, when she wanted. He never pressured her. They had time, he told her. There was no hurry.

Weeks went by before he touched her, and at first she reacted to his caresses as if she had lost layers of skin and her nerve endings were rubbed raw. Moistening his hands with lotion, he tried to soothe her, massaging her back, her flanks, her legs, then between them. Her spine arched, her breathing died, her stomach muscles quivered tight as wire. She never came, not even much later when she asked him to make love with her.

Tonight, David raised his weight above her on the strength of his arms, moving against her gently, slowly. Leaning down, he kissed her shoulder, her neck. Splayed against the pale pillowcase, her dark hair appeared to be suspended by a violent wind. When he couldn't hold back much longer, he withdrew and, still making no abrupt moves, pressed his lips to her belly, then lower. She slipped a hand behind his neck, murmuring, "No, you go ahead."

Afterward, Stephane said, "I'm so glad you're back. So glad about your book." Then she drifted into a fitful sleep.

Although he felt the full weight of this day, the long flight, and the last six weeks settling over him, David couldn't sleep. He thought of Stephane and how much she depended on him, how he had come to count on her in ways he had not acknowledged. He thought of what he had done in New York, of what he had to do in Rome. He couldn't waste time justifying his decision; there was no point reconsidering the risks. He had to concentrate on making it work.

CHAPTER II

ITALO BIANCHI SAT in a folding chair in the enormous, empty nave of S. Andrea della Valle, an isolated figure in an operatic setting. He knew this baroque church best as the scene of the first act of *Tosca*. Only recently had it become his favorite rendezvous point. Overhead arched high vaults of gleaming gold leaf; in his lap lay the chrysanthemum David had brought Stephane, a flower for the dead, a flower Italo had borrowed for a friend. It was two years to the day since he had killed Piero Galganni.

Since then, he had spent a great deal of time in churches, very little of it praying. The dim, cool cathedrals of Rome, abandoned except for tourists, were excellent spots for clandestine meetings, for exchanging coded messages, for dropping ransom notes, for contemplating the monstrous betrayal he had committed, an act that had cut him off from Piero and God and the people whose dogmatic beliefs he was supposed to share. Now he was like a monk locked in a cell, continuing to worship a divinity he had come to doubt. David, Stephane, and Marc were his last innocent contacts, and he meant to employ all his well-practiced powers of deception to preserve their ignorance. Otherwise, he feared, they would wind up like Piero Galganni.

For Bianchi it had begun harmlessly with the donation of a few thousand lire and an expression of sympathy for causes his students espoused. In the collective delirium that existed after the '68 upheaval of universities, it had been quite common for professors of a leftist persuasion to identify with the young. When students asked for advice or small favors, he saw no reason to refuse. He regarded it as his pedagogical duty to provide them with a historical analysis of revolutionary movements and to summarize the intellectual justifications for direct political action, radical self-defense, and terrorism.

Expressing admiration for his lucid assessments of Herbert Marcuse and Carlos Marighella, they invited him to play a more active role. Nothing violent, nothing overt. They needed reports on professors and university officials, so that fascists might be monitored and fellow socialists rewarded. Then they wanted him to spread disruptive rumors, both in the academic community and the country at large, by planting stories with journalists he knew. They considered this a means of combatting the government's campaign of disinformation with one that was every bit as false and sometimes as pernicious.

Before long Bianchi was delivering messages, placing telephone calls and repeating cryptic combinations of letters and numbers, codes to which he was not allowed the key. He dropped sealed envelopes near newspaper offices and anonymously alerted editors where to pick up these propaganda leaflets or ransom notes. Because he was a bachelor and had his own apartment, he was asked to let people stay with him. Although he inferred that they were fugitives, he didn't know what they were running from until he saw their mug shots in the newspapers. They were wanted for bombings, bank robberies, kneecappings, and killings.

Soon they no longer bothered asking to use his place. They

simply showed up and demanded to be let in. Even if Italo had been tempted to turn them away, he didn't dare try, no more than he dared report them to the police. There was no power in the country capable of protecting a traitor from reprisals.

Moreover, at the start, he had no inclination to betray members of the Red Brigades who sought refuge in his apartment. Theoretically, he agreed with them; reform was impossible in Italy. As one fellow, a firebomber, told him, "There is a cancer devouring this country. That leaves us no choice. When there is cancer, you don't waste time asking, 'What shall we put in its place?' You amputate. You cut away the rotten flesh."

Of course there were dangers, but that was part of the attraction. Bianchi had faced far greater risks climbing mountains. And for what? A rich man's hobby, a vain, personal satisfaction. Now he was working for a cause. He and hundreds, perhaps thousands, of above-ground, above-suspicion operatives were creating a Second Society, an Autonomous Area, the sheltered space necessary to sustain a terrorist campaign against the state. Providing safe houses, documents, information, and money, they were, in the words of underground newspapers, "witnesses to history, makers of it."

The problem was, Italo witnessed very little, felt he accomplished less, and enjoyed none of the camaraderie he had expected. He had two contacts—one with a disembodied, sexually ambiguous voice called Giovanni, the other with his friend Piero Galganni.

Like him, Piero was a university professor, an expert in economics and an above-ground operative. Also like Bianchi, he harbored a desire to play a more dramatic role in events. Given his background, he naturally believed the greatest threat to revolutionary success was financial; the greatest need was not for arming the masses, but for money. An urban terrorist required about fifteen thousand dollars a year to survive. This meant the Red Brigades had to meet an annual payroll of over eight million dollars. Petty larceny, "people's expropriations," were neither enough to destabilize the state nor to cover the movement's operating expenses. For that, Piero pointed out, they had to rob banks and squeeze the richest families in Italy.

"Like your own."

"There are richer ones."

"But we have an advantage with yours."

While Bianchi was uncertain which tone to strike, Piero sounded as if he had given the matter serious thought. "Unfortunately, very little of the money belongs to me."

"Someday it will. In a sense it already does."

There was no need to speculate how the Galganni family would react if their oldest son were abducted. They had millions of dollars in land, in apartments, in olive oil and vines, in factories in Turin and a resort in Sicily. They would spend whatever was required to ransom Piero.

Up to a point the notion was purely hypothetical, a half-formed idea. But gradually, as it assumed the dimensions of a plan, bold yet plausible, he concluded that Piero viewed it precisely as he did—or would view it that way if Italo told him what he was thinking. Why shouldn't Piero claim his patrimony a few years early, when it could accomplish something worthwhile? It was a way of playing the dramatic role he craved. While objectively he would be innocent of the details of his kidnapping, subjectively he would be a willing accomplice. Hadn't he said that the richest families should be squeezed?

In a series of phone calls to Giovanni, Bianchi described Piero's apartment, his routine, his family's fortune, and his presumed willingness to be kidnapped.

One warm autumn afternoon he heard the news on television at a tennis club on the banks of the Tiber where David and he had just won a doubles tournament. Piero had been jerked out of his Lancia at a traffic light and tossed into a van.

Three days later the police discovered a body in the trunk of a car on the parking lot at Fiumicino airport. Piero had a single gunshot wound at the base of his skull. The autopsy mentioned traces of chloroform and concluded that he had been dead for more than forty-eight hours. The Galgannis had already paid a ransom whose size they wouldn't reveal.

Italo was listening to this news in his apartment when Giovanni called and, without identifying himself, urged him to telephone his uncle. Too shattered and saddened to take any precautions, he hurried out to a pay phone.

"Why?" he wailed, not waiting for a code word. "Why did you kill him?"

"An accident. You said he wouldn't resist. He did. He got an overdose of chloroform. They were just trying to quiet him down."

"Goddamnit, don't lie. There was a bullet in his head."

"After he was dead they had to make it look like a Mafia operation."

"Why should I believe you?"

"We had no reason to kill him. If we had, why would I call you? Why not kill you too?"

"It doesn't matter if you do." At that moment, he had meant it. "He was my friend, my best friend. He trusted me. I trusted you."

"It was a mistake. But his death served a purpose," Giovanni said. "His family paid millions."

"I'm finished," Bianchi said. "I want out of this."

"Calm down. Don't talk like a fool. No one quits. You said you wanted to do more. Now you're doing it."

For two years he had done more—more of the same. The lone difference was that he had one less contact. Now there was only Giovanni's distorted voice to encourage him and an occasional sullen, pathological *brigatista* to keep him company.

He recognized the logic of this system of isolated underground cells and secret above-ground sympathizers. He realized why they never used real names and why he wasn't told how to reach anyone except Giovanni. The less any one person knew, the less vulnerable the entire column was. But Italo didn't feel safe. Alone, as ignorant of his own position as of the overall picture, prey to doubts about Piero's death, plagued by guilt over his part in it, he felt as he would if scaling a cliff blindfolded. He sensed cold air sucking at his spine and suffered the nightmare of climbers—the urge to lean back, release, and abandon himself to emptiness. No one quits, Giovanni had said, meaning no one leaves alive. So why not leave on your own terms, he wondered? Let go before you do more damage?

Still, he stayed. Although he no longer believed in the dogma, he found some small reassurance in the rituals. Coding, decoding, memorizing new telephone numbers and names, picking up notes, burning old notes, backtracking, zigzagging, double-checking. Like a bad priest mechanically muttering his breviary, he retained some murky hope that salvation depended upon adherence to the forms of his shattered faith.

Italo carried the chrysanthemum to a side altar, advancing over oblongs of polished marble. Placing the flower on the altar rail, he knelt, reached under a tray of devotional candles, and removed a scrap of paper twisted to resemble a taper. On it was scribbled a question: "Alison Lopez, Is she intelligent?"

Bianchi touched the paper to a lighted candle. When the message had burned down to his fingertips, he let it fall onto the metal tray, shriveling to ash. Then he lit a candle, dropped two hundred lire into the slot, and bowed his head. He couldn't bring himself to pray; that seemed a profanation. But he thought of Piero, just as he did every day, and begged his forgiveness and wished him peace.

CHAPTER III

AFTER THE CAFÉ across the street blew up, raining needles of glass and splotches of blood around her feet, Alison Lopez decided to leave Beirut. The bomb hadn't frightened her into fleeing. During her months in the Middle East she had seen a lot of things blow up—buildings, automobiles, people—and if she was afraid of anything, it was of turning away too soon. But with an obscure sense of sadness and failure that showed itself as impatience, she realized the shots she had snapped of the café were as good as she would get.

When the bomb went off, the camera had been at her eye and she had caught the explosion in isolated stop frames. One moment the crowd was sitting there eating croissants and sipping coffee in the cool morning sun. The next moment everything was airborne—metal chairs and tables lifting and twisting, severed arms and legs lifting and twisting, blades of glass scything through anything that stood up to them.

As the debris settled and the scene, for an instant, turned static and absolutely silent, Alison stared at her feet, at the jagged glass that glinted in lurid shades of red, green, and yellow. The sight set her trembling so badly she feared she'd lose her breakfast. She brought the camera back up to her eye; she could face any catastrophe that was framed. Through the lens the lethal glass, gleaming with warm body juices, looked like brightly colored confetti. She snapped a few shots to steady herself before advancing to the café and finishing the roll.

That afternoon she flew to Paris and dropped the film at the agency, feeling the same sadness, the same dull sense of predictability that showed itself as impatience. She had no desire to see what developed; she knew what she had shot and could guess what would sell. She caught the next plane to Nice where in September the Riviera was still balmy and fragrant with flowers.

The balcony of her hotel room presented a postcard view of the cobalt blue Mediterranean, but Alison didn't bother to uncap her camera. It wasn't her sort of picture.

After a few days, the Côte d'Azur wasn't her sort of place either. She soon lost her taste for French food, for sightseeing, for sitting idly in the sun. At night in bed she found it disconcerting not to hear artillery or small-arms fire, and during the day as she swam off the stony shore, it disoriented her to stare back at the overbuilt hills of Provence, not the bombed-out ruins of Beirut. She realized it had finally happened, just as so many journalists, soldiers, and mercenaries had warned her it would—she now preferred war to peace. She could cope with fear and make it work for her, letting it add a malevolent subtext to otherwise mundane shots. But boredom, this sense of aimless drift, unstrung Alison. Ordinary life was the enemy; it brought ordinary emotions for which she had little practice and no outlet.

It was a relief then when she switched on the television and discovered she was less than thirty miles from what sounded like a new front line. As the commentator panted about riots and killings in Italy, she decided to go shoot the country's disintegration.

She tried to rent a car, but when they heard where she was headed, most agencies didn't welcome her business. She had no luck until she found an outfit in Cannes that had a Fiat that needed to be dropped in Milan. Hoping to reach Italy by midday, Alison rushed over to sign the papers—then had to tarry while an officious agent in a splotchy red blazer instructed her in the intricacies of the car's theft-proof, double-lock device.

Two keys were linked by a long, jangling chain, and the plump man grunted as he bent forward to reach under the dashboard and insert one key before shoving the second into the ignition. "Remember, please," he said, "turn the left key first, then the right. Now you practice."

"I'll remember."

"Please, it's company policy. You must practice."

While Alison demonstrated her dexterity, the agent warned her, "Italians steal everything," and to dramatize his point, he repeated a story which had run on the wire services. Twenty-two German dentists, Mercedes owners all, had recently driven to Milan for a convention. Eighteen of them had returned home car-less.

"Now, let me show you the boot," the man said.

"Look, I'm pressed for time."

Clutching the registration papers, he waddled to the rear of the Fiat and waited there until she joined him. "I trust all your baggage will fit here. If you leave anything in the backseat, they'll break the windows."

She slung her suitcase into the trunk. "Good enough? Now give me the goddamn papers."

To get the feel of the small, underpowered car, she followed the coast road through Juan les Pins and Cap d'Antibes, past glinting high-rise condos, crowded cafés, and pastel villas half hidden by hedges of cypress. In Nice she drove the length of the Boulevard des Anglais, which was bustling with Germans, then swung inland, laboring uphill to the *autoroute*. At the border there was surprisingly no bottleneck. After a cursory glance at her passport, an Italian customs officer waved her through. In the westbound lane, cars were being let out just as casually as she had been let in. Considering what she had heard on the news, she had expected police to search for weapons and terrorists entering Italy, and fugitives and currency fleeing it. Financial analysts estimated that fifty billion dollars in private capital had been smuggled from the country.

When she stopped to trade her francs for lire, Alison reckoned the smugglers must have hauled their loot out in small change. There wasn't a single 50- or 100-lira piece to be had. At gas stations, snack bars, and toll booths she listened to the same line, *"Non ho spicci."* Everybody offered postage stamps or bags of candy instead of change. Yet when she went to pay with candy and stamps, nobody would accept them, and she began to do a slow burn.

It wasn't just petty annoyance about the *spicci*. She feared she was wasting her time. There seemed to be nothing happening in Italy except the usual inefficiency. Still, she pushed on to Milan, where, by all accounts, the Red Brigades were strongest and the country's collapse most advanced.

Next morning, leaving the car at the hotel, she set off on foot through a city that was staid, grey, and prosperous, more Teutonic than Italian. With its blocks of modern office buildings and expensive boutiques, Milan had neither the look nor the edgy feel of a freefire zone. No checkpoints for cars and pedestrians, no sandbagged gun emplacements, no crosshatched tape on windows, no blast-shields in front of doorways. Although an occasional carabiniere, cradling an automatic weapon, lounged on a corner, the place seemed positively soporific, smug and self-satisfied in the manner of wealthy cities everywhere.

Of course, at times Saigon and Beirut had also appeared peaceful, and Alison had learned that the greatest menace was the one you weren't aware of until it was too late, the danger that didn't manifest itself until someone died. But there had been no tourists in Viet Nam or Lebanon, nor on any other battleground she had worked. Here in Milan, however, dozens of gleaming buses disgorged groups of Japanese, Germans, and Americans who docilely followed their guides. The living parody of platoon leaders, these guides led their charges with bright plastic flags.

She attempted to avoid them, but wherever she went, the tour groups had arrived first and were fiddling with their cameras. Finally, in despair, she fell into step with them, thinking they presented as attractive a target as a terrorist might ask. If there was trouble in this town, she figured it would find them.

Tall, slender, and deeply tanned, dressed in khaki slacks and one of the wrinkled linen jackets which were in fashion that fall, Alison Lopez passed easily as a tourist. Her blond hair had been braided and pinned up in a bun as if in imitation of some prim hardworking secretary who couldn't relax even on holiday. But there was nothing prim or plain about Alison and, at a glance, nothing except her surname to suggest she had Hispanic blood.

Unlike others in the group, she never trained her eyes where the guide pointed. She scanned the area ahead and off to the sides. From time to time she glanced behind her.

With a single Nikon dangling by a web strap from her neck, she carried less elaborate equipment than many of the tourists. She didn't like to be pegged immediately as a professional photographer and she didn't want a panoply of cameras and lenses to come between her and what she was shooting. Insisting on the simplicity of her aspirations, admitting to no theories, no "philosophy of the visual," no favorites or influences, she always told interviewers her goal was to get in as close as she could and let the picture speak for itself. Let others call it art or sensationalism. She knew what she wanted.

What Alison wanted was for people to look at her photographs and not only see what she had seen, but feel what she had felt. A watery weakness in the belly that rendered you powerless to shut your eyes. Fear that left you empty as a gourd with pebbles rattling inside. The emotion she meant to generate had nothing to do with ideas. Or rather all ideas had to be measured against that emotion. If people claimed some principle was worth dying or killing for, then she viewed it as her responsibility to show them what death was like. Afterward they could do as they pleased—call for revolution or repression, sell arms or cut off medical supplies, pledge allegiance to a flag, an ideology, a god, or to themselves, just so long as she had put the stamp on the meat and left no mistake about the price. She had been called a vulture, a carrion bird. But she considered herself a witness, someone whose job was to bring back the bad news and keep the body count.

Still in step with the tourists, she strolled past la Scala and entered la Galleria, a cruciform shopping arcade—more boutiques, bookstores, bars, stalls full of silk scarves and ties. In Beirut she had grown accustomed to the smell of urine, eastern spices, disinfectant, decomposing corpses in the rubble. Here, the air was redolent of leather goods, burnt toast, wine-stained tablecloths, cappuccino at Biffi's café.

Outside on Piazza del Duomo, she lifted the Nikon, tested the light, and clicked off a shot of pigeons circling the sooty spires of the cathedral. Then she broke away on her own, heading down a side street, her long stride and the loose carriage of her shoulders revealing none of the impatience she felt. The melancholy annoyance was on her again. Why the hell was she here?

When she raised the camera next, it was a reflex. She heard a backfiring engine, swung the Nikon up to her eye, and twisted the lens into focus. Two men on a motorcycle accelerated toward her. Over the high torque of the engine, they couldn't have heard the shutter click, but they saw the camera. Bumping up over a curb, they parked on the sidewalk in front of a bank and stood there staring at her.

Having watched men react to cameras many times in many countries, she knew when to stay close and stay ready. On the sidewalk opposite them, she passed behind a wall of parked cars, only her slim shoulders and head exposed. The camera hung down at her chest, her hand on it as she paused to glance into a shop window, poised to change the setting and shutter speed by touch.

Reflected in the glass, the two men stood beside the motorcycle which radiated wavy lines of heat. One man had his back turned. The other was talking to his friend and watching Alison. They wore dark clothes. Couriers, she wondered?

Several doors down from the bank, she stepped into an antique shop and signaled to the owner that she was just looking. What she was looking at was the two men. Although she doubted they could see her, they watched the shop front for almost a minute before starting toward the bank. As the tinted glass door swung shut behind them, one man pulled from his back pocket what appeared to be a red knit cap.

Alison left the shop, moving in a crouch to keep below the roof line of the cars. Across from the bank, she hid behind a Peugeot. From this position, she couldn't miss. Standing up, she'd have an unobstructed view of the bank entrance. The instant the men came through the door, she meant to start shooting. If she'd made a mistake, if they were couriers or nervous customers withdrawing money, they'd work it out later. She didn't intend to blow a chance by being careful.

Down the block a door opened. The antique shop owner craned his neck and peered at Alison. She waved for him to duck back inside. Just then the bank door flapped wide and the two men, wearing red ski masks, charged out. They spotted the antique dealer and squeezed off a few rounds, smashing the shop window.

Elbows propped on the roof of the Peugeot, she snapped her shots in rapid succession. As the men scrambled aboard the motorcycle, they saw her and the camera and opened fire again. Slugs tore through the interior of the car, ripping ragged holes in the door panel beside her. She felt her stomach fall away; she wanted to drop to her knees and scuttle to safety. But she kept herself locked in place and shot as if answering their fire, increasing the shutter to freeze the action.

The man in front had both fists on the handlebars, twisting

for speed. The one in back hung onto a money satchel and a pistol. They were rumbling toward her when suddenly a third man, a uniformed guard, raced from the bank.

He ran straight at the motorcycle, then stopped in mid-stride. The gunman aimed at him; the guard's head snapped back and his hair stood on end as if he'd been paralyzed by an electric shock. His body still looked bold and purposeful, but his face had changed, fallen in on itself, shriveled. A chunk of his skull fluttered to the street; it might have been a cap blown off by a gust of wind. As the guard fell, the motorcycle accelerated as though it had sucked speed from his dying breath.

Alison watched it all through her lens and got it on Tri-X black and white. When the motorcycle was out of sight, she circled around from behind the car and finished the roll of film on the guard sprawled on the pavement, blood pumping from the raw pulp of his brain.

Slowly shop owners and bankers emerged along the street, still jittery, sniffing the air for danger. Someone asked Alison if she was all right. She nodded yes, though she acted unsure of herself, unsteady on her feet. She stumbled along the sidewalk, the image of a woman in shock struggling to control her emotions. When she reached the corner, she wheeled around it and ran. She wasn't going to wait here and take a chance that the cops might confiscate her film.

Half an hour later she had packed and paid her hotel bill and was at the wheel of the rented Fiat. In her haste, she forgot to turn the left-hand key first, and the mistake set off a shrill alarm. She feared the worst—that she'd spend the night in jail and lose the film. At the very least she thought she'd have to explain to the police why she was sitting in this car deafened by a burglar alarm. She yanked out the key; the noise died. No one had bothered to glance her way. By now, Italians were inured to alarms.

Reinserting the keys and turning them in the correct order, Alison drove north out of Milan. On the *autostrada* she forced the Fiat up to 110 kilometers an hour and held it there even after it started to shimmy and screech. At the border, she paid her toll, accepted a shower of candy as change, and was waved into Switzerland. From Lugano she airfreighted the film to Paris. Then she swung around and set off for Italy again, as elated as someone returning to the land of her heart's ease, a country where she had been happy and had enjoyed great good luck.

CHAPTER IV

ON HIS FLIGHT to the States, David Rayborne had read the
August 1 issue of *Newsweek*, which featured a cover story on
Italy entitled "Living with Anarchy." Focusing on what it called
the country's "vicious street crime, the wave of bloodshed," and
illustrating the text with grisly photographs of kneecapped
carabinieri and assassinated public officials, it maintained "the
incidence of shootings and firebombings has grown out of all
proportion"—and by not specifying out of all proportion to
what, it let each reader fill in his most gruesome nightmare.

David had lived in the country long enough to recognize that
the article was grossly exaggerated. He also had enough friends
at the Press Club who told him how much heat *Newsweek* had
put on its stringers and correspondents to produce this pastiche
of bloodcurdling paragraphs. If you were a journalist assigned
to Italy and cared about your career, you concentrated on political corruption and violence. For variety, you might file a

human interest piece on the Turin Shroud, or a peasant woman who loomed clothing out of dog hair, or a priest who managed a pasta factory. But mostly you stuck to meat and potatoes—the bloody meat of corpses, the warmed-over potatoes of old scandals—and you disregarded statistics that showed the rate of homicide and violent crime in America was more than five times as high.

When he arrived in New York, anxious to arrange free-lance assignments, David had no illusions that he would be asked to do articles on those aspects of Italian life that were always ignored. On the other hand, he hadn't expected that the sole topic to prompt the faintest flicker of interest would be the Red Brigades.

As if quoting a prepared statement, editors at six magazines in succession told him they'd like an inside story on urban terrorism. Could he land an interview with the Red Brigades? No, not with those busted *brigatisti* awaiting trial in Turin. To preserve his pedigree and merit media attention, a terrorist had to be rampant, bloody-clawed, fully fanged, on the loose.

David tried to explain that what they asked for was impossible. But they didn't want to hear it, they didn't care to listen to his article proposals, and they had no intention of reading samples of his work.

In the evening, after each day of dismal failure, he walked from midtown Manhattan to the Lower East Side, where he was staying with a friend. Later he told Stephane and Italo that the heat, noise, and tumult of New York had reminded him of Italy, but, in fact, the city and its dispirited population looked as if they had been lifted intact from newsreels of the Depression, the decade of dirty, pinched faces, of desperate men and women. Just as the wild spree of the twenties had brought on the hangover of the thirties, this bummer in the seventies seemed a direct result of the sixties and its overdose of speed, of unrealistic hopes. Everyone talked of hard times and nobody expected them to get better soon.

The friends he had made here after college had planned to

become actors, artists, writers, political organizers. Now they worked, if they were lucky, as taxi drivers, part-time file clerks, waiters. The fellow he was crashing with, an aspiring playwright, supported himself by typing address labels for a bill collector. Because they had no clear image of the *American News* and his life in Rome, they envied David. Children of their time, they didn't describe him as anything so corny and middle-class as a success. They said his job sounded "interesting"; they said he was "free."

It occurred to David that they were right, although in ways they didn't realize. Living in Rome, he was free from the unwieldy baggage of memories and thwarted dreams they were fated to carry from youth into early middle age. But to remain in Italy, he needed money—not much, just enough to supplement the risible salary de la Chasse paid him under the table, enough to cushion the fall if he was fired or the paper folded, enough to bribe some petty bureaucrat if he was caught without a work permit. He hoped a few free-lance articles might lead to regular assignments and, eventually, to a job with a wire service. He couldn't afford to fly back empty-handed.

If forced to return to America permanently, he knew what was waiting for him and knew he didn't have the willpower to avoid it. Every evening, he passed a row of town houses in the Village and paused in front of a tapered building of poured concrete and tinted glass which had been inserted like an ax blade between two dignified brownstones. There was no explanation for this obtrusive piece of architecture, no bronze plaque proclaiming that on this spot, in 1971, the sixties had ended. Or, since that was just David's opinion, a plaque might have cited the brutal facts. On this spot, three people had been blown to bloody shreds in an explosion that had reduced a four-story house to heaps of smoky rubble.

He had known one of the women killed in the blast. He had thought she was a graduate student at Columbia. He had thought he loved her. He had thought her name was Elizabeth Anderson.

In those days David had worked for a counterculture tabloid which, while styled along the lines of the *Village Voice*, prided itself on being more aggressively antiwar, more forcefully in favor of the Black Panthers and the Weathermen, an earlier advocate of Feminine Liberation and Gay Rights. Although it favored mass demonstrations and encouraged a politics of confrontation, it was not much more extreme in its rhetoric than staid journals such as the *New York Review of Books*, which during that time ran on its front page illustrated instructions for manufacturing Molotov cocktails.

One afternoon as Elizabeth Anderson, a part-time secretary at the paper, reached for the dictionary on an upper shelf of the bookcase, David noticed she didn't shave her underarms. A mist of blond hair as fine as cornsilk—it was this incongruous detail that first caught his attention. He asked her out, then asked her back to his apartment. She came and stayed there several nights a week. The arrangement was loose, improvised. She kept her own place up near Columbia and occasionally had to leave town for Washington—to do research at the Library of Congress, she said. She was writing a dissertation on Henry Wallace and the 1948 presidential election, which she refused to let David see until she had polished it to her satisfaction.

She insisted, however, on reading early drafts of every piece he wrote and never hesitated to make suggestions. Sometimes, without telling him, she cut words, reorganized his leads, deleted passages of exposition, and rephrased his conclusions. David didn't like this and told her so, but then backed off when she accused him of resenting editorial advice from a woman. Since their disagreements were always over style, never content, he assumed they were in essential harmony and granted her the final say about diction and syntax. He laughingly chided her, though, for working toward a degree in political science when her real talent was as a literary critic.

When the bomb factory blew, David felt the blast in his office ten blocks away and dashed over with a note pad and a cassette recorder. Soon the forensic experts showed up and started sifting the debris, working with tweezers and tiny brooms, like the archaeologists he would see years later in Italy. The town house had been headquarters for a radical cell. Three people—two women and a man—were mangled in the wreckage. Two others had fled, their clothing and hair in flames. No one had been identified. At first, even the name of the group was unknown.

Next morning, two FBI agents arrested David. In contrast to the new breed of narc and agent provocateur who dressed and acted hip, these guys looked like a pair of linebackers from the early days of pro football, dense men who had played the game without helmets. Thickset, ham-handed, burr-headed, wearing brown brogans and baggy suits, they went at him with an earnestness that he found humorous and, at the same time, flattering. He thought he'd get a good story out of this, enough for an article, enough to amuse Elizabeth and his friends at the paper.

"What do you know about Darlene Spaulding?" one agent demanded.

"Nothing."

"She's your girl, isn't she?"

"Never heard of her."

"Darlene Spaulding." The other agent spat it out. "A great name for a hairdresser or a whore."

"You'd know more about that than I would."

Over and over, they badgered him with the names of groups and people and peace committees and communes, all of which they insisted he was associated with. They accused him of treason, insurrection, sedition, and conspiracy. They recited a long list of federal laws he had violated and described in Technicolor what he could expect in prison.

"Ever been fucked up the ass? Yeah, I suppose with the people you hang around, you probably have. Tender, young white meat. They'll love you in the slammer."

When it stopped being funny, he refused to talk again until he had telephoned the paper and asked them to hire a lawyer. The fellow they sent over was no older than David—mid-twenties, recent law school graduate, left-wing, cool, transparently pleased with himself. He explained that Darlene Spaulding had died in the bomb factory.

"Where do I fit in?" David asked.

"You knew her."

"Never."

"Yeah, you did. You knew her as Elizabeth Anderson."

"That's bullshit. She's in Washington. I would have known if—"

"She had a perfect set of IDs as Elizabeth Anderson. But dental records don't lie."

"I don't believe this."

"You better. They've had her under surveillance. They know she shacked up with you. They know she was sending messages to other underground cells through your articles."

For an instant, he took heart, convinced there had been a mistake. "That's ridiculous."

"Let's not dick around," the lawyer said. "Maybe you didn't know what she was doing. We'll float that as a defense. But there's no fucking doubt about it. It's in every article—simple codes, anagrams, acrostics. People at the newspaper said she was always fiddling with your stuff."

David couldn't speak.

"Did she revise your articles or didn't she?"

He nodded.

"Okay, you'd better be sure of your story and stick to it. We'll claim she did it without your knowledge or consent. The feds have her involved in some bombings where people got wasted. Now that she's dead, they'd love to dump those charges on you. Tell them everything you know. Don't worry about playing dumb. That's how you're going to look anyway."

A stranger died and it turned out to be his lover; his lover died and proved to be a stranger. David couldn't decide how to express this and so, at first, stayed silent and let the FBI fill in the blanks.

She had dropped out of college in California and never enrolled at Columbia. The days he thought she spent in Washington she was making bombs or planting them. Her greatest talent was not as a literary critic, but as an electrician handy with wires, timers, and detonators.

For a while he clung to intimate details, evidence he had verified with his own eyes and hands. He recalled that she took tea and lemon every morning, never coffee, and wouldn't eat red meat. He remembered the mist of cornsilk under her arms, much lighter than the tassel between her legs. He remembered the fair freckled skin of her face and how his beard left it reddened when he kissed her. Her entire body appeared to blush when she was excited, and she came to a climax with a muffled cry, a young girl's deep, slow rush of exhilaration.

But gradually the agents, working in teams, invaded his memories, pillaged his emotions, violated his intimacy with Darlene—even he called her that now—and exposed it as another lie.

"She fucked niggers," the FBI told him, "she fucked women, she fucked everybody in the commune. Know what their slogan was? 'People who fuck together, fight together.' They did it everywhere. They took dope and held orgies in churches to get ready for riots. They called it 'Wargasm.' Why protect a cunt like that? Tell us what you know."

When he had accounted for every hour in the last six months, they finally believed he didn't know anything and couldn't possibly have participated in bombing missions with Darlene Spaulding. After a month, they released him, and David returned to his apartment, which resembled the rubble-strewn lot where the town house had stood. His belongings, like his life, had been ripped inside out; clothes, letters, notes for articles lay tangled on the floor. Although the cops had taken nothing of his, they had removed every trace of Darlene down to her empty tubes of lipstick.

He turned and walked away from it all. Abandoning the apartment, New York, and the newspaper, he wanted never to hear certain expressions again—"the Movement," "the Revolution," "guerrilla tactics," "gone underground." He wrote for a slick city magazine in Texas, drank too much, and smoked more grass with cowboys and shitkickers than he ever had in the Village. Still he found himself tense, expectant, playing out painful fantasies that she would reappear, that she had been one of the two who had fled the fire storm alive.

Yet if she came back, would it be as Elizabeth Anderson or Darlene Spaulding? And why would she return? He had served his purpose; the sixties were over and there were no more coded messages to send through him. Darlene had gone underground for good. He was above ground and wanted to stay there. But to do that, he had to find something to fill the ragged, bleeding cavity her death had created. For David, it took more than a tall building of poured concrete and tinted glass to plug the empty space. It took all of Rome, loud, swirling, dirty, ferociously alive.

After a few weeks, he started making appointments with agents instead of magazine editors and, by a process of elimination—the major agencies had declined to represent him—he met Meg Diggins. A plump redhead in a shirtwaist dress, she wore a pair of horn-rimmed glasses pushed back to the crown of her head and did business in her home on the West Side. When she bustled David up to the second floor where a bedroom had been converted into an office, he couldn't imagine anything good coming of this. A few glossy book jackets had been thumbtacked to a bulletin board behind her desk, but he didn't recognize the names of any of the authors.

Lowering the glasses over her eyes as though they were an arcwelder's visor, she sat beside him in a canvas deck chair, screwed her face into an unconvincing show of concentration and glanced at his article proposals and a few pieces he had done in the past.

"You write well," she said pertly and shoved the glasses back up onto her head. "I think you're right. I think we're not getting the full picture from Italy. Take this terrorism thing," she said, reaching for a cigarette from a silver box on the desk. "There's been a lot of sensationalism. And you know why?"

"I have a few theories."

"Fine. You're a theory person, David." She pointed the unlit cigarette at her plush bosom. "Me, I'm a people person. Most readers are people people. And that's what's missing from so much writing today. People! A reader can't get behind a story that lacks a people angle. Take this terrorism thing," she repeated. "Who are these Red Brigades people? Where are they coming from? What kind of trip is it to go underground? What I'd like to see—what any reader really wants to see—is the human face behind the mask, the man behind the gun. Know what I mean?"

Unfortunately he did. He told Meg he had been acquainted with a few Italian journalists who attempted to show the "human face behind the mask." Two of them now had knees that bent in every direction. The third had been shot in the head and left to die on the sidewalk in front of his wife.

Meg swore she appreciated the dangers. But rolling the unlit cigarette between her thumb and index finger, she added, "Believe me, it'd be worth the risk."

He reminded her that nobody—not a single antiterrorist agent, much less a journalist—had managed to penetrate the Red Brigades.

Far from viewing this as a problem, she broke into a radiant smile. "That's the beauty of it! Nobody's done it before. You do it, and you can forget about nickel and dime articles. I see this as a book. A big book. I see a potential advance in the six-figure range. I see the possibility of a major paperback sale and a major, major movie deal."

"All I have to do is infiltrate a terrorist cell."

"No, what you have to do first is draw up a proposal. Give a bit of background about the Red Brigades. Describe all the exciting revelations this project could produce. You don't have to be specific. After all, you've not finished your research. But you can suggest. And remember, be personal. These terrorists are people!"

Meg had no more intention of listening to reason than she did of lighting her cigarette. And if she wasn't worried about putting him in danger, he knew she wasn't going to be dissuaded by the fact that he loathed journalists who exaggerated the importance of the Red Brigades, raising them to the status of a liberation army.

"Don't give me an answer now," she said. "Think it over. Talk to your contacts. But before you go, David, can I be completely frank? These article proposals, they won't fly. They don't have any punch, and you don't have a reputation. What you need is a book. And you're in a great position to write one. After all, who knows more about the Red Brigades than you do?"

He held his silence as she showed him to the door. Then unable to face another lonely, defeated hike downtown, he hailed a cab he couldn't afford. His anger at Meg's obtuseness and at himself for wasting the afternoon were exceeded by his mounting anxiety. He wanted to do the right thing, but realized that wouldn't keep him in Rome and wouldn't prevent him from going broke. Even at the *American News* he liked to believe he had retained certain standards, but he wondered how long he could afford this luxury.

Alone in his friend's apartment, he sat on the lumpy sofa and entertained the idea of doing what Meg seemed to suggest. Not that he had made up his mind. But, as if mulling over a chess problem, he pondered how he might orchestrate his moves.

Immediately, he stumbled headlong into an obstacle. He had no contacts in the underground and doubted any of his friends did. Meg was right about one thing: nobody knew more about the Red Brigades than he.

After chewing that thought for an hour, he dialed her number. "Could the book be done under a pseudonym?"

"Sure," Meg said. "Why not?"

"I'd have to have anonymity. I intend to go on living in Italy. There'd be trouble, a real shit storm, if I wrote under my own name."

"I get your drift. We'd demand it in the contract—different name, no picture. Anything else?"

"The same would have to hold for my sources. If it leaked that they had talked to me, they'd be executed."

"That's standard procedure. A journalist has to protect the confidentiality of his sources. Every publisher accepts that. It's like part of the Constitution. You go ahead and get the story. I'll make sure you're covered on this end." Then after a pause, "When can I see the proposal?"

"Let me check out a few facts first."

David did his fact checking in the New York Public Library and began by reading best-selling fiction. He leafed through Frederick Forsythe's *Day of the Jackal* and Jack Higgins's *The Eagle Has Landed*, both of which he had read before. Then he skimmed a few clones of these thrillers.

By now the formula was immutable. Its contours might change, but, like a piece of accordion luggage, its basic shape remained the same as it expanded to accommodate new filler. Into a historically accurate context, among real people, some still living, an author introduced fictional characters who were purported to have played major roles in imaginary events in the real people's lives. The convoluted plots were set into motion by fiction's oldest ploy. What if . . . ?

What if an ingenious international assassin had been hired to murder Charles de Gaulle? What if the Nazis had sent a commando squad to kidnap Winston Churchill? What if Hitler wasn't dead? What if John F. Kennedy had engineered his own assassination?

Behind these questions loomed larger ones about credibility, but the books all possessed a raw narrative verve which suspended a reader's disbelief until after the last page. Partly, this was a function of style. The prose scuttled along at ground level, the language subservient to subject matter, the author assuming a pose as mere conduit of "facts." The novels worked, he realized, because they sounded like newspapers.

When he glanced at best-selling nonfiction, he discovered just the opposite. Whereas so many novels now presented themselves as thinly veiled fact, nonfiction had adopted the devices of the novel. There were long stretches of dialogue, interior monologues, and personal insights of obscure origin. Names were said to have been changed to protect the innocent; "composite characters" had been constructed from dozens of interviews; chronology, quotes, and events had been altered, sometimes to "shield confidential sources," at other times simply "in the service of readability."

In this blurring of the genres, David believed he could find camouflage for himself. As he recalled from his literature courses in college, prose fiction had begun its long-endangered existence under false colors; many a famous author had passed off his novel as truth. And as he knew better from experience, many a journalist enlivened his articles with dubious information, unverifiable quotes, unnamed sources, and pure—or impure—invention. Why shouldn't he do the same?

One excellent reason was that he might get caught. Staying in the library, he pored through the periodicals catalog, studying recent literary scandals and hoaxes. Clifford Irving's "autobiography" of Howard Hughes had a morbid fascination for him; the author had not only been found out—he had been indicted for fraud, fined, and imprisoned.

Yet, after some reflection, he decided that case didn't remotely resemble his. For one thing, Irving had received an advance of more than six hundred thousand dollars, which had subjected him to intense public scrutiny. For another, he had written about Hughes assuming the millionaire was either dead or too loony and reclusive to emerge from hiding and denounce the book. As soon as Hughes had called a long-distance telephone press conference, Irving's charade had collapsed.

If David wrote about the Red Brigades, it would be under a pseudonym and few people would be aware of the book before its publication. Once it was out, who could contradict him? Presumably, the terrorists themselves could, but they were in no position to hold press conferences. If they leaked word that his story was a lie, who would believe them? Even imprisoned Red Brigades members couldn't refute what he wrote, since he would contend that he had infiltrated an underground cell with the help of a contact who could scarcely be expected to have informed his superiors of his betrayal.

As he drafted the proposal, David tried to salve his conscience by regarding this fraud as his revenge against those magazine editors who weren't interested in the truth about Italy, against journalists who filed copy every bit as bogus as his book would be, and against "the underground" in all its self-congratulatory, self-aggrandizing incarnations. If the notion of terrorism satisfied some worldwide psychic need, much like the need of children to believe in monsters as well as good fairies, he would give people what they craved. As for his own needs, he recognized more every day how much it meant to him to remain in Rome, between the lines, off the books, leading his own version of underground existence, disappearing from his old life no less completely than Darlene Spaulding had.

The book, he maintained in the proposal, would be an inside account of an urban guerrilla cell, centering on several men and women who had agreed to discuss their daily lives, political goals, and recent operations, including a bank robbery and kidnapping. It would reveal among other things whether the Red Brigades received weapons and money from Russia. Claiming access to sources throughout Italy, especially among left-wing fringe parties, he predicted a major terrorist attack in the near future and promised he would be an eyewitness to it if he got adequate support from a publisher.

In her unbridled enthusiasm, Meg wanted to submit the proposal to a dozen houses and auction it to the highest bidder. But David's nerve had limits. Afraid he would be found out if he overplayed his hand, he asked Meg to show it to one house at a time, with instructions to hold the matter in strictest confidence.

The first offer was fifteen thousand dollars—half in advance, half upon delivery of an acceptable manuscript. David was inclined to take it, on condition that he could remain anonymous even with his publishers. When Meg snapped that he couldn't expect anybody to risk money on an author he had never met, he reminded her he was risking his life.

This appeared to impress her. It must have impressed the publishers too. They tentatively agreed to meet his conditions. But then the senior editor insisted on talking to him by telephone and his first question caught David by surprise. Prepared to be cross-examined about his confidential sources, he found himself momentarily tongue-tied when asked why he was willing to accept such a meager advance.

"I just need enough to get started and—"

"If you've got what you claim, you could name your price. Why not go for the jackpot? Let's have lunch and work out what the book is really worth."

"Look, I don't claim to have anything except access to some important sources. If they let me down, I'd rather pay back seventy-five hundred than seventy-five thousand. Another thing, I don't want a lot of noise and publicity. The wrong people get wind of what I'm doing, I'm dead."

The editor said he'd have to think it over. When Meg called the next day, David feared bad news. But she was exuberant. "You told him what he wanted to hear. If you'd gotten greedy, he'd have killed the deal. We'll settle for small money up front, then really score on the paperback and the foreign rights. They've agreed all communications can pass through my office."

The check passed by the same route. Once he received his advance, minus Meg's fee, he carried it to Rome in cash.

Autumn in Italy is a season measured by climate rather than the calendar, commencing after the last blistering day, ending with the first slashing cold rain. Unlike Indian summer in the States, there is no frost and the leaves don't flame with color. The change is in the sky, in the depth of light, the play of shadow. No New England forest radiates more brilliant reds, oranges, and purples than Rome in October, yet these intensifying colors reveal themselves on the buildings, not the vegetation. But when the drab leaves, taking their own lazy good time, spin to the ground and are swept into heaps and set ablaze by the *spazzini*, the city's street sweepers, they yield the same sweet smoldering scent that marks autumn in America, the smell of melancholy, loss, and memory.

David remembered fall in Virginia, his years as an undergraduate in Charlottesville. He recalled days when the air had been crisp and cool, but the countryside, the campus, and his mind had seemed on fire as he charged through tumbling leaves to the library where he sat daydreaming and calling it research. What he had daydreamed about back then was becoming a writer. Now, as the season brought on an attack of nostalgia and profound longing, he thought some essential aspect of his earlier self had been restored to him. His job at the *American News* remained what it had always been—a parody of newspaper work. But he found from the start that his book, fraudulent though it was, fascinated him, stirring up a youthful sense of excitement, of open-ended possibility.

Suddenly every street in the city served as a classroom and every hour offered its lesson if you were careful to learn it. He studied the sky and the acute angles of advancing shadows and the mist rising from the river each morning as he walked to work. He plotted the course of the sun which burned without focus until it achieved its milky golden apogee at noon, and he watched a waxy moon wane against an evening sky the color of *vino bianco.*

People gained new gravity in his mind and he read them in a new way, trying to remember how they moved, how they held themselves, how what they said and what they did was sometimes a mirror of what they thought, and sometimes a screen. Each voice had a distinctive inflection and he struggled to capture it on paper. The essence of Italian conversation, where so much meaning was conveyed by gestures, was especially elusive, but he refused to resign himself to a flatfooted translation.

Both by professional experience and personal temperament David was persuaded to emphasize the eye and ear over the "I." He was a compiler, not a creator, an observer and an arranger, not an inventor. This posed problems now that he needed to create characters. In newspaper work, all the criminals, politicians, and celebrities came ready-made—interchangeable loaves of white bread from a mold. But with no confidence that his imagination could conjure up the population of a Red Brigades cell, he became a kind of literary cannibal, picking over the bones of the people around him, tearing away their names and faces and physical attributes to flesh out his terrorists.

Like any competent journalist, he was sure he could present a convincing picture once he had amassed enough facts. And facts lay close at hand, nowhere more so than in the Red Brigades' own house organ, *Contro Informazione*, which baldly stated the group's goal, "to destroy democracy and build a dictatorship of the proletariat." The means toward that end were abstruse, however, as expressed in the peculiar jargon of radical theorists who described violence as the "coagulant of the movement's subjective energy."

An earthier expression of the same idea was embodied in the aphorism *"Tanto peggio, tanto meglio"*—so much the worse, so much the better. For what the Red Brigades meant to do was make conditions in Italy unbearable, especially for the official Communist Party, which had drifted from revolutionary orthodoxy into a position of quasi-respectability. Through a program of "intensive provocation," the terrorists, in their words, intended to "violate the law openly . . . challenging and outraging institutions and public order in every way. Then, when the state intervenes as a result, with police and the courts, it will be easy to denounce its harshness and repressive dictatorial tendencies."

Radical newsletters weren't alone in providing source material. In *L'Espresso* magazine David discovered a chart which, according to unnamed but reliable sources, corresponded to the secret structure of a Red Brigades column.

To guard against infiltration and the domino effects of a single mistake, each column was comprised of units that could be sealed off like the chambers of a leaking ship. Since at the lowest level the cell operatives knew no more than was absolutely necessary—their only contact was with the cell commander above them—their arrest or defection wouldn't carry repercussions vertically in the column.

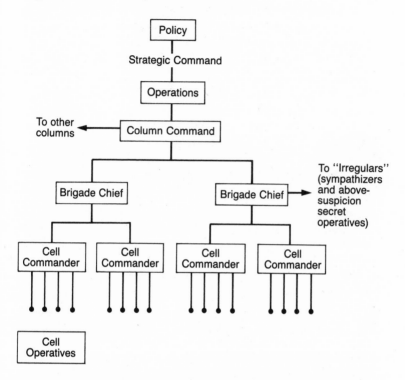

After tracing the chart, David scribbled in his notebook, "Unlike a snake which can be decapitated and killed, the Red Brigades resemble an earthworm which has the power to regenerate the segments it loses."

The image returned to mind when this year's batch of aspiring reporters arrived at the *American News.* They were all—David included himself—utterly replaceable segments in a scheme devised by the worm-in-chief, Pierre de la Chasse.

As the editor delivered his unvarying welcome-aboard address, the new employees huddled together in the dingy office and stared in bewilderment at the paint-blistered desks, the ancient

Olivettis, the army-surplus file cabinets, the wire service machine which fell silent as often because of delinquent payments as because of mechanical difficulties. If de la Chasse was aware of their stunned expressions, he didn't acknowledge them—no more than he acknowledged the disparity between the exuberance of his speech and the seedy disrepair of his newspaper. Emphasizing the rare opportunities his employees enjoyed, he failed to mention that most of their experience would be acquired not in the streets hustling for scoops, but right here, with scissors and paste in their hands. Even his capsule autobiography and history of the *American News* were marvels of omitted information.

Despite his name, de la Chasse was not French, and his idiomatic English to the contrary notwithstanding, there was serious doubt whether he was American. Some said he was an Italian who had worked with U.S. Intelligence during the war and had been rewarded afterward with language lessons in Langley, Virginia, and a sinecure at the *American News*.

Amid the welter of contradictory opinions about de la Chasse, one fact remained irrefutable. The CIA had started the paper in the fifties for the dual purpose of supporting Christian Democrats in print and with cash. While its editorials vociferously attacked Communist and Socialist party candidates, a substantial portion of its budget was spun off to the Christian Democrats by virtue of some adroit bookkeeping.

Although few Italian leftists believed it, this arrangement was supposed to have ended in the early seventies when the CIA was brought to heel by Congress, and for a while it looked as though neither the *American News* nor its editor would survive. But nobody had bargained on de la Chasse's genius for improvisation. Realizing he could no longer afford a staff of seasoned journalists, he sent bulletins to every J-school in the States announcing that he would award fellowships to talented graduates who desired on-the-job training as international correspondents. With thousands of journalism majors madly clamoring for work —in the wake of Woodward and Bernstein, every boy and girl with clear ideals and murky ideas longed to be a reporter—students from Texas were not the only ones who rose to de la Chasse's tainted bait, but for some reason they far outnumbered "the prizewinners" from other regions. Every fall they arrived with their accents, their cowboy boots, their craving for Mexican food, and their cassettes of country music. Eventually the term "Texans" came to be generic for the entire group.

The "fellowship" consisted of a flat three hundred dollars a month. With no overtime, no medical insurance, no vacation, and no benefits, the Texans made less than a fifth of what a union Italian journalist earned and half of what David was paid off the books. Bewitched by the city and baffled by the fluctuating currency rates, they seldom complained at first. They hurled themselves into the work with the same furious, inefficient energy they must have squandered during the early weeks of every college semester. It wasn't until the weather turned cold and they had gone hungry for a while that some of them grew surly and left. Others survived on bread and pasta, swilled cheap wine, shared rooms in *pensioni*, and pursued the mirage of supplementing their income with free-lance assignments. David noticed the more desperate ones at the Sunday flea market at Porta Portese, hocking their books, blue jeans, and cassettes.

Still, de la Chasse maintained they were having the time of their lives. "So I work them hard all day. So what? They screw all night."

Whether he had any legitimate insight into their sex lives, they did keep coming—a new crop every season. Only David stayed in place, clearing out the desks of the old ones, greeting the new ones, hoping for good tennis players and, back before he met Stephane, attractive young ladies. This year he kept his distance and barely registered their faces and names.

On October 13 a Lufthansa airliner was hijacked. After landing in Rome to refuel, it flew off to the Middle East and the four hijackers announced that they were allied with the kidnappers of German industrialist Hanns-Martin Schleyer. They threatened to blow up the plane unless the government released two Palestinian prisoners and eleven members of the Baader-Meinhof Red Army Fraction.

The news excited the Texans, who hovered around the wire awaiting word of developments. But David's thoughts took a tangent toward his book. From his research, he had learned of the importance that revolutionaries placed on liberating their imprisoned comrades, preferably through an attack that "frightened and enlightened." If executed with military skill and splashy violence, such an operation not only demonstrated the group's ability to move with impunity against the state, it convinced its members and potential recruits that it could protect them if they were captured.

In Germany, Ulrike Meinhof had once broken her lover, Andreas Baader, out of jail. Now his comrades were struggling to liberate him again.

In Italy, Margherita Cagol had freed her husband and co-founder of the Red Brigades, Renato Curcio. Four months later, however, the carabinieri had killed "Mara"—some claimed they dispatched her at point-blank range while she lay wounded on the ground—and Curcio had been recaptured. He and several dozen *brigatisti* were still awaiting trial in Turin on charges that ranged from membership in an armed gang to murder. The trial had had to be postponed when the Red Brigades carried out a bloody campaign of terror, intimidating magistrates and prospective jurors. Now, nearly two years after Renato Curcio's arrest, there was fear that no one in Italy dared sit in judgment of him.

To David, it seemed obvious that during the long delays in Curcio's trial the Red Brigades must be formulating plans to spring him. Given their bellicose public statements, how could they avoid the revolutionary responsibility of liberating a comrade?

On October 16, the hijackers shot the Lufthansa pilot and dumped his body onto the heat-warped tarmac of the airport in

Mogadishu, Somalia. They threatened to begin executing passengers one by one unless their demands were met.

Next day, a squad of German Grenzschutzgruppe 9—the elite "Leatherheads"—stormed the plane. Hurling stun grenades that temporarily blinded and deafened everybody on board, they blew off the hatches, killed three terrorists, wounded the fourth, and rescued eighty-six passengers and a Yorkshire puppy.

Within hours of the rescue, German authorities released word that Andreas Baader and several members of the Red Army Fraction, depressed by the abortive hijacking, had killed themselves in Stammheim prison. There was no satisfactory explanation of how they had succeeded in smuggling pistols into their maximum security cells, nor how they had managed to coordinate their suicides.

Days later, just across the border in Mulhouse, France, Hanns-Martin Schleyer was found dead in the trunk of a car. The Red Army Fraction announced that it had executed him in retribution for the assassination of its imprisoned comrades.

Like a graduate student, David diligently took notes.

CHAPTER V

AS THE SKEIN OF WARM, palmy days stretched into November, Pierre de la Chasse committed an extraordinary violation of his fiscal policy and invited everybody at the *American News* to a cocktail party at his villa. While the jubilant Texans caught a bus out to the Appia Antica, David lingered at the office late that afternoon, digging through the files. Then he violated his own fiscal policy by hailing a cab that sped him up Via dei Fori Imperiali, past a phalanx of tour groups and a rampart of buses around the Forum and Colosseum. What was it, he wondered, about crumbling, dun-colored ruins that induced tourists to dress the way they did? Perhaps some intuition that if *tempus fugit*, they wanted to be poised to fly with it, disguised as bright birds of paradise.

He hadn't considered bringing Stephane with him. Because of his slippery position at the *American News* and their fear that Lucio might make more trouble, they had long ago agreed it was better to be discreet, even secretive, about their relationship. They seldom went out, and when they did it wasn't to socialize with people from the newspaper.

The taxi circled the Circo Massimo; where chariots had once raced, portly bureaucrats from FAO jogged off their lunches. They passed the cavernous shell of the Baths of Caracalla, then rattled through Porta S. Sebastiano. Shafts of evening sunlight slanted through pine branches, illuminating oleander and ilex bushes. As the cab bounced over the broad, convex stones that paved parts of the Appian Way, David heard the dry chirring of locusts, busy as the click of the cab's meter.

The road narrowed, turned one way, and was hemmed in on both sides by brick walls bristling with broken bottles, by hedges of cypress, by fences of rusty iron spikes laced with ivy and bougainvillea. As always, Romans kept their lives screened off, sealed in, secret. He liked that.

The gates to one villa were open, but an armed security guard stopped the taxi and checked David's name against an invitation list. He paid his fare and proceeded on foot up a gravel drive on which each white pebble, the size and shape of a lima bean, looked to have been set in place by hand.

As usual he wore blue jeans and a shirt unbuttoned at the collar. His lone concession to the occasion was a denim sport coat which hadn't quite faded to the color of his trousers. After collecting the first half of his advance, he had debated whether to splurge on new clothes. But the last few years had driven home many hard lessons in caution, and he had decided to wait until he got all his money.

Ahead of him loomed de la Chasse's villa, a pink stucco extravaganza with *trompe l'oeil* pilasters painted on the facade and statues of questionable provenance displayed in obtrusive spots on the lawn. Since the Appia Antica was a historical zone, the *Belli Arti* commission had declared it off-limits to new construction. Ruins discovered on private property, however, could be reconstructed. So de la Chasse had bought a parcel of land, salted it with ancient bricks and slabs of marble, and bribed some impecunious archaeologist to excavate the stones and attest that at the height of the Roman Empire an important *palazzo* had stood on this spot. Then he ordered built to his specifications the monstrosity he had long had in mind. The place recalled Beverly Hills or Miami Beach rather than the grandeur that had been Rome.

. Like most social events *all'Italiana,* a cocktail party was free-style. Hosts were apt to be vague, inattentive, even absent—which scarcely mattered to the guests, who invariably arrived late and brought half a dozen uninvited friends. While a host's motives were always subject to speculation, everyone else was candid about his intentions. The object was to eat and drink until the restaurants opened and one could move on and continue eating and drinking.

At de la Chasse's, most guests remained outdoors in the cool dusk, thronging a bar that had been set up in an olive grove. Others clustered on the patio, teetering at the lip of a swimming pool as if making up their minds whether to take the plunge. David suspected he and the Texans had been asked as an afterthought. In a group this size, their presence barely registered.

He recognized people from various embassies, from the American Academy, from the bureau desks of wire services, newspapers, and magazines. Hovering around the hors d'oeuvres trays were out-of-work actors, their faces dimly familiar, poets and novelists, their book titles now forgotten by everybody but them, and dozens of hangers-on who mysteriously appeared at every function where there figured to be free food and drink.

He also noticed newcomers he couldn't place, for the city that fall was full of disaster tourists. Having heard rumors of the country's imminent collapse, they had rushed to Rome to enjoy the spectacle. It was like a championship fight or the Super Bowl; what the poor had to content themselves with watching on television, a fortunate few could come and witness firsthand.

When he spotted de la Chasse at the far end of the pool,

draped in a billowing sport shirt, his bald pate gleaming, David was inclined to keep his distance. Better yet, increase it. But then he saw the woman with de la Chasse. Grabbing a Cinzano from a passing waiter, he waded toward her, shouldering through the crowd.

Tall and blond, she carried herself with the poise of an athlete or dancer, and wore one of those peasant dresses from Guatemala, white cotton with bright flowers embroidered on the bodice. Beneath it her brown legs were bare, slightly spread for balance, flexed at the knee. As David drew near he noticed the lightest dusting of freckles across the bridge of her nose and a fine tracery of wrinkles—laugh lines—around her green eyes. The sculptured column of her neck was whorled with a mist of minute gold hairs.

Since de la Chasse was notoriously maladroit with introductions, it was possible he never mentioned her name. Or maybe David didn't hear it over the other name that resonated through the throbbing bell of his skull. It wasn't so much that this woman resembled the dead girl feature for feature as that her coloring, the broad planes of her face, her self-containment, suggested what Darlene Spaulding might have become if she had lived ten more years.

Already disconcerted by her appearance, David received a second high-voltage shock when de la Chasse said, "Here's our expert on terrorism. He'll tell you whatever you need to know about the Red Brigades."

The editor's fleshy paw fell on his shoulder, and he leaned toward David with the kind of leering intimacy that precedes an off-color joke. "She wants to meet them in person," de la Chasse said. "I told her she already met them. But she wants to renew the acquaintance. See what you can do for her."

While the editor waddled away, David sipped his bitter Cinzano to hide the commotion he felt. Had somebody seen him digging through the dead files? Was there any way de la Chasse could have discovered he was doing a book? No, just a coincidence. Just another instance of de la Chasse letting someone else cope with questions he was too ignorant or embarrassed to answer.

"Are you one of the new Texans?" David asked, although he knew she wasn't.

"I'm an old Texan," she said with an exaggerated arch of the eyebrows. Smiling, she showed slightly crooked front teeth— less a flaw than an asymmetry he found attractive.

"Sorry, I thought I recognized you from the office."

"I bet you say that to all the girls." She held out a firm, dry hand. "Alison Lopez. I *am* from Texas. Nuevo Laredo by way of Odessa."

Suddenly he felt the transcendent stupidity of someone who has mistaken a celebrity for an old acquaintance. Her photographs of the bank robbery in Milan, followed by pictures of her, had run in newspapers and magazines everywhere in Europe.

"You have to forgive me. Forgive everybody at the *American News!* A prerequisite for working there," he said, "is to have spent your childhood eating lead paint off windowsills."

"Come on now. It can't be that bad," Alison said. "De la Chasse is pretty well connected. My agent knew him after the war. He thought your boss might have contacts with the Red Brigades."

"Not unless they hang out at the Press Club." He was raking his fingers through his beard.

"What about you? De la Chasse said—"

"The only thing we run about the Red Brigades is what we clip off the wire service. And most of what the wire service sends out is slightly refined gossip."

"Ever do free-lance articles on Italian politics?" she asked.

"I'm a broken-lance journalist. Every once in a while, I interview a writer who interests me. Nothing more than that."

"Which writers?"

He was as disconcerted by her questions as he had been by her appearance. She listened with the same single-minded intensity as most people put into talking, and as she listened, she bit at her lower lip, leaving the print of her crooked teeth.

"I've done Gore Vidal here in Rome," he said. "Graham Greene in the south of France. James Jones before he left Paris."

"Which should I read first?"

"You've probably already read the one with Greene. People keep ripping it off and printing it under their names."

"Plagiarism is the highest form of flattery. Did you like Greene?"

"Sure. He's a very funny man, full of jokes and sly tricks."

"I don't see him that way," she said. "I thought he'd be serious, kind of heavy and lugubrious."

"Maybe I'm such a lightweight I bring out the prankster in everybody."

"Oh no, more self-deprecation. It's the vice of the truly egotistical. Tell me about Greene."

"I interviewed him at his place in Antibes, and to prove I'm not your average American barbarian, I made a big production of admiring his paintings and *objets*. On the coffee table, there was this *maquette* of a Henry Moore sculpture."

"I'm impressed," Alison said.

"That he owned it? Or that I recognized it?"

"Both."

"Well, I'm no connoisseur, but when I see a reclining woman shot full of holes, I always guess Moore. There was this other piece, though, this tall, cylindrical, chrome-plated job, that gave me problems. I picked it up and admired it, turning it this way and that, sweating for something to say. Tell you the truth, it looked just like a vibrator. But I maundered on and on about how it seemed to show the influence of Brancusi, with maybe a little Jean Arp thrown in on the side."

"Yes. And then?" She watched him over the rim of her glass as she sipped a vodka and tonic.

"Greene said he had no idea who'd done it. He said he bought it from a chemist in Nice. I knew he meant a guy in a drugstore, but, dumb me, I played it straight and said the chemist must have had papers for the sculpture. Greene claimed the only papers that came with it recommended using it in case of inflammation and itching. He explained he had just had an operation for hemorrhoids and this chrome-plated number was some sort of medicine applicator. 'It's so decorative'—David did his best to imitate a British accent—'I couldn't bear to throw it away.' "

She laughed so hard her drink splashed over her wrist. "What'd you say? What'd you do?"

"I set it back on the coffee table and resisted the impulse to wipe my fingers on my pants. Then I asked him if he typed or wrote longhand."

She let out another laugh. "I'd love to meet Greene. Love to spend days with him talking about Viet Nam. You know, when I was in Saigon, I made it a point to rent his old apartment."

Since anything he said on this subject was apt to leave her feeling like a fool or a liar, David steered the discussion to her work. "I won't kid you, I can't claim I like your pictures. They're too disturbing, too terrifying. But I always look at them. Then I go back and look at them again. You never forget them."

"Thanks. That makes up for some of the frustration of the last two months."

"Frustration? Why? I've seen your shots from Milan in dozens of magazines."

"There hasn't been anything since. I want to do the Red Brigades. But it's like chasing smoke."

"Like de la Chasse said, you've already *done* them."

"I'm after something different. Something from their point of view."

"You mean looking down a gun barrel?"

"That might be part of it. I'd like to do a feature, maybe a whole book, on terrorism from the inside. All we see is the aftermath, the consequences. I'd like to show—"

"The human face behind the mask."

"Who knows? Maybe it's a monster behind the mask. Whatever it is, I want to be the first one to get it on film."

"That's how journalists get kneecapped." He glanced briefly at her firm, tan legs, then raised his eyes. "Or killed."

The warning didn't ruffle her in the least. "How long have you lived in Rome?"

"Five years."

"So you know the city?"

"Yeah, a bit."

"Say you wanted to touch base with the Red Brigades, how would you go about it?"

"They're not our home-fried radicals. They haven't hired a booking agent."

"I'm serious. You must have contacts here. People you trust."

"Keep poking around, asking questions, and maybe they'll come to you."

"Hey, you're no help. What are you doing, saving them for yourself?" Although she was smiling, the set of her jaw reminded him again of Darlene.

"The best advice I have is stay away from the Red Brigades."

In the villa, the lights flashed on and an instant later the patio and pool, too, were flood-lit by bulbs tucked away in treetops. A breeze strummed through the foliage, stirring up the scent of the Mediterranean countryside, an amalgam of rosemary, eucalyptus, and pine.

Alison drew a deep breath. "Wonderful smell." Raising a hand, she ran it through her loose hair. He was relieved to see she shaved her underarms. Then it troubled him to realize he had been looking for that.

"Let me get you a fresh drink," he said.

"I can get one for myself."

"I'll bet you can. But I want to test my masculinity. Have you seen the mob at the bar? Only a real man would risk fighting it." He took her glass.

By the time he returned, a dark, stout man had moved in on Alison. Undaunted by the fact that she was a few inches taller, the fellow bent forward as if sniffing the flowers on her bodice. It was Italo Bianchi, wearing a black velvet jacket and a silk shirt unbuttoned to his hairy sternum. As he spoke, his eyes flared with innuendo, his lips fluttered with suggestive grins. Yet what he said was so wildly out of synch with his flirtatious manner, it was as if the sound track from a foreign intrigue film had been superimposed on a romantic farce.

"Now, *cara*, you must explain to me about those photographs from Milan."

Although Alison leaned away from him at the waist, creating a sinuous tension in her upper torso, she held her ground. "There's nothing to explain. The whole story's in the pictures."

"Yes, they're marvelous. But how did you happen to be there just at the right time, just when the Red Brigades arrived?"

"I was taking a stroll."

"Imagine stumbling onto something like that. You were very lucky."

"I wouldn't say it was luck."

"Oh?" Italo grinned. "Did you know the bank was about to be robbed? Do you share a party line with the *brigatisti*?"

She turned to David. "Have you two met?"

"Everybody in Rome knows David. He's my entrée into the fascist mind of America." He embraced David and clapped him on the shoulder.

"What Italo means is he's my mole on the Italian Left." He handed Alison her vodka and tonic. "Any time I need a snappy quote about communism, he's happy to sow the seeds of disinformation."

Bianchi's nose swung back to her bodice. "Perhaps you would like to hear my analysis of the historic compromise between the Christian Democrats and the Communist Party. That *cretino* Aldo Moro calls it a policy of parallel convergences. But I believe—"

"I've listened to this lecture before," David said. "Excuse me if I don't stay and take notes."

He thought it wise to move away from Alison Lopez. His affair with Stephane was already complicated and the best measure of his fidelity was to refuse to test it. Drink in hand, he drifted through the crowd, occasionally pausing to speak to friends, mostly listening to strangers lament the nuisance strikes that plagued the country, idling trains, buses, and planes, shutting off water and electricity. He also heard animated debates about where to obtain the best black market exchange rate, how to buy counterfeit gasoline coupons, and who had the better commissary—FAO or the American Embassy. "Let's face it," somebody asserted, "there'll never be another PX like the one in Saigon." No voice was raised in contradiction.

Holding court on the patio, Pierre de la Chasse was enthroned on a rattan peacock chair, surrounded by sycophants. The portly Mrs. de la Chasse had squeezed in beside him so that they resembled the royal couple from some Polynesian archipelago, stuffed with poi, brown skins supple with coconut milk. "I wouldn't use the Italian post office on a bet," the editor announced. "It's a nest of pinkos. The bastards see an envelope with an American address, they toss it in the trash. Me, I always use the Vatican P.O. Or if it's anything urgent, I airfreight it."

As David headed in the opposite direction, Bianchi fell in beside him, grabbed his elbow, squeezed. "Why did you run off?"

"Thought you might like to be alone with Alison Lopez."

"I don't know her."

"Sounded to me like you were trying to."

"Of course, I know she's a photographer. But who does she work for?"

"Herself. Magazines let her do pretty much what she wants."

"Always political violence?"

"No, she does ads and fashion layouts, too. Funny thing. Even they have this sort of S and M sheen. The way she sets up shots, with models sprawled all over, their clothes torn, legs and arms twisted, faces contorted, they look a lot like the pictures she took in Viet Nam and Lebanon. Ever see the stuff she did during the fall of Saigon?"

Italo shook his head. "She's well-known in the States?"

"Very. She's our Oriana Fallaci. Naturally, since it's a na-

tion of illiterates, she works with pictures, not words. But she
gets what she's after. She puts people on the spot, she puts
herself on the spot."

"May I ask a personal question without insulting you?"

"That damn well depends." Despite his bantering tone, David
was on guard.

"Are you and *la bella bionda* lovers?"

"Jesus, Italo, what makes you ask that? I just met her."

"She's interested in you, full of questions. She wanted to hear
about your work."

"What'd you tell her?"

"That you don't do any work worth discussing."

"Great! You couldn't have done me a bigger favor."

"If you're not interested in her"—he sounded serious now
—"I may be."

"*May* be! You're drooling."

"Why aren't you? Have you been struck blind? Are you
suffering a calcium deficiency?"

"You're forgetting Stephane."

"Oh, you Americans, monogamous even when you're not
married. I assure you, I have no such compunctions. But one
thing worries me. What is this obsession she has with the Red
Brigades?"

"She wants to meet them. Wants pictures of life in a terrorist
cell."

"My god! I have changed my mind. I don't care to lie between her beautiful legs. Not when she is bound to be kneecapped."

They walked a few moments in silence, circulating through
the crowd as aimlessly as the breeze. Italo said, "Do you think
there is anything more to her fascination with terrorism?"

"What more could there be?"

"What are her politics?"

"I've tried to tell you, Americans don't have politics. We
have Visa and Diner's Club."

"She asks an awful lot of questions."

"So do you, *amico*. Should I assume you're working for the CIA?"

"David, don't say that, not even for a joke. Someone might hear."

Ahead of them, Alison approached the edge of the pool. With one hand she smoothed the white dress to the back of her thighs, crouched with a swift grace that sent an ache through David, and dipped her other hand into the opalescent water.

"It's warm," she said.

Abruptly the lights blinked out and the party, after a child-like cry of wonder and delight, fell into a silence so profound they could hear crickets in the grass and wind soughing through the trees. It was a dizzying, upside down night, the sky brightly lit by stars, the earth shrouded in darkness.

Then a car, its headlights dim, rumbled up the gravel drive. It halted close to the crowd and its high beams burst on with dazzling force.

"What the hell is this?" de la Chasse demanded.

Alison moved over beside David as half a dozen men scrambled out of the car. Five wore ski masks and carried Uzi submachine guns. A sixth man, the security guard from the front gate, was handcuffed.

"Don't move! Don't talk! Stand right where you are," one man hollered in Italian. "We're the Red Brigades."

Several people panicked and dashed blindly into darkness, dodging statues, lurching across the lawn toward the back fence. There was a burst of automatic gunfire from that direction, then a short volley of answering fire from the men around the car. Amoebalike, the crowd contracted, huddling close, rigid with fear.

Four more armed men marched across the lawn, herding in front of them the handful of guests who had tried to escape.

"We're the Red Brigades," the man repeated in accented English. "It's time you rich people paid your taxes. Who owns this house?"

No one answered. David darted a glance to his left. De la Chasse and his wife had abdicated the peacock throne.

The man grabbed the trussed-up security guard by his shirt collar and gave him a vicious shake. "Who's your boss?"

The guard wouldn't say.

The man jabbed an Uzi into his belly. "You want to die for him?"

The guard mumbled something, and two gunmen rushed the editor, who screamed, "First you don't do your job. Then you betray me. *Stronzo! Cazzo! Froscio!* Turd. Prick. Queer."

De la Chasse dropped to his knees, cowering. One man seized him by the nostrils and jerked him to his feet so fast he might have been no more than a flashy sport shirt swinging from a wire hanger. They ripped his wallet and keys from his pockets. Then, still leading him by the nose, they shoved him, bellowing, into the pool where he bobbed up and down in the deep end, spouting water and blood.

"Now, while some of my friends explore your host's villa, the rest of you will have a chance to contribute to our cause," said the man who did all the talking. "When my comrades come by, please be generous and quick. We are not as patient or in-efficient as Italian tax collectors."

Alison pressed close to David, slipping her arms under his jacket, clinging to his waist. For an instant, she had him fooled; he thought she was terrified. Then a hand slid inside his shirt, her tightly balled fist warm against his belly. With a deft downward motion, she stuffed the hand under his belt, into his pants, and quickly yanked it out again. David felt something cold and metallic in his underwear.

The men bustled through the crowd with plastic trash bags, snatching wallets, rings, wads of cash, wristwatches, bracelets, earrings, and necklaces. A few guests argued and attempted to hold back their belongings. They were roughed up and heaved into the pool with de la Chasse.

For once, David was grateful he didn't have more than fifteen thousand lire on him. Although the men told him to turn his pockets inside out, they didn't frisk him and find whatever was lodged in his underwear.

Alison asked to keep her IDs, but they refused. They ripped

her purse from her hand and ordered her to unscrew her earrings.

"Watch?" One man grabbed her wrist which bore the precise,
white shadow of her wristwatch.

"I didn't wear it tonight. It's broken," she said.

They pushed on to Bianchi, who promptly deposited his
wallet and watch in the plastic bag as if this were a benefit.

In less than ten minutes they were finished. While one team
of burglars trotted down the drive, lugging the trash bags, the
leader ordered people to remain where they were. He warned
them they would be watched; the first person who moved would
be shot. He and the other team clambered into the car and,
keeping the high beams trained on the crowd, rolled backward
toward the gate. There they swung around and accelerated onto
the Appia Antica, speeding away from the city.

For a moment, there was no sound except for those in the
pool treading water. Then de la Chasse floundered onto the
patio, sputtering like a beached whale. A woman started sobbing. Somebody said, "Stay calm. Don't give them an excuse to
shoot." A married couple was bickering. "I told you never to
wear that diamond bracelet." "Why have it, if I can't wear
it?"

David saw a man scuttle crablike across the lawn toward the
house. Although her arms were no longer around him, Alison
was close by his side. A breeze brushed gauzy strands of her
hair against his cheek.

When the lights snapped on, one of the new Texans, a boy
named Joe Bob, strode out of de la Chasse's villa and announced proudly that he had called the police. This produced as
much consternation as would the return of the Red Brigades.
Guests raced for their cars. Those who had arrived in taxis
fought to reach the telephone. Some set out on foot, desperate
to get away.

"What is this?" Alison asked.

"They don't want to be here when the police show up."
David hustled her toward Italo's red Alfetta GTV.

"Why?"

"They'll hold us all night, asking questions."

"But if that helps get our things back—"

"No chance of that. The cops'll never catch them. They'll be too busy taking statements, demanding identification, making sure everybody's papers are in order."

"I have little fear of burglars," Bianchi said. "But God save us from bureaucrats."

CHAPTER VI

HURTLING UP APPIA ANTICA toward town, bucking the traffic running against him, Bianchi sounded his horn, blinked his high beams, and swore at startled drivers as though they, not he, had broken the law.

"The logic of the Italian Left!" David exclaimed.

"Don't label my political beliefs," Italo said. "I go my own way."

"Yes, always the wrong way up a one-way street. And take a gander at the radical professor's car." David was in the back seat, speaking to Alison in front. "It's a plank in the Party platform—pasta in every pot and an Alfa Romeo in every garage."

"Trotsky wrote, 'You don't have to believe in the trolley company to get where you want to go.'"

"You two are pretty damned good-humored for people who just got robbed," Alison said.

Italo shrugged and gave a gesture with his fingers signifying monumental indifference.

"I didn't have much on me. At least not that belongs to me." David pulled the metallic object from his pants. A watch—a gold Lady Rolex worth about five thousand dollars. He handed it to Alison. "They'd be very unhappy if they knew they'd missed that. Of course, they'd have made me even more unhappy if they'd found me hiding it."

"Thanks. This means a lot to me. It was a gift."

"Hope you didn't lose much in your purse," Italo said.

"A few hundred dollars. It's losing all my cards that kills me. It's such a pain replacing them."

"I believe it was identification papers more than money that the Red Brigades were after."

"That wasn't the Red Brigades," said David. "When they're short of cash, they knock over a bank or kidnap a millionaire. As for IDs, they've got printing presses that run off all they need."

Alison turned to him. They were close enough for him to inhale her perfume and notice again in the oncoming headlights the fine trembling whorls of down on her neck. Wind lashed her hair at her face. "So you *do* know about the Red Brigades," she said.

Italo chuckled. "Like all of us, he knows what's in the newspapers."

"Right, and from what I've read, they wouldn't be carrying Uzis. Not when they're getting arms from the PLO and the eastern bloc."

Bianchi laughed again. "Ah, the dauntless reporter and his great expertise."

"Did you notice how they dressed, Italo? That should tell you something."

"I was too busy marveling at the new batch of Texans. How is it that they have such extraordinary names—Lance, Betty Sue, Merlee, Joe Bob, Orbert—yet they can never pronounce my name? And why do they all look the same, so bland, as if they were raised on a diet of nothing but dairy products?"

Unswervingly single-minded, Alison said, "What about the way those men dressed?"

"That's Italo's specialty. He can glance at a crowd of thousands and tell you what their politics are. It's the haberdashery school of sociology. Everything depends on how they crease their pants."

Tired of their jokes, she asked Bianchi, "What did you make of the men who robbed us?"

"I would bet they were the Red Brigades," he said.

"I think they were your garden variety Italian thugs," David said.

At the end of the Appian Way, a swarm of cars, whirring like so many venomous wasps, snarled at one another as they nudged through the gate in the city wall. Showing more concern for his Alfa than others did for their Fiats, Bianchi nosed along an inch at a time. Then the line of automobiles lurched to a stop and stood throbbing in coils of exhaust fumes and smoke from the bonfires lit by whores beside the road. Fed up with waiting, a VW bus full of nuns passed in the left lane, honking madly against oncoming cars. The Holy Spirit sped with them; at least there was no crash.

When the traffic started up again, they made it beyond the Circo Massimo before a boy on a Vespa sideswiped the automobile in front of them. The driver wanted to climb out and fight, but his wife held him back. He belted her instead while the boy on the Vespa puttered away. As Bianchi eased past the couple in their dented car, they were screaming and clawing at each other.

"Just another evening of *commedia dell'arte*," David said.

"Don't listen to our cynical friend," Italo warned Alison. "He hates Italians. He fears our warmth and spontaneity."

They entered the *centro storico* where the clamorous streets reminded Alison of the Orient. At bus stops, newsstands, and telephone booths, people formed arabesques—never lines—and the traffic described patterns no American would imagine. One-way streets mysteriously switched directions, sidewalks metamorphosed into exit ramps, alleys into cloverleafs. Red lights and pedestrian zones signified protection to the deluded and the soon-to-be-dead.

"Are you going home?" Bianchi asked David.

"No. Let me off near Largo Argentina."

"And you?" he asked Alison.

She hesitated before saying, "Drop me the same place."

"Careful of the company you keep. With David, you're a marked woman."

"I'm capable of keeping myself company, thank you."

"Such independence!" Italo said. "Just the quality for a free-lance photographer."

At Largo di Torre Argentina, a large square opened in front of them, the fenced-in, sunken space at its center punctuated by truncated pillars, fluted columns, a tower, and tall cypress and pine trees rooted in stone. As always in the land of the Janus face, there were two ways of regarding the square—as a harvest of Roman antiquities, as meticulously cared for as a backyard garden, or as a blaring chaos of converging traffic, one of the city's black lungs. Cars, buses, and cabs careened around the ruined temples with the brutal indifference of scavengers scuttling past meatless bones.

Bianchi stopped next to a newsstand where magazines and posters, clipped to nylon cords like the flags of many nations, flapped in the breeze. "You must visit the university and let me show you around," he said to Alison.

"I'd like to meet your students."

"I'll introduce you."

"Think any of them are in the Red Brigades?"

The question clearly caught Italo off guard, but he attempted to conceal his surprise by doing a comic double take. He lifted her hand to his lips. "Come and visit me, *cara*."

He let the Alfa slide, sleek as an eel, into the hissing stream of traffic and reached into the ashtray for a handful of *gettoni*, the copper slugs used in pay phones. When through a clump of pine trunks and shattered pillars he saw David and Alison start down

Via de' Cestari, Bianchi bumped up onto the curb in front of a café and spent several minutes securing his car. First, he set the burglar alarm. Then he looped a heavy chain, encased in clear plastic, through the steering wheel and bolted it to the floor. Finally he climbed out and locked the doors.

In the café, he descended the stairs to an alcove beside the W.C. Italians were so sadly consistent, he thought. Jolly on the surface, pessimists at heart. They installed public telephones next to shitholes to demonstrate that although they owned sophisticated equipment they had no confidence in it or in the notion of progress. Throughout the city he had stood breathing the smell of stale piss, trying to calm himself and recall the right number.

At the third ring, a thin, high-pitched voice answered, "Pronto?"

"Giovanni?"

"Who?"

"Giovanni?"

"There's no Giovanni here."

Italo hung up, relieved to have spent less than a minute on the line. But this was only the first, the easy, step. He had no great eagerness to take the second.

Outside, he checked his Alfa. Although it might appear to be an improbable place for a thief to strike, that was when you had to remain most alert. His abiding image of Bologna—the Communists' model city, for Christ's sake!—was of an orange Porsche Targa perched on cinderblocks beside the train station, stripped of tires, radio, windshield wipers, muffler, and detachable engine parts. In full view of passersby, the thieves had worked with a speed and efficiency unparalleled anywhere in the country.

Criminals were always more industrious, he thought, and the Red Brigades had been wise to imitate their example, as they had tonight at the party. He could guess what they had been after—information on Alison Lopez. The cash and jewels were a bonus.

It pleased Italo that David wouldn't have suspected that.

Although he worked for de la Chasse, a man reputed to have CIA connections, David was apolitical, as devoid of curiosity about Bianchi's ideological entanglements as he was of personal ambitions. Aside from Stephane and tennis, his single passion seemed to be staying in Italy.

Italo had ceased attempting to understand this. So many foreigners said they loved Italy, so many had forsaken families, careers, and homelands to settle in a country for which he found it impossible to feel much except disgust. Still, he sometimes wondered. . . . He was living a lie. Why not David? Bianchi could ooze bogus charm at every pore, pretend to be a womanizer, pretend to be carefree. Was it conceivable David, too, had adopted protective coloration, disguising himself as a cheerful, naïve American?

No, he didn't believe it. He realized his contact would regard this as bourgeois self-indulgence—worse yet, a punishable offense—but Italo longed to preserve at least one friendship uncomplicated by politics, unmarred by suspicion. He needed someone to joke with, to play tennis with, someone like David who demanded little, who knew nothing about Piero Galganni and had no appetite for involving himself in events, who minded his own business and expected him to do the same.

He sprinted through heavy traffic to the sidewalk surrounding the ruins. Close enough now to dredge in the rank, fecal stench of cats, he watched them slink from one chunk of marble to the next, pools of oil dissolving, then reappearing on widely spaced blocks of white. Crazy old crones had set out dishes of pasta for the animals, like offerings to reincarnated deities.

Circling the ruins, he made certain no one was following him, then crossed the street and entered a *gelateria* where a girl dreamily clung to the telephone, gabbling to her boyfriend. Crowding her, he made a show of peering at his wrist where his watch should have been. When she ignored him, he suffered an attack of nerves and stepped over to a display case packed with tubs of ice cream.

It was nothing, he told himself. If he was late, if he missed a connection, he'd start over. His contact had to understand he couldn't foresee every contingency. Still, he experienced a deep disquiet, a stinging abdominal pain, and decided to coat his empty stomach.

Paying with *gettoni*, he bought a strawberry sherbet cone, took one lick, wished he hadn't. The sweetness did not mix well with the whiskey he had drunk. If Giovanni ever learned how much he had been drinking lately, how undependable he had become, Italo feared he would be dismissed. And this wasn't a job with severance benefits. To be dismissed by the Red Brigades meant being stuffed into the trunk of a car and rolled into a lake.

Sidling close to the girl again, he took audible licks of the cone, rubbing his leg against her skinny behind. She whirled around. When he gave her a sharklike grin, she hung up and hurried away.

He dialed and someone lifted the receiver at the other end before the second ring.

"*Pronto.*" The high-pitched voice quavered against a background of traffic noises.

"This is Scarpe."

"This is Giovanni. You're late. What the hell is wrong with you?"

"The phone here was busy. There was no time to reach another."

"You leave me hanging in the open. Quick, tell me."

"The woman does not appear to be intelligent. She doesn't act intelligently, she doesn't speak intelligently."

"That could be cover."

"I think not. I've talked to her. She's curious about our friends, but knows very little. For one thing, she has only a few words of Italian."

"Our friends in Milan, they say she showed up at exactly the wrong time. As if she knew where they'd be and when and why."

"A coincidence. I asked my journalist sources. They said

she's a photographer, nothing more. She used to do pictures for fashion magazines. What she does now is just another kind of fashion."

"I want you to keep watching her. I want to know more."

"What more can I find out? You have her purse, her identity cards."

"What are you saying?" A siren shrieked above Giovanni's hermaphroditic voice.

"Our friends, when they crashed the party, they carried off everybody's money and papers. The woman's purse must contain far more information than I could discover."

"What's this shit? Our friends weren't at any party."

"They claimed to be with us. I thought you sent them. They stole my watch and a hundred thousand lire." Italo's cone was leaking; sticky liquid dribbled between his fingers.

"Every crook in the country is hiding behind us."

"Look, about the woman," Bianchi said, "we're wasting our time. If she knew what was going to happen in Milan, why didn't she tell the police? Why did she just take pictures?"

"That's what we need to find out. We can't run the risk she'll show up again with a camera."

"Why don't you grab her and question her?"

"It's dangerous. She's American. If we grab her and she's not intelligent, we're liable to attract the attention of those who are. Keep an eye on her. I'll call in a couple of days."

Outside, he dropped his cone into the gutter and followed a circuitous route back to his car, crossing and recrossing streets. He knew he wasn't being tailed. He hadn't stayed on the line long enough for the call to be traced. But his hands trembled and his tongue, despite its sheath of sweetness, tasted like blood, just as it would after a near miss in the mountains.

CHAPTER VII

ALISON SLIPPED HER ARM through David's and, despite her better judgment, let herself lean on him as they walked. The robbery, the reckless drive, the maddening banter with Bianchi had left her feeling wobbly. Or perhaps it was just Rome that disoriented her.

She couldn't call it culture shock—she was accustomed to exotic cities—and since arriving here, she had been struck less by the strangeness than by the eerie correspondences in the place. It was as if after so many miles, so many years away from her home and family, she had gotten nowhere, had escaped nothing.

At de la Chasse's, she had listened to Bianchi describe Italy as an undeveloped country, a long drain leading to the Third World. "People are afraid of slipping down into the muck," he had said. "That's why Italians act crazy. Living on the brink produces schizophrenia."

Alison understood that; she knew what it was to live at the

edge. But back in Laredo, there had been the tea-colored river and a chain-link fence between her and that seedy, desolate section of the city which was called Nuevo, yet looked ancient. Now it seemed she had stumbled over the edge and into the muck.

The thought nagged her, This is Mexico. Familiar sights and smells and sounds assaulted her—garbage in the streets; diesel fumes fouling the air; shriveled old women in black shuffling through alleys; boys with their shirts unbuttoned and gold crosses gleaming against their chests. Everywhere she looked, there were too many churches, too much history, too many people.

On buses and street corners, men rubbed against women and let their hands rove, their caresses perfunctory, almost impersonal. Like Mexicans, Italians appeared to be unsure of the contours of their own bodies, unable to judge where theirs ended and someone else's began, and so they had to submit all flesh to a crude Braille.

With David, she felt something of this same vacillation between intimacy and coolness, curiosity and detachment. Although his arm was linked with hers, he kept his distance and didn't react as she shot him a look of blunt appraisal. His curly hair was nearly as blond as hers and his features were fine-boned. He might have been too pretty for her taste if his reddish beard hadn't given him a rough edge she liked.

What she didn't like was the way he talked. Incapable of dealing with routine exchanges of conversation, pausing at every sentence and weighing his words, he passed his remarks off as jokes, glib put-downs, often of himself. Alison could only guess what he was holding back, and why.

Pasted to the walls of the narrow street they were going down were garish posters—broadsides from the Left, shrill calls to arms from the Right, gory photographs with which each side accused the other of atrocities. One picture in particular caught her attention. A man had been hit by a Molotov cocktail that had scorched off all his clothes. Naked, he sat dying in a café chair, a handkerchief draped decorously over his penis. She supposed the photographer had covered the man's sex to ensure that the shot wasn't spiked. To print an incinerated body was one thing. A cock was quite a different question.

"What does the caption say?" she asked.

"He was an informer. The Red Brigades found out and executed him."

Continuing toward the Pantheon, they passed a shop that specialized in ecclesiastical clothing. Mannequins modeled nuns' habits, priests' vestments, cassocks, and surplices. Alison nibbled her chapped lips. "Is there any place I can buy Blistex? Oh damn, I forgot. I don't have any money."

"They cleaned me out, too."

They paused near Piazza della Minerva. In front of the church, amid a cluster of haphazardly parked cars, stood an odd monument. Atop a tall pedestal rested a marble elephant sculpted by Bernini, and on the elephant's back an Egyptian obelisk was balanced upright. The scene had the skewed logic of a dream.

"Where are you staying?" David asked.

"Palazzo Vertecchi." It was a residence hotel for high rollers, movie stars, and expense account bandits.

"I'll put you in a cab and explain the situation to the driver. He'll wait while you get money from your room."

"I'd rather walk. Which direction are you headed?"

"I have to meet somebody," he said. "You know your way from here?"

"I never get lost."

"Maybe we'll bump into each other again."

She shook the hand he offered and said nothing.

"If I were you, I wouldn't go walking around alone. Let me get you a taxi."

"I'm a big girl."

"I'm serious."

She laughed. "You really are scared of the Red Brigades, aren't you?"

He glanced down at her knees. "I just hate to think of nice legs wasted."

"Don't worry. I won't waste them."

He left her in Piazza della Rotonda; she didn't watch him go. She gazed up, as if deeply absorbed by the lighted pediment of the Pantheon. It was ridiculous. She recognized that, yet couldn't help feeling furious at David—and at herself. She wasn't used to being the one dismissed. Who was he anyway? Some small-time smart-ass hack.

The hell with it and the hell with him. She could catch a cab to the airport any time she wanted. As always, it was important to know she could leave. There was nothing to keep her here—not unless it was the reminders of home and her mother; the cool dark quiet of churches, street corner shrines where the Sacred Heart was lit by neon bulbs and pierced by seven swords, articles of an old faith, faint outlines of a former self. . . .

The past had an ache for Alison like a phantom limb. She thought she had amputated it all, cutting away the gangrene of a messy childhood, the family confusions, the resentment of relatives, old friends and lovers who refused to understand. But this fall the past had overtaken her at odd moments, undermining any satisfaction she might have derived from the photographs in Milan, calling into question what she should do next, what she should do now.

She fought the same battle against the same instinct that urged her to give in. Or if not give in, then go back. Remain in one place and indulge in the kinds of emotions she had come to equate with weakness.

She refused to do that. If she stayed in Rome—and she knew she would—it was for the challenge. She liked to believe she was a woman to whom things happened. Her guiding principle was to gravitate to places where things were bound to happen. That was why she had first flown to Viet Nam, carrying a camera as a kind of visa.

What she had discovered there was a complex, deadly game with shifting boundaries, arbitrary rules, and multiple levels of

skill. What she liked best about the game was the one constant
—to play well, she thought, you had to put yourself on the spot.

Like everyone else, she swore she hated the war; she claimed
she was haunted by it; she told tales of atrocities so sick-making
she said she could never live in America again. But a raw
nerve in her had vibrated in response to a stronger rule. Deep
down she admitted she loved what she was doing. Otherwise,
why was she there? Why were all of them there—the soldiers
who signed up for second tours, the reporters, the camera
crews, the congressmen? And at home, why was the appetite for
pictures insatiable? Why was no American meal complete unless the evening news served up dead bodies? Of course, everybody decried what they saw. But that didn't account for why
they kept looking. The fact was, for every peacenik, Alison
knew two or three war junkies, and she was one of them.

At first, she had counted on the brute power of that inex-
plicable impulse and was convinced you couldn't fake it. Now
she knew better. The game had begun to seem fixed, the payoff
as punchless as cocaine cut with baking soda. With her last shots
of Beirut and the bank robbery in Milan, she had understood
how heavily the odds were stacked in her favor. The camera
came between her and the action. She wanted to break through
to the other side. Although she realized she might be mixing her
personal and professional motives, she believed David Rayborne had information that could take her where she needed
to go.

Hiking to Stephane's apartment, he thought of Alison Lopez—
her appearance, her aplomb, the single-mindedness that painfully recalled Darlene Spaulding. He tried to take her measure
as Bianchi might. Although she asked a lot of questions, David
didn't share Italo's suspicion that she might be CIA. She was
too direct, too impatient, and he doubted she would jeopardize
her reputation by snooping on the side. The hallmark of her
work was a cold, uncompromising eye and while she was in the
business of selling what she saw, she pursued what she, not the

Company, wanted. She was simply after a story and couldn't believe that he wouldn't help her. David was grateful she didn't know how tempted he had been.

At Stephane's, ascending in the elevator, he debated what to tell her about tonight. Like Alison Lopez, she would be brimming with questions; most of her social life consisted of his secondhand accounts. Since she was sick of Rome and apt to magnify its dangers, he was reluctant to mention the robbery. And there was nothing he felt safe in saying about Alison. By now he had hidden so much from Stephane—he had never told her about Darlene Spaulding—their lives reminded him of Aldo Moro's geometrically impossible definition of the "historic compromise"; theirs was a relationship of "parallel convergences."

He decided to describe de la Chasse being shoved into the swimming pool. He'd narrate it like a newspaper story, long on drama, short on analysis, a humorous anecdote without motive. It would delight her to imagine the fat editor floundering in deep water.

But then Stephane opened the door, her eyes swollen and red-rimmed.

"What's the matter?" he asked.

"Everything." She led him to the living room and sagged onto the sofa. "My lawyer called. I've been in court." She skinned her hair back from the angular bones of her face, then let it fall to her shoulders. "Then I came home and have been arguing with Lena ever since."

He reached for her hand. The palm was rough from work. "Calm down. Tell me what happened."

She sucked in a ragged breath. "Lucio's demanding custody of Marc. He filed some sort of paper. My lawyer asked the magistrate for an immediate hearing so we could reply."

"I don't get it. Why now? On what grounds?"

"He claims I'm not providing a moral environment because you sometimes spend the night here and that's a bad influence on Marc. I suppose he thinks it's better for his son to watch him beating me."

"Christ, I should have been careful. I should have known."

"I have the right"—her voice broke—"to have a man in my house. I don't object to his women."

"How did he find out?"

"Lena. She denies it, but she's lying. I fired her. Probably she'll take me to court too, but I won't have her spying on me."

"Can't anything be done in this country without a goddamn lawsuit?"

"Nothing. Not a thing. I think for Italians a legal process is entertainment, something elaborate and full of ritual like opera or Midnight Mass at St. Peter's. You should have seen the courtroom today. It's as bad as the post office. Everybody crowds around the magistrate and screams, and the person who yells loudest gets heard first."

"I'm sorry, baby." He put his arms around her and kissed the pink shell of her ear.

"It's all right." She amended that to, "It'll be all right. My lawyer promises me Lucio won't win. No Italian judge would take a child away from his mother. But it'll be long and ugly, and without Lena, it'll be hard to keep up with my translating jobs and the housework and these court hearings."

"You'd better hire somebody else."

"No, I'd rather be alone for a while." She forced a smile. "I don't mean to complain so much. I'm tired. I'll be fine after I've had some sleep."

"Of course."

"There was one funny thing today," she said. "My lawyer asked the magistrate if he realized Lucio had been beating me systematically the whole time we were married. The magistrate acted shocked. 'This is very grave,' he said. 'I knew there had been beatings. I assumed they were spontaneous.' My lawyer said, 'They both cause pain.' But the magistrate shook his head and made a special note about the new seriousness of the offense."

"Anything systematic must be a rare crime in Italy," David said, and Stephane laughed.

"The trouble is, for a while, just until the custody is settled, I think you'd better not spend the night. My lawyer warned that might go against me."

"I understand."

"This doesn't mean we can't make love. When I'm not so upset, I want to be with you. It's just that now . . ."

"I understand."

Although it was late and he had work to do, he walked home, hoping that that would lift his spirits. He didn't blame Stephane for feeling low. Women like her, divorced foreigners with children, were Palestinians in this country. They lived on sufferance, perpetually dependent on the whims of other people.

And to love a Palestinian? Did that ensure nothing but *lotta continua?* Constant struggle? No, don't start the self-pity, he thought; you knew what you were getting into. Regardless of the setbacks, no matter how many corners of his past remained sealed compartments, he was where he wanted to be.

The streets hummed with life. This late in the season, no one knew when the weather might break and chase people indoors. So it was urgent to seize the last warm hour, eat a final meal *al fresco*, enjoy an ice cream or *granita di limone*. Couples strolled hand in hand. Kids whirred by on skateboards. Young bloods cruised in their cars, radios thrumming to a disco beat.

Everybody was eating something—pizza, *suppli, gelati, cannoli,* candy. Restaurants pulsed with noise and motion. Romans might make a mess of things in a courtroom, but they could certainly choreograph a meal. As in France, eating in Italy was a religious ceremony. The difference was—and David thought this sometimes explained Stephane's irritation—it was low church rather than high, more a fundamentalist revival than a solemn benediction. Each course was heralded not by a sacred hymn, but by profane outbursts of praise and blame, the clatter of dropped cutlery and plates.

He passed the Cancelleria en route to Campo dei Fiori, which smelled of fish, dying flowers, and overripe vegetables from the daily market. Trash was piled at the base of the statue of Giordano Bruno, as though he were about to be burned at the stake again. The dilapidated buildings lining the square looked like they might have collapsed if they hadn't had each other to lean on.

By contrast, Piazza Farnese appeared indestructible. Although the French Embassy with its uniformed guards and formidable walls was an austere fortress, something about its impregnability attracted teenage lovers. The more demure among them sat and kissed on the stone ledge out front. Others stretched out full-length, undaunted by dirt or gawking pedestrians.

At the Tiber, he had his choice of bridges and picked Ponte Sisto. Off to his right, the dome of St. Peter's gleamed like a bishop's miter; down below, the river ran golden-green under the lamps along the embankment. He was beginning to feel better now and thought that if a man kept his eyes open in Rome, it was possible to accept almost anything as long as he could go on living here.

In stories filed by foreign correspondents, Trastevere, David's neighborhood, was invariably referred to as one of the most dangerous in the city. "A staunchly Communist, tough, working-class enclave, seething with violence," the cliché ran. Yet by all appearances, a clutch of fashion-conscious capitalists had made deep inroads among the proletariat. In Piazza Trilussa, he passed Hippy Hairstyles and a store that advertised hand-tooled Texas cowboy boots. Farther on, there were boutiques called Twiggy and Ariel Unisex Casuals, and discount outlets specializing in scented candles, recycled jeans, and incense. If David had ever harbored any doubts that accuracy of observation in Italy required keen peripheral vision, they had vanished the first time he noticed that the local Communist Party headquarters were flanked by a posh Brazilian supper club and a pricey shop that retailed Oriental jewelry.

His apartment building on Vicolo del Cedro was the color

and shape of a wedge of cheddar cheese, its thin edge aimed at a staircase that led up to Via Garibaldi. Across the cobbled street from it, a stable offered all the joys of a barnyard right here in a residential area. He had made friends with a carriage driver, Massimo Manfredi, who lived with his wife above the horse stalls.

Near the entrance, David had left his car, a battered Fiat 850, which he used for weekend trips into the countryside. Legally, it didn't belong to him. Legally, he didn't know to whom it belonged. For over a decade, it had passed from person to person in the expatriate community, a loan between friends, a gift from a lover, the payoff for a poker debt. When it fell into his hands, he had received no title, no registration, no documents whatever.

On the rear bumper was bolted a Maine license plate that had been invalid since 1968. The front plate was a wooden plaque painted and numbered to resemble the one in back. Without a residence permit, without an owner's title, David couldn't buy Italian tags. Although the Fiat wasn't worth stealing, he had taken the precaution of displaying on the dashboard a plastic sign sold everywhere in the city. "This car is unlocked. Don't break the windows. Open the door and have a look."

In the courtyard, he pressed the time-light and trudged up a staircase whose ancient, scalloped stones and iron railings reminded him of a prison sketch by Piranesi. The hall reeked of garbage cans and cooking oil, and behind one door somebody was screaming as if in answer to the inquisition of television sets throughout the building. The ticking of the time-light urged him on, but he knew better than to hurry. It clicked off long before he reached the fifth floor.

His door had three massive locks, and he inserted the keys by touch, untumbling the bolts. The living room tapered at an acute angle to the far wall and, beyond it, the bedroom lay at the tip of the triangle. When she first saw his apartment, Stephane said it must be like living aboard ship. "Yeah, a garbage scow," David replied.

Actually, he liked the place. It was reasonably warm in winter and cool in summer, and through the hall staircase, it had access to the roof, which he used as a terrace. But what most appealed to him was that, officially, it didn't exist. The blueprint of the building identified the apartment as storage space. Throughout Rome there were rooms like these—crannies, crawl spaces, and attics that had been transformed into living quarters by the ingenious and the needy. He hadn't the vaguest notion who owned it. His dealings were with a scruffy man who appeared once a month to collect ninety thousand lire in cash. David knew better than to ask for a contract or a receipt.

When he first arrived in Italy, he had been troubled by this constant finagling and subterfuge. It seemed not just to cast him into some unfathomable legal jeopardy, but to erode his sense of self. Like those jumpy tourists he saw slapping at their pockets to make sure their cash, keys, and credit cards were safe, he had groped for a fixed point of reference. Yet this side of the grave, where was that point? Whether you went underground for political or personal reasons, you had to depend on your wits and take your chances.

David did, however, have one nervous tic in common with jittery tourists. He felt compelled to check periodically on his money, squeezing into the tiny kitchen, shoving aside the refrigerator, and lifting a loose floor tile. In a hollowed-out space, he had hidden his passport and more than six thousand dollars, the balance of his book advance. He didn't open a bank account for fear of leaving a paper trail; to sign your name once was to risk having the police demand other documents.

Besides, with so much cash on hand, he believed he had more room to maneuver. If things threatened to cave in on him, he could buy a plane ticket out of Italy. He had no intention ever again of being the one left behind to sift the rubble.

In the bedroom, he switched on a gooseneck lamp and settled at the desk which he had fashioned with a door and two file cabinets. His transistor was tuned to Radio Onda Rossa, an underground station that prided itself on broadcasting "war bulletins" about "proletarian raids" and "fascist reactionary violence." Although the disc jockeys professed to revile everything about America, they embraced its pop culture with no qualms. Amid their anticapitalist, anti-imperialist diatribes and celebrations of terrorist attacks, they played records that had been hits in the U.S. during the sixties. Just as it had in college when David was plugging away at dull courses to finish his degree, the music distracted him precisely enough to prevent him from asking too many questions about what he was doing.

Opening the spiral notebook, he reviewed what he had written in the last few weeks—or rather, what he had paraphrased from the Bible of the Red Brigades, "The Resolution on Strategic Direction." The document contained long pages of practical tips for surviving underground, and he had cribbed from it as he recreated a typical guerrilla cell.

The *brigatisti* were clean-shaven, well groomed, well dressed, polite and soft-spoken with outsiders. The group I infiltrated had rented an apartment in a middle-class neighborhood in Monte Mario, and they were fastidious housekeepers. They paid their bills promptly and in cash so as not to leave a paper trail; they treated their neighbors with respect; they kept regular hours, rising early each morning, rushing out as if to jobs, returning for meals, getting to bed by midnight.

Yet despite this display of domesticity, they were battle-hardened and vigilant. Required to carry sidearms at all times, they maintained an arsenal of guns, grenades, and high explosives in their apartment. They also kept large caches of medical supplies, bulletproof vests, police and military uniforms, forged IDs, walkie-talkies, gas masks, stolen license plates, and short-wave radios tuned to police frequencies.

Men and women mixed freely and were to all appearances equal. But sex, like every other aspect of their lives, was monitored by the Strategic Command. Before they began sleeping together, *brigatisti* were expected to discuss "the modality of these relationships with their column superior."

This revelation had given David a long pause, both because it contradicted what he had learned about Darlene and because he believed his publisher would be disappointed that there were no orgies in the *covo*. These *brigatisti* sounded as ascetic as he was likely to be during Stephane's custody battle with Lucio. Shave my beard and give me a gun, he thought, and I'd fit right into the Red Brigades. Outwardly, a man of moderation leading a stolid bourgeois life, yet secretly plotting deep into the night. . . .

Uncapping a Bic ballpoint, he wrote:

By birth, religion, and upbringing, Stephane Von Essen didn't figure to turn to terrorism. She was born into a wealthy family with noble ancestors. Her father was a manufacturer of printing equipment. Her mother raised her to be a devout Catholic, an obedient daughter, and a good German. When they sent her to the university in Munich it was less in the expectation that she would receive an education than that she would meet and marry a man from a family like her own—or, they hoped, one much more prominent.

Instead, she fell in among student radicals who encouraged her to ask her father for a printing press, with which they intended to run off reams of propaganda. When he refused, she dropped her courses and joined the Red Army Fraction. With the Baader-Meinhof gang, she made a bombing raid on a U.S. Army depot, then went underground for months of guerrilla training in South Yemen. She returned to Germany to participate in the kidnapping and execution of Hanns-Martin Schleyer. When I met her, she had just crossed the Italian border with a forged passport and traveled to Rome to rendezvous with the Red Brigades for a joint operation.

Her contact was Pierre de la Chasse, who worked aboveground. As editor of an English language newspaper once financed by the CIA, he enjoyed perfect cover. Far from being suspected of radical sympathies, he was excoriated by the Italian Left. Yet his position allowed him access to information which would be crucial to the success of the operation.

David couldn't help recalling how de la Chasse had constructed his bogus Roman palazzo, for he was compiling his book in much the same manner. Once he had collected the building blocks of the story, dragging them into place from disparate sources, he "discovered and reassembled" them.

There were other ironies. Although he believed the dangers in Italy had been overstated, here he was making the country sound as tumultuous as a banana republic. He detested those journalists who bestowed upon the Red Brigades the status of a national liberation army; now he was their accomplice.

But the greatest irony, he realized, was that after demanding anonymity for his "sources," he had given them the names of real people. It wasn't a simple failure of imagination that led him to shanghai friends and enemies into this first rough draft. It was wish fulfillment, a way of dealing at night with people who presented problems during the day. He knew he would never have a better chance to settle the score against de la Chasse—at least on paper—and for the next few months, he was likely to spend more time with Stephane Von Essen here at his desk than in her bed. These were temporary measures, of course. He meant to make changes before anybody read the manuscript.

Long after midnight, he heard the clip-clopping of hooves and the rolling thunder of carriage wheels on cobblestones. From the window in front of him he watched Massimo Manfredi negotiate the narrow length of Vicolo del Panieri. Judging by the racket, it might have been a cavalry charge, but Massimo was advancing slowly, yanking the reins and applying the handbrake as he approached Vicolo del Cedro. Singing to himself, to his horse, and to his sleeping neighbors, he eased the carriage around the corner and through the stable doors which his wife, Osvalda, had rushed to open.

He decided to go down and say hello. He left the notebook open on the desk.

The rough-hewn planks of the stable doors didn't quite cover the arched space in the wall. At the top, a half moon was open; at the bottom, the splintery boards stopped about two feet above the cobblestones. David had seen neighborhood kids scuttle under them.

Thick-walled and sturdy as a bunker, the stable had a vaulted ceiling and several alcoves which served as stalls. In the far wall, a tunnel led to a second set of doors and Via del Panieri. This saved Massimo the trouble of backing the carriage out the same way he entered.

Osvalda and he lived upstairs in one large room which, unlike the dim earth-toned stable, gleamed with Formica, linoleum, and plastic. At the head of the bed stood a shrine to the Blessed Virgin; at the foot was a different sort of shrine—a television set with a twenty-seven-inch screen.

The horse had been unharnessed, and Massimo was currying its flanks while his wife forked hay into a trough. A fat, grinning woman, she had strapped on each stout ankle a shiny flea collar, the kind that dogs and cats wear around their necks. She had explained to David that, having despaired of ridding her home of fleas, she had devised this method of warding them off her.

Her husband seemed impervious to fleas, impervious to all petty annoyances, including his own poverty. By this hour of night he was always drunk. He swore he never drank on the job; he would not endanger the tourists he chauffeured through the traffic-choked streets of the *centro storico*. But on the ride home, he let the horse have its head and uncorked a liter of wine "to ready myself for sleep."

Spotting David, Massimo cried out, "*Ciao, professore,*" and continued talking. Tipsy and tired, he lapsed into Romano, a local dialect as unintelligible to David as Arabic. Still, there was no mistaking his friendliness. He offered wine, and David drank it straight from the bottle, then watched them work. He had often asked to help, but they refused even when he said he hailed from Virginia and felt it was time he learned about horses.

"Look and you'll learn plenty," Massimo had said. "But take care to stand clear. This bastard has the bite of a rat."

Tonight he grabbed the horse by the bridle and brought its head close as if to kiss its muzzle. The horse bared long yellow teeth. "You see," he exclaimed, "I'm good to her, but she treats me like a *cornuto con tre punti*." A cuckold with three horns.

David always enjoyed dropping by this dark, odoriferous place. He liked Massimo and Osvalda, admired their good humor in the face of hardships that far exceeded his own, and believed he had discovered in them that rarest of rare quarries, one that foreigners sought as avidly as they did pheasant or wild boar—a brace of real Romans. He didn't want to romanticize them; he wished he could help them. But all he could do was remember what he had observed of their lives and recall the colorful expressions with which Massimo flavored his conversation.

Wishing them *"Buona notte,"* he climbed the stairs to his apartment, turning a phrase in his mind—*cornuto con tre punti*—and thinking about Darlene. All day, he had been thinking about her. Or trying not to. Now Massimo had summed it up. A cuckold with three horns, that was what David had been. Not merely deceived, but self-deluded.

At his desk, he let the shameful, self-lacerating questions overwhelm him. Had anything he did or said touched her? Leaving love aside, had even the sex been a lie? For her was it only another aspect of ideological activity?

It required an act of the will to stop and pick up his pen.

Massimo Manfredi is a carriage driver, like his father and his grandfather before him. Although he has the complexion of a hard drinker and, at times, the temperament of a mud dauber, the two aren't related. He is never a mean drunk.

When soused he becomes sweet and melancholy, and sings the songs he learned as a child. But when sober he remembers all that has gone wrong in his life, all that has left him venomous and ripe for violence.

He has long considered himself a Communist and, although an uneducated man, he thought he understood the Party line. Eventually, the PCI would seize power and throw out the Christian Democrats. Eventually, the capitalists in their cretinous greed would sell the Communists the rope with which to hang them. During rallies Massimo always waited for some speaker to paint that pretty picture of a fat capitalist dancing in a noose of his own design.

But then the Party line changed just when it appeared its prophecy was about to be fulfilled. With the government, the church, and the economy in shambles, the PCI could have yanked the trapdoor out from under the Christian Democrats. But no! Incredibly, they had let the enemy tiptoe down from the scaffold. Tricked and manipulated by Aldo Moro, they had chosen to prop up the Christian Democrats!

Massimo still considers himself a Communist, a true one, not a political opportunist. Through students in his quarter, he has become a recruit in a terrorist cell. He is not afraid to kill a carabiniere, but the students have asked him to continue as a carriage driver. He delivers messages and carries weapons, explosives, and important passengers.

When he first met Stephane Von Essen he guessed by her accent that she was German, and it buoyed his confidence to think his group had such allies. Germans got things done.

Although he hasn't been told the reason for the arrival of the people he has picked up in the last few days, he has gathered that they are in Rome to make plans to free a *pezzo grosso*, a big shot. Massimo figures that must mean Renato Curcio, the Red Brigades founder who has been imprisoned for nearly two years.

CHAPTER VIII

IN THE EVENING after work when David stopped to see Stephane, they seldom spoke about it, but both assumed that in some dusty, paper-littered office Lucio's petition to gain custody of Marc ground on and on, like one earth plate pressing inexorably against another. There was no sense asking for interim reports. Progress was too slow, too infinitesimal, to calibrate. Nothing could be done, little of significance could be said, until the land buckled and a crevasse opened.

They also assumed they were being watched—if not by Lucio himself, then by somebody he had hired—and if David stayed the night, Stephane would be hauled into court and forced to relinquish her son. David felt their lives were controlled by unseen presences, by a legal system no one pretended to understand, and by obscure institutions as chambered and complex as a nautilus.

After Lena left, Stephane tried to arrange her translating

assignments so that she could pick up Marc after school, then
do the shopping, cleaning, and cooking. In another country this
might have been manageable, but in Italy the mechanics of daily
life taxed the muscles and will to the breaking point. Each
day there were new strikes interrupting essential services.
Demonstrators blocked off the streets downtown, and the bus
drivers walked off in protest. Right-wingers shot a student, and
left-wingers demanded that shops be closed in mourning. Every
political event offered Romans another excuse to stop working.

Even under what passed as normal conditions, something
as simple as cashing a check or mailing a package could devour
an entire morning. Forms had to be filled out in triplicate, there
was the perpetual shortage of change, and while customers
clogged the aisles shouting for attention, the clerks and tellers
performed in hallucinatory slow motion some ballet of aimless-
ness which would exhaust the patience of a Buddhist monk.

Inevitably Stephane escaped the post office or bank just as all
the shops closed for lunch, and when they reopened, Marc returned from school. Dragging him with her, bribing his cooperation with candy and ice cream—and cursing herself for spoiling
him—she hiked from bread store to meat stall to vegetable
stand, buying their dinner.

By the time David arrived, her face was pale with strain and
fatigue. After he bathed Marc and she read him a bedtime story,
they had a glass of wine and a bowl of soup or a salad, something quick that dirtied no more dishes than absolutely necessary. Then, less and less often, they made love.

In bed, he sensed the tension augmenting inside her, the
buried earthquake of her emotions. When it ended with her
pulling back as if in pain, she assured him, "It's not your fault.
It's just that my body is all mixed up." But he began to suspect
otherwise.

Eventually it seemed better not to make another futile attempt, better not to coax her to the brink, then watch her fall
away, frustrated, sometimes in tears. He told himself he was
being reasonable; there were other ways of showing love. Still,

he wondered whether the fault wasn't his. Would a man with more tenderness, more competence, have satisfied her?

It was a question that, in slightly different forms, had gnawed him after Darlene's death. Would a more perceptive man have guessed what she was up to? Would a better lover have succeeded in turning her away from a dead end?

He recoiled from these questions. They weren't just a lash to his pride. They threatened the plans he had for their lives. Although he had mentioned nothing to Stephane that could be construed as a commitment, he wasn't cutting corners just to stay in Rome. He wanted things to work out for them.

The weather remained mild well into December, and on days after the sirocco had blown, David watched housewives reenact the familiar rituals of summer—watering down the cobblestones in front of their buildings, walloping the grit of the Sahara from carpets they hung over their windowsills. One wine-scented afternoon, when a few fleecy clouds had coalesced against a tall autumn sky, he had a date to play tennis with the director of the American Academy. Leaving the office early, he hurried home, changed into cut-off Levi's and a sweat shirt with an orange armadillo stenciled across the chest—a gift from the Texans—and jogged up the Janiculum Hill.

On Via Angelo Masina, a team of gardeners was trimming shrubbery, slashing away with blades attached to long bamboo poles, sculpting hedges into oblongs, ovals, and obelisks. From the shredded leaves on the sidewalk, there rose a false promise of spring, of foliage oozing to life again.

He waved to the *portiere* at the Academy gate and went up the stairs, past the fountain in the courtyard. Spider plants in baskets dangled from arches of the portico; shards of marble bearing Latin inscriptions were embedded in the pumpkin-colored walls. In the *salone* someone played the piano—a piece by Vivaldi, a quiet counterpoint to the splashing water.

Waiting for his partner, he wet down the clay and cleaned the cracked plastic lines. The court, in terrible condition, needed to be resurfaced. After baking all summer, the pulverized brick had turned the consistency of talcum powder, and the faintest breeze sent dust devils dancing along the service lines.

Still, he liked playing at the American Academy. Set in a copse of umbrian pines, the court had a backdrop of ivy at one end and the Aurelian wall at the other. The light was apple-green at this hour, and sometimes David became so engrossed in the sweeping progress of shadows across the red clay, he lost track of the score.

He had been good enough at tennis to win a scholarship to the university. But after his sophomore year, he quit the team, having discovered that he didn't care for the clear-cut emotions brought on by losing, or the more complicated ones that went with winning. He especially didn't like to regard the guy on the other side of the net as an enemy. This was back in the sixties when competitiveness had fallen into low esteem.

It wasn't until he settled in Rome that he started playing again, and then, on slow courts, it was like learning a new sport. He enjoyed the running, the long rallies, the premium on strategy and steadiness. He claimed he didn't care whether he won. Still, he seldom let himself lose. This was after he had fallen in love with the city and with Stephane and realized how tireless, how tenacious, he would have to be.

Alison Lopez strode out of the Academy wearing a purple velour warm-up suit, carrying a canvas shoulder bag and two fiberglass Prince racquets. Her hair had been braided and pinned up in back, and she had a headband holding it in place. "The director couldn't make it," she said. "I'm filling in—if you don't mind."

"Lucky me." David's voice was as thick with sarcasm as hers.

"No luck. I went to a lot of trouble to arrange this. Bianchi told me you're a terrific player. I want to see for myself."

"Glad to get a chance to prove Italo right."

She stepped over to the fence and did a series of stretching exercises. Clinging to the chain-link, she lifted her long legs, bending to touch her head to her knees. Everything about her seemed supple, relaxed—everything except her face, that is. Her jaw was set, her front teeth had worn a groove in her lower lip.

Once she had loosened up, she opened a new can of balls and hit him a forehand with a lot of whip to it. Her backhand was basically a chop, but it had deceptive pace.

"Ready whenever you are." She removed her warm-up pants. Her legs had a nicely muscled flex, but David noticed tender-looking hollows behind her knees and the paler flesh of her inner thighs. "You serve," she said. "I want to break to a lead right away."

As he hit a few half-speed practices, Alison blocked the balls at her feet and caught them in her free hand. On his first good serve, she slapped a return to his backhand and rushed the net. Surprised, he hit wide. She laughed and stuck out her tongue. "Come on. Show me something," she shouted.

He served to her backhand. She chipped a low return and rushed the net again. Unable to find his touch, he hit a few more wild passing shots, each punctuated by a taunt from Alison.

After he dropped serve, David paused at the bench to dry his racquet handle. She took off her jacket, then removed her gold wristwatch and laid it on her spare racquet. "I think you're coasting," she said, her breasts rising and falling under a tight tank top. "Just toying with me because I'm a woman."

"You're merciless. I'm doing the best I can."

"You'll have to do better or I'm going to beat you."

He was tempted to rush the net and sweep the set 6–1. But he stayed on the base line, trying to make it amusing.

That was a mistake. Alison could serve and volley. She hit a flat, wide ball and moved in behind it. Her shots weren't overpowering, but the sheer audacity of her tactics put her ahead 2–0.

"You ought to be ashamed," she said.

"I am."

He served an ace to open the third game, then hit two clean winners. Then Alison got a bad bounce and grumbled, "Shit shot." She wasn't really angry. She wanted to needle him, wanted him to play hard. But as his feel for the ball improved, he fell into the game he preferred, any hint of aggression concealed. Alternating top-spin and backspin, drop shots and lobs, he chased her around the court and at times took such joy in jerking her back and forth, he lost the point. He didn't, however, lose another game.

Afterward, as they sat on the bench and Alison caught her breath, he praised her speed, her agility and fighting spirit. It was his way of apologizing for the pleasure he got from beating her.

"Bianchi was right. You're not half bad." She smiled, slipping off the headband and shaking out her damp hair. "But I demand a rematch on a hard court, if I can find one in Rome." She snapped the Rolex onto her wrist and pulled on her warm-up pants.

Ever since she showed up, he had been on guard, and her friendly razzing didn't reduce his wariness. It was too close to flirtation, too full of reminders of Darlene. "You staying at the Academy now?" he asked.

"I'm still at the Palazzo Vertecchi."

He stood up. "Call me if you find what you're looking for."

"What's that?"

"A hard court."

"Oh yeah. Where are you headed?" The weight of her full attention was like one of her tennis strokes—flat, penetrating, impatient.

"Down the hill."

"I'll give you a lift." She was stuffing things into her shoulder bag. "I've been in the library reading your interviews. They're first-rate."

It wasn't her flattery that convinced him to accept a ride. He wanted to find out what she was after.

The esplanade around Fontanone dell'Acqua Paola was crowded. Tourists, clutching purses and cameras and ice cream cones, climbed the Janiculum Hill to admire the foun-

tain, which with its gargoyles spouting water and its towering
Corinthian columns was hailed by the guidebooks as "the baroque at its most serene and loving." Then they turned and gazed
down at Rome, which glowed rosily in the fading light. A landscape of cupolas, arches, and red brick ruins, the city stretched
toward the Alban hills like one vast lesson from an architecture
manual.

Oblivious to the view, Italo Bianchi sat alone in a Mini
Cooper, gripping the steering wheel with callused palms, doing
isometric contractions to relieve his tension. He had his eyes
on a grey BMW parked on Via Giacomo Medici. Afraid his
Alfa Romeo would give him away, he had borrowed the Mini
from a student, followed Alison Lopez to the American Academy, and seen her meet David. Then, after long hesitation, he
had called his contact.

"I don't know the American Academy," Giovanni had said.
"Is it guarded?"

"There's a *portiere*."

"Could our friends reach her and get away?"

"Reach her?"

"Lay hands on her."

"She's playing tennis."

"With whom?"

"A man. I thought you said it was too risky to grab an
American."

"We're not going to grab her. You remember the three methods of flushing a mole out of hiding?"

The answer came to mind like a response from catechism
class: Make the mole feel safe. Offer some irresistible inducement. Scare him.

"We're going to employ the third method," Giovanni said.
"When moles are scared, they make mistakes. They leave their
holes. They contact their superiors."

"The American Academy is the wrong place for that. There'd
be witnesses. And there's the man she's with."

"Call me when they're in the right place."

"You don't expect me to scare her?"

"No, Scarpe. You sound scared yourself."

Italo was more heartsick and soul-weary than scared. Once again he was faced with the prospect of putting a friend in the rough hands of his political allies. As he saw it, he had no choice.

As she parked at the staircase leading from Via Garibaldi down to Trastevere, Alison said, "That profile of Graham Greene, that's the best piece you've done. But I wish you'd asked more about Saigon. When I was living in his apartment, I wondered whether the first chapter of *The Quiet American*—"

"Greene didn't have an apartment in Saigon."

"What?"

"Greene never lived in an apartment in Saigon."

"Like hell he didn't. I rented the place. Cost me a bundle. Every journalist in the city wanted it."

"That's what you said that night at de la Chasse's. But Greene told me he stayed in hotels. He thinks it's funny how many writers claim to have rented his apartment—each one putting it in a different part of Saigon."

As she stared at him, the skin drew tight across the broad bones of her face, her crooked front teeth clamped down on her lip, and for the first time, he could believe she had Hispanic blood. Her high cheekbones and green eyes reminded him of an Aztec mask. Pawing in her shoulder bag, she brought out a tube of Blistex, applied a dab of it to her chapped lips. The car filled with a medicinal scent.

"I'll be goddamned," she said. "The landlord swore Graham Greene had lived there. Guess I've been had."

"Hope the place had something else going for it."

She capped the Blistex and dropped it into her bag. They both paused a beat, then another, and during the silence he decided Alison wasn't entirely displeased to be confronted by an embarrassing truth. Just as on the tennis court, it seemed to matter more to her to try to force him to play her game, to transform every encounter into a blood sport. He preferred to put things on an easier footing.

"Like a beer?" he asked.

"Sure."

They locked the BMW, stowed their tennis equipment in the trunk, and locked it too.

"Now watch, somebody'll steal the whole damn car," Alison said, starting down the stairs.

"They might."

"Doesn't matter. It's rented."

"Ever hear about the German dentists who had their cars ripped off in Milan?"

"Jesus, how many times do I have to listen to that story?"

David laughed. "I never claimed my material was original."

The crumbling staircase smelled of urine and burnt sugar, and the brick walls on either side were scorched black. Needles and syringes spiked the ashes heaped up in the corners. On the bottom step, three teenagers, two boys and a girl with the angelic air of a Botticelli madonna, huddled around a pile of burning twigs, heating something in a spoon.

The girl rolled back her sleeve and tied off with a belt that she yanked tight with her teeth. The veins in her arm jumped up. She probed the pasty flesh on the inside of her elbow, found the vein she wanted, and jabbed in the needle. Almost at once, she swiveled her head and vomited. The two boys continued cooking.

Alison stopped dead. David took her elbow. "Just keep going."

"Jesus Christ, did you see that?" Walking backward, she watched the boys shoot up. She didn't sound dismayed so much as excited. "Aren't they scared of cops?"

"They've decriminalized personal possession. First time I saw a kid mainlining, it floored me. I tried to talk him out of it. He pulled a knife and told me to fuck off."

"Are they there every day?"

"Somebody's always there after school."

"I'll come back tomorrow with a camera." She turned and followed him to Piazza di S. Maria in Trastevere. "You live around here?"

"Yeah." He motioned vaguely. "I think it's warm enough to sit outside."

In the square a few boys were kicking a soccer ball, banging it against the grillwork that caged the portico of the church. The rest of the crowd was listless, lifeless. A couple of maggoty characters with runny noses and filthy jeans lounged around the fountain, their bodies molded bonelessly to the marble. Others stood in scattered clumps, whispering, eyes panning the piazza. These freaks—*frichettoni*, as they referred to themselves —stared hard at Alison in her purple warm-up suit.

They took a table at the Bar di Marzio facing the gold leaf facade of the church, a gleaming mosaic of the Virgin and attendant figures. Alison soon let her eyes stray from it.

"These kids," she said, meaning the *frichettoni*, "are they political?"

"Everybody in Italy is political."

"You think any of them are terrorists?"

"No. They're junkies or dealers or hustlers. They might swipe your purse or break into your apartment and call it a political gesture. But the guys doing the kneecapping and killing, they hide out in middle-class neighborhoods. You don't see them."

She stirred impatiently in the chair. She hadn't touched her mug of beer. "You read about Rome and it sounds ready to bust loose. Then you get here and . . . and you can't find it, can't put a finger on it. Doesn't it bum you out not to connect with what's happening in this country?"

"I never have any trouble finding what I want in Italy. But then I don't feel any desire to grab a live wire."

"Come on, you're a writer. A good one. How can you not go after the big story?"

"I'm busy with other things."

"I've seen the *American News*. What you do there doesn't use half your talent."

"I've been applying most of my talent to tennis."

"Don't hide behind these wisecracks. You sound like a refugee from the sixties."

"My least favorite decade."

"I'm surprised," she said. "I thought you would have loved it."

"Ten years of phoniness. A decade-long circle jerk."

"So you're not what you look like," she said dryly. "The last hippie dropout."

"Dropout? For Chrissakes, I didn't move to Marin County. I didn't kick back and mellow out in a hot tub. I dropped *in*. I moved to Italy."

"You'd never know it from what you write."

"You haven't read everything I've written."

"Sorry. I just think you're blowing a lot of terrific opportunities."

"Look, I don't have any contacts in the Red Brigades, if that's what you're driving at."

"I think we could work together and get exactly what we both want."

He looked at her, and she looked back. Unlike Stephane with her narrow face and oblique glances, Alison stared straight at him. He imagined an economy of motion, a quick and uncomplicated response. He recognized the fantasy he was indulging and told himself nothing that easy could be worth having. But he told her, "I'll think it over."

She sipped her beer, then rolled the sleeves of her jacket and draped her left arm over the back of the chair. The gold Rolex glittered on her wrist like a lure flashing in a school of barracuda. David was about to warn her; to wear gold in Rome was to invite trouble. But he didn't care to rekindle her inflamed notions. That might bring on more questions about the Red Brigades.

Behind them, two burly men stumbled out of the bar, laughing and jostling for space as they squeezed past the wrought-iron tables. One of them tripped and blundered into Alison.

Both men made a clumsy show of groping for balance, as if to catch hold of a chair to keep from falling. But they wound up grabbing Alison's wrist.

The three of them were trapped in an awkward tangle of arms and hands, and it took David an instant to decide what they were doing—stealing her watch. Acting on impulse, he splashed beer in one guy's face and followed up with a roundhouse right that landed flush on the fellow's jaw. It sent him spinning down the aisle, knee-walking into the piazza.

With her mug Alison was flailing at the other man. David barged up behind him and tried to collar him in a hammerlock. But the man broke free just as she swung the beer mug again. It smashed against his face, slicing the cheek in a long, clean slash. At first, no blood flowed. Then a torrent of red spurted from the blue gash, and the fellow's knees turned liquid. David let him sag to the cobblestones.

Whirling around, he feared he'd see the other guy flying at him with a knife or wine bottle. But the man had scrambled to his feet and sprinted past the fountain, barreling through clumps of befuddled *frichettoni.*

"Go get him!" Alison shouted. "I'll stay with this one."

The wounded man was flat on his back. A waiter rushed over with a towel and pressed it to the cut. Blood soaked through the cloth, blossoming into an enormous, dripping rose.

"Let's get out of here." David dragged Alison with him, backing away as the crowd shouldered forward.

The man on the ground was struggling to get his alibi straight. "I was looking at her watch. I wanted to know the time."

"What are you doing?" she demanded.

"We're not waiting around." David led her past the overturned chairs and tables and across the piazza, oblivious of Italo Bianchi deep under the church portico, peering through iron bars.

"Hold on a minute. I want to get his name and why he—"

"The cops'll be here in a minute," he said.

"They'll make him talk."

"No. What they'll do is run us in." He heard a siren and quickened his pace down Vicolo del Piede.

"They were stealing my watch."

"That's your story. The fellow whose face you fucked up claims he was asking for the time."

"Bullshit." She dug in her heels.

They stopped in front of the Pasquino theater. Woody Allen gaped at them from a faded poster. Swaying overhead on wires, Virginia creeper quaked in the wind, the last spade-shaped leaves of the season fluttering like tongues.

"I'm not going to stand here and argue," he said. "You don't believe me, go back and see what happens."

"I don't speak enough Italian to explain."

"Exactly. So who are they going to listen to?" He headed toward the Tiber, his hand at the small of Alison's back, urging her on.

"You could interpret for me. Is that such a goddamn big favor to ask?"

"There's nothing to interpret. What we did is just as illegal as what you *think* they were doing."

"I was protecting myself." The street lights burst on, and beneath the taut skin of her face her cheekbones revealed their broad yellow shapes.

"In Italy they have different ideas about self-defense." When they reached the Lungotevere, he doubled back into the dim, enfolding labyrinth of streets. "The cops could charge us with assault. At best, they'd hold us until they had the story straight. I don't know about you, but I can't afford to spend a couple of weeks in jail."

Everything he said was more or less true. But one point, the most important to him, he didn't mention. If he returned to translate for Alison, the cops would realize he was a foreigner and might demand his papers. When they learned he was living in Rome illegally, they'd deport him—which for David would be worse than jail.

"My arm hurts like hell," she said. "I think that creep wrenched it out of the socket."

Hearing sirens again, he was anxious to get off the street. "Let's stop at my place and make sure you're all right."

"I wouldn't want to put you to any trouble."

In spite of the sarcasm, in spite of her sullenness, she went with him to the wedge-shaped building and followed him up the five flights of stairs. Once they were inside with the lights on, they saw that they had both been splattered with blood. It didn't show up so gruesomely on her purple velour jacket, but David had dry flecks of it all over his sweat shirt, and the armadillo looked like its throat had been slit.

"I could use a stiff Scotch on the rocks," she said.

"There's Scotch, but no rocks."

"I'll take it straight." She glanced at the shabby living room and, beyond it, the triangular space that contained his desk and bed. As he poured her a few fingers of whiskey, she unzipped the jacket, baring her lean brown shoulders. "You think it's dislocated?"

He put a hand there. Her skin was warm, smooth, small-pored. He massaged the sorest spot, the heart-shaped curve of her deltoid muscle. She leaned her head against his chest. At the nape of her neck the hair had curled into moist gold ringlets.

He moved his hand. "It may ache a few days. It's nothing serious."

"It helped when you were rubbing it."

"I have to change this shirt." He gave her wide berth going to the bureau, picked up a sweater, and went into the bathroom, where the warped mirror over the sink reflected a face even more perplexed than hers. He was angry—mostly at himself—for the effect her close, warm presence worked on him. She was beautiful, and he wanted her. Nothing bizarre about that. But after the incident in the piazza and her barbed remarks, after the rush of memories about Darlene, after so many failures with Stephane, he was aware of a need that exceeded desire. He wanted to prove something to Alison and himself.

No, the hell with that. He wasn't sixteen. He'd had enough of proving things.

When he stepped out of the bathroom, she wasn't in sight. His first thought, followed by no small relief, was that she had left, fed up with his fecklessness. Then he spotted her in the bedroom. Backlit by the glow of the gooseneck lamp, she stood at the desk, drink in hand. She might have been staring out the window. Or skimming a page in his spiral notebook.

He was stunned by the strength of the panic that poured through him, wave after wave. But just as quickly he regained his composure. He'd been gone no more than a minute, not enough time for her to realize what she was reading.

"So now you know," he said.

She smiled. "Yes."

"Now you know why I'm marking time at the *American News* and not doing any free-lance work. I've been tinkering with a novel."

"Is that what it is? I came in here to admire the view. The notebook was open. I couldn't resist. Tell me about it."

With a flick of a finger, he shut the notebook. "I don't mind talking about my articles, but I feel uncomfortable discussing a piece of fiction I'm nowhere near finishing."

"I'd love to read it."

Although uneasy under her sharp scrutiny, he refused to shift his eyes from hers. "Guess I'm not sure I can bring it off. I don't want anybody reading it until I'm satisfied with it."

"When will that be?" Alison sipped at her Scotch.

"Hard to say. I may never get it the way I want it. Meanwhile, I'd appreciate it if you didn't mention it to anybody. You know the wisecracks people make about closet novelists."

"Yeah. Just the kind you make when I ask about the Red Brigades. But what an attractive combination," she mused. "A man with a top-spin forehand and an artistic sensibility." She set her glass on the desk and advanced a step, slipping her arms around his waist. When she went to kiss him, he turned away.

"I'm involved with somebody," he said.

"So what?"

"So I'd rather not."

"Is that right?"

"That's right."

"I'm beginning to doubt it's a novelist in that closet of yours."

"Okay, I confess. I'm gay." He led her into the living room. "Finish your drink. I'll walk you to your car."

"No need," she said. "I know my way."

After she left, he dropped the notebook into the bottom drawer of one of the file cabinets that served as the foundation for his desk. Slamming the drawer shut, he shoved in the metal cylinder that locked the cabinet. To open it he had to insert a key; the cylinder would pop out like half an inch of a small-bore pistol barrel. David hid the key on the window ledge above the desk.

Bianchi waited until the police and the ambulance had gone and the crowd at the bar cleared off. He waited until he was certain someone else had called Giovanni first. He waited until he had made up his mind how much to say about David. Then he waited until he found a telephone far from Trastevere.

"Who was the man with her?" Giovanni demanded at once.

"I don't know."

"You saw what he did?"

"I told you she was with somebody. You should have waited until she was alone."

"You didn't recognize him?"

"It was the guy she played tennis with. That's all I know. When our friends showed up, he protected her."

"Why?"

"Maybe he's her lover. Maybe it was instinct. You're with a woman, she's attacked, you protect her. Anyway, it was she, not he, who cut our friend. I thought they were supposed to be specialists."

"Call me if you see her with that bastard again."

. . .

That night, David decided it had to be a kidnapping. For weeks, he had circled the subject, stalking it, studying it from all angles, attempting to imagine how the Red Brigades might break Renato Curcio out of jail. Last time, "Mara" Cagol and a five-man commando unit had blasted their way in and out of Casale Monteferrato prison. But he doubted the guards in Turin could be caught napping; no small team of sappers would stand a chance this time.

Although in his book the plan need not be carried out, it had to sound plausible, and the trouble was, he couldn't plot a prison break for the same reasons the Red Brigades were unlikely to pull one off. He didn't know the layout of the jail, the location of Curcio's cell, the daily routine of prisoners and guards.

Kidnapping was a different question. All that fall, he had read articles that constituted one long primer on abduction. First, there had been the Hanns-Martin Schleyer case. Then digging back through the files, he found that the Red Brigades had had ample experience in holding people for ransom.

They had snatched Ettore Amerio, a personnel director at Fiat, and imprisoned him for eight days in a small windowless room paneled with sheets of soundproofing. He had been interrogated by two men who wore hoods—"like hangmen," he said. When Fiat agreed to reconsider its layoff of workers, Amerio was released unharmed.

Then Mario Sossi, a prosecutor from Genoa, had been hurled into the back of a truck and drugged. He woke in a "people's prison" much like Ettore Amerio's. Floor padded with mats, walls and ceiling paneled with soundproofing, the room was actually a huge wooden box built inside a farmhouse.

Sossi had also been subjected to the inquisition of two hooded men who, in police parlance, "Mutt and Jeffed" him. They called to mind David's cross-examination by the FBI. While a tall, thin fellow remained unfailingly polite, a short, stocky one came on as a crude bully. "He was uncouth," Sossi reported, "and he often used the word 'prick,' even when he was not in a bad humor; he said 'prick' to show he was sincere."

After thirty-five days, the Red Brigades freed Sossi and portrayed themselves as Robin Hoods, capturing venal public figures, subjecting them to a people's tribunal, and exposing their corruption.

Just this past summer, in June 1977, they had captured an armaments manufacturer and held him for eighty days—releasing him only after Lloyds of London coughed up two million dollars in ransom insurance. Now they had the money, David reasoned, as well as the practice, to mount a more ambitious operation.

From accounts of these cases he appropriated details for his book, confident no reader would spot the seams and zippers in this Frankenstein he was fashioning out of spare parts. The kidnapping of an important public figure, the getaway in a stolen car, the victim's imprisonment in a soundproof box, the people's trial conducted by hooded inquisitors, the demand for the release of Renato Curcio—he could envision these scenes and was convinced he could dramatize whatever he saw clearly.

What he still needed to do was choose a victim and learn as much about the man's habits and his bodyguards as the Red Brigades would. He also had to invent the Grand Inquisitors, the Mutt and Jeff in hangman's hoods.

The gentle one might be Stephane Von Essen. Better yet, a composite of Stephane and Alison Lopez—a beautiful woman working to extract information by seductive means, while behind her lurked some greasy baboon, threatening to break bones. David conceived of the female character as full of high ideals, yet capable of low cunning and deception.

This suggested not just Alison, but Darlene, who had moved with a sense of unswerving purpose, always challenging him to live up to her expectations, yet never truthfully divulging what they were. Explicit about her physical desires, she had been a shroud of secrecy about her deepest feelings and beliefs, a volatile compound of unfathomable impulses. As David infused Stephane's character with some of Alison's qualities, then Darlene's, he realized he wasn't coming any closer to comprehension. That would have required an artist. He was a mere craftsman, strengthening a rope by braiding coarse strands in with finer material.

Palazzo Vertecchi rose above the Tiber. Although from her room she didn't have a view of the river, Alison felt its damp proximity and sometimes late at night heard it purling along between its deep, marble-faced banks.

She heard something like that muffled sound now as she sat at the breakfast bar in her efficiency, thumbing through a sheaf of credit card receipts that had arrived from her accountant. Still dressed for tennis, she computed how much she had spent since coming to Italy, since getting that shot in Milan. It wasn't that she feared running out of money. She could live for months on the picture of the bank guard being blown away. But it annoyed her to have gotten nothing since—and to have gotten nothing today from David. The sound she heard was the angry pulse of her blood, not the river. Having glanced briefly at his notebook, she believed Rayborne was doing a number on her.

Turning a receipt to the blank side, she paused, concentrating, trying to remember the little she had read. Around her in the stark, modern room, there was nothing to distract her; no article of her private life on display, no surface with enough texture to slow the eye. Furnished in chrome, Formica, and glass, the room resembled an air terminal. Because they carried no reminders of her past, because they were uniformly impersonal, Alison had always found such places appealing. They demanded no energy, no involvement, they didn't delay her in her transit. She liked to travel light; her bags were always half-packed, her passport in order, her credit cards up to date, her cameras, film, lenses and light meters ready. Once she had used up a city, she could discard it and move on to the next. But Rome, like Rayborne, eluded her grasp and she resented that.

On the scrap of paper she scribbled:

—Red Brigades
—Stephane something
—The carriage driver. Marcello?
—Pierre de la Chasse

On the back of a second receipt, she wrote:

—Photo of bank robbery in Milan
—Rayborne's reaction to questions about Red Brigades
—Robbery at de la Chasse's party
—Attack today in the piazza
—Rayborne's refusal to wait for the police
—Rayborne's book
—Rayborne's reaction to me

Intuiting a pattern she couldn't explain, she struggled to locate the connection. Even assuming David knew more about the Red Brigades than he admitted, the facts didn't add up. She had a hunch somebody meant to scare her away from the story. But where did Rayborne fit in? He couldn't have arranged the robbery at the party; he hadn't known she'd be there. And if he had planned the attack today, he wouldn't have defended her.

Yet after defending her, why had he run off and dragged her with him? At his apartment, why had he left the book where anyone could see it? And why, when he was obviously attracted to her, did he turn away? She didn't buy his excuse about "being involved" any more than she believed he was gay and writing a novel.

Having tracked down contacts many times in other countries, she knew it was mostly a matter of staying patient and gaining the trust of someone who could carry you a step closer to a score. She had passed the call to leftist friends in Italy, to members of the PLO she had met in Beirut, and to a few American mercenaries who did contract work in Libya. The response from every quarter had been the same; the Red Brigades were impenetrable.

This didn't entirely disappoint her. She viewed it as proof

that her instincts had been accurate. It wasn't inertia or lack of resolution or attraction to Rayborne or all the troubling reminders of Laredo that kept her in Rome. It was a determination to accomplish something that people said was impossible. If it would help carry her that crucial step closer, she was willing to risk making a fool of herself and follow David.

In the bathroom, she ran the shower and, waiting for the water to warm, stripped off her tank top and shorts. Her body bore the pale negative imprint of a bikini. One breast was slightly larger than the other—an imperfection only Alison would notice—and her nipples were inverted. When she was a teenager, her mother had advised her to rub them, to squeeze them right side out. Otherwise, she would never be able to nurse a baby. To shock and hurt her mother, she had said she wanted no babies. Now, in her mid-thirties, she wasn't so sure, and this uncertainty sometimes swept through her in a wave of weariness and general regret.

Standing under the shower's stinging spray, she scrubbed her belly and breasts, then between her legs. She knew David had been ready. So had she. The bar of soap squirted from her hand; she didn't bother picking it up. She fluttered her fingers back and forth, doing what the nuns had warned her was a violation of the temple of the Holy Ghost. She recalled their admonitions, yet continued touching herself. Far from the simplicities of Laredo, she was in Rome, where the Holy Ghost had loaned His name to high finance—Banco di Santo Spirito.

She thought of Rayborne and imagined her hands were his. But that fantasy infuriated her. She refused to accept that some girlish crush had brought her to this. She was lonely and depressed and this felt good. That was all. She would rather forgo pleasure altogether than fall into confusion about her motives.

BOOK TWO

CHAPTER I

SOMETIMES IN ROME the seasons advanced so slowly, so subtly, their changes couldn't be felt any more than could the rotation of the earth. Only the achieved effect, not the process, was palpable. One morning you woke up and finally noticed it was winter.

But this year the weather broke with all the abrupt emphasis of a slamming door and winter arrived with cold, soaking rains and high winds that stripped the trees to skeletons. When the sun reappeared, it was faint and depleted, too feeble to offer warmth, too wan to deepen the city's pastels. Dead leaves and pine needles matted the streets, temporarily hushing the traffic, and pedestrians congregated in amazement on bridges, gaping down at the flood tide of the Tiber which had crested in white-caps over the quais.

Along the river and the main thoroughfares, gangs of workers with roaring chain saws pruned the plane trees. Afterward, the bare limbs looked like hands uplifted in agony, the fingers amputated at the first knuckle. Beneath the trees, looking no less tormented by the gelid weather, street-corner whores and vendors of black market cigarettes danced from leg to leg next to bonfires they had built of twigs.

When the temperature dropped, snow fell on the Castelli Romani, and from his terrace David saw it glowing like molten gold on the hills above Frascati. One icy day, walking to work, he passed under a clothesline where, next to trousers and socks, two thin filets of veal, pale as underpants, were pinned to the wire to keep them fresh for dinner.

Because it was too wet and cold to play tennis, several days slid by before he realized he had left his racquet in the trunk of Alison's car. He went by the Palazzo Vertecchi each morning on his way to the *American News,* but he didn't stop. He preferred to buy a new racquet than to confront her cool green eyes.

Still, he thought about her, and one afternoon he flipped open *Who's Who* to her entry. It didn't surprise him that Lopez wasn't her last name. He supposed he'd never again be surprised to learn he didn't know a woman's real name. Alison's father was listed as Archie Dove of Midland, Texas. She used her mother's maiden name.

When bagpipe players from the Abruzzi appeared on the streets in sheepskin vests and slouch hats, blowing their baleful, skirling tunes, Romans regarded them as a joyous sign that Christmas was near. But to David they seemed to signal a season of mourning, and although he attempted to be cheerful around Stephane, it was difficult for either of them to pretend to be happy that December.

Lucio had demanded that Marc spend the holidays with him, and a magistrate had granted his wish. Stephane's first impulse had been to protest and she was at the point of instructing her lawyer to file papers when she got word that her father was sick. Lonely and worried, her mother wanted her home. Stephane discussed it with David and they decided to send Marc to Lucio's while she flew to France.

"That leaves you alone," she said. "What will you do?"

"I'll be fine."

"A Frenchman would never put up with this."

"Do I look like a Frenchman?" He pursed his lips and puffed out his cheeks, imitating Charles de Gaulle. "For Americans, de Gaulle was kind of what Jerry Lewis is for the French—a really serious comedian."

"I'm the one trying to be serious, David. I'm ashamed of the way I've treated you. My mother raised me to be a wife *bien bourgeoise*."

"I don't want a wife *bien bourgeoise*. I want you."

"But you don't get to spend the night here and I don't even cook your meals. I always give you quick food *à l'américain*."

"Quick food?"

"You know, like in a little shop beside a road. Hamburgers and *frites*."

"Ah, fast food! I crave it. I'll eat at Wimpy's while you're away."

David made Marc an Advent calendar, and every evening after work he brought a small present—a cap pistol, a plastic racing car, an action figure from *Star Wars*. Then together they would peel away another window on the calendar and count how many days until Santa Claus came.

One Saturday, he cranked up his rusty Fiat, and the three of them drove to a winter resort in the Abruzzi, an hour outside Rome. They couldn't afford to spend the night there or to ski. But they rented a sled and took downhill runs with Marc until their clothes stiffened with ice and their fingers turned blue.

On a clear evening, he hired Massimo to drive them in his carriage down Viale Trastevere, across Ponte Garibaldi, and into the city's historical center, past shop windows resplendent with candy, toys, and cakes. Above them, strung from street lamp to street lamp, giant stars of gold foil shivered in the wind and strands of lights blinked green and red and blue. Marc said the carriage was Santa's sleigh and he sang them carols he had learned at his American kindergarten. In his version of "Hark the Herald Angels Sing," God and cinders were reconciled.

The night before she flew to France, Stephane and Marc announced that David needed a Christmas tree for his apartment. It was to be their going-away gift. He told them not to bother, but Stephane wouldn't relent. Normally shy about asserting herself, she had attached a magnified significance to this idea, and he saw something unsettling in her eyes, a fragility of mood which prompted a rare determination.

They made an expedition of it, marching through boisterous crowds to Campo dei Fiori. They entered the square at the end that smelled of seafood and where at this season eels, Rome's traditional Christmas Eve dish, writhed in plastic basins, some of the greasy creatures the size of fingers, others as long and fat as a man's arm. Marc led the way past vegetable bins, meat stalls, and kitchen equipment to a flower stand that was aflame with poinsettia plants. There he picked out a spruce that, if laid on its side, would have filled David's triangular bedroom from wall to wall and floor to ceiling.

"Let's look for something smaller." David chose one he could set on an end table.

"No, that's not big enough," Marc protested.

"Sure it is. And we'll buy some holly."

"Don't," Stephane said. "All the holly here is fake."

He touched a clump of prickly leaves. "Feels like the real thing to me."

"Look closer."

He leaned forward as if to sniff a bouquet of flowers. Was this why Stephane had insisted they come? To play a joke on him?

"The berries," she said. "Look at the berries."

Both the leaves and berries were genuine, but they hadn't grown on the same bush. With an effort and meticulousness that were unimaginable to him, somebody had plucked each glistening red berry from one shrub, then fastened it with piano wire to a sprig of leaves from another. Not a single berry was out of place, not a centimeter of wire was visible unless one nudged aside the leaves.

Grinning, he turned to them, thinking they would laugh at his gullibility. But Stephane said, "Isn't that just like Italians? Always cheating."

"They're giving people what they want."

"If people knew it was fake, they wouldn't buy it."

"I know and I'm going to buy it."

She eyed him narrowly. "You don't mind being fooled?"

He glanced at Marc, who appeared to be as puzzled as David was.

"I don't understand why you admire everything Italian," she said.

"I admire people who make the best of what they have."

"And if they lie and cheat?"

Suddenly he wondered whether they were talking about holly. "Look," he said, "no problem. I won't buy it."

He gathered her into his arms. She tucked her head under his chin, her sleek black hair like satin against his neck.

"I'm sorry," she murmured. "I'm just sick of Italy. Sick of having to live like this."

"What's wrong?" Marc asked.

"Everything's fine." David put a hand on the boy's shoulder. "Your mother's tired from packing for her trip. And she's worried about your grandfather."

"It'll be better when I get back," she promised.

After they had eaten dinner and Marc was in bed, David confronted the usual quandary. Would Stephane rather he leave or make love? He did neither. He prolonged the dilemma, silently debating. One way or the other, he feared he'd ruin their last night together—leaving her unsatisfied if they made love, insulting her if he didn't try.

Finally he said, "You'd better get to sleep or you'll miss your flight."

They exchanged brightly wrapped packages, promising they

wouldn't open them until Christmas morning. But twenty minutes later, as he climbed the stairs to his apartment, he heard the telephone ringing. It continued ringing while he unlocked the door and crossed the living room.

"It's lovely," Stephane said.

"You broke your word."

"It's lovely," she repeated. "But it's too expensive." He had bought her a silk blouse at Beltrami's on Via Condotti.

"I wish it was more. I wish—"

"I wish you were with me now. Why did you leave?"

"To give you a chance to look at your gift."

"Have you opened yours?"

"I have infinite will power." He tore the foil off the box as he talked. It was a red Fila warm-up suit. "I refuse to yield to temptation. Nobody could make me break my word to you."

"You're a good man. I love you."

"I love you too. See you after New Year's."

Then he was alone, adrift. It had not occurred to him before that without Stephane and Marc he would feel less anchored to Rome. In the morning he walked to the office through ghostly tatters of fog, feeling ghostly himself, watching tattered and foggy winos emerge from movie houses that let them sleep on cracked plastic seats. In the afternoon, the ruins on the Palatine appeared to hang suspended in the distorting light of an aspic. After work, as he strolled the darkening streets, night roused the city rather than eased it toward sleep, and the noise came on, rising in volume, like some mechanical appliance controlled by a timer. Nobody paid attention; it was an aspect of the environment, the Muzak of the Mediterranean. On the wrong side of the glass, David went by the windows of local cafés and working men's bars where the light was brutal, the smoke deep blue, the heat nonexistent. All the drinkers were bundled up like Eskimos.

Once, rounding a corner, he thought he saw Darlene, the dead risen to life. Then he recognized Alison Lopez, her long hair sustained by her brisk forward motion. He hurried on and didn't look back. He didn't trust her or himself. Although he wanted more than a warm body beside him, he was afraid he would settle for that.

Coming out of the Vatican post office, he bumped into Italo Bianchi under the long colonnade that curved away from St. Peter's. Italo had his foot on the plinth of a column, scraping his sole. He had stepped in dog shit, supposedly a sign of good luck.

"Now you're set for the New Year," David said.

Italo was unamused. "Animals shit on our monuments. People step in it. Friends assure them that means good luck. I tell you, Italy isn't just cynical, it's uncivilized."

"Jesus, it seems all I do these days is defend the country against defamation. What are you upset about? Have a hard time in the post office? Still mad Italy lost the Davis Cup to Australia?"

He stopped scraping his shoe. "Our leaders are criminals. We are failures at everything except certain marginal activities, such as making industrial waste products palatable and selling them in liquid form labeled as wine. And you ask why I'm upset? You're hopeless, David. If Italy were worth the shit on my shoes, you wouldn't have to come here to mail your Christmas cards."

"I grant it can be inefficient."

"That's what foreigners believe." Bianchi buried his fists in the pockets of his camel's hair coat and stamped his feet as the wind howled across the piazza. "They think there's some flaw in the system. What they don't realize is the system's designed to be flawed. That keeps a lot of bureaucrats working. And it means nobody can live entirely within the law. To survive, we must break it. That leaves everybody vulnerable. Including you, my friend."

Startled by Bianchi's vehemence, David stared at him. Had he learned David didn't have working papers and a residence permit? Worse yet, had he heard about the book? No, Italo appeared to be absorbed by some private grievance and today he looked less like a decadent aristocrat than a very tired man fast approaching middle age.

Suddenly, he realized how little he knew Bianchi. Though they had been friends for years, they always met in public places—restaurants, tennis clubs, the university. Italo had stopped by his apartment once or twice; he had never been invited to Bianchi's and had no idea where he lived.

"Why don't we have Christmas dinner together," he said. "You can raise my radical consciousness."

"*Natale con tuoi, Pasqua con chi vuoi,*" he responded, and promptly translated the aphorism. "Christmas with your family, Easter with whomever you like."

"I speak the language," David said, disappointed.

"Sorry. It's something I can't get out of." He clapped David on the shoulder. "Don't become Italian," he added ambiguously and set off across the piazza, scattering pigeons.

He liked Roman churches and sometimes stopped to sit for a few minutes in a quiet spot, drenched in the smell of beeswax, incense, and wine, convinced that the closest he could come to prayer was to cease being preoccupied with himself, cease worrying about mundane matters. On Christmas Eve, David paused in a tiny, unprepossessing chapel on Via di San Gallicano. It opened through its transept onto a hospital ward, and ambulatory patients in baggy pajamas shuffled through the aisles as if this were a recreation room. Some prayed out loud; others crawled along on their knees, kissing their fingers and touching statues; still others chatted companionably among themselves.

Sitting with them, he felt less lonely and recalled a line from *Rome and a Villa* which he thought accounted for his fondness for religion in Italy: ". . . it is all physical and close; God is not up in the Gothic shadows but to be touched and smelled and fondled."

Later that night at his apartment when he phoned Stephane in

France and his parents in the States, their echoing attenuated voices were more distant, more difficult to communicate with, than God in that crowded chapel. He was seized by a desire to touch them, to be with them in a place he felt belonged to him. In the past he had assured Stephane he had no interest in moving back to America. He told her the longer he stayed away, the more he preferred to sample the crackling high voltage of his country in small doses, at one or two removes, like a piece of familiar music overheard in the street, all the more appealing because it is half-remembered, half-imagined. But now he wanted to be there. He wanted to marry Stephane and he wanted Marc with them. He missed the boy and, what's more, missed some part of himself which Marc touched, a deep-down memory of childhood which called to mind his parents and left him longing for kids of his own.

Over the holidays his fabrications about the Red Brigades acquired an eerie shimmer of reality when he read the wire service reports about a German woman named Gabriele Kröcher-Tiedemann who had been arrested in Switzerland enroute to Italy. In constant trouble since the early seventies, a member of the June 2 Movement, she was once sentenced to eight years in prison for wounding a policeman. But her comrades had kidnapped a prominent politician and demanded Gabriele's release. The German government capitulated, allowing her to fly to South Yemen with several other convicted terrorists.

After months of advanced guerrilla training, Gabriele had returned as part of a commando team, led by the legendary Carlos, that raided an OPEC meeting in Vienna. There, she shot another policeman, executing him with a bullet in the neck. But once again authorities had let her flee to the sanctuary of the Arab world.

Now Gabriele Kröcher-Tiedemann was back in Europe and back in jail for shooting two Swiss border guards. Traveling on forged Austrian papers, she had been carrying a secret report on the Hanns-Martin Schleyer kidnapping, several ordnance maps of Italy, and twenty thousand dollars in cash, part of the ransom from yet another political kidnapping. Among many coded documents, she had a sheet of paper with "Rome" written at the top and two enigmatic abbreviations—"Al. Mo."—in the text.

Police professed to be ignorant of her intentions. But David, sensing that the story had begun to pursue him now, believed he knew them. This woman was the model for his Stephane-Alison-Darlene character. Or was it the reverse?

On New Year's Eve, while his neighbors ignited fireworks and slung saucers and cups out their windows, dashing them against the cobblestones, he invented a hostile, unstable guerrilla named Lucio to serve as a foil for Stephane. Then, creating the impression he had been there in person, he scribbled notes on a heated debate among the *brigatisti*.

Stephane Von Essen dominated the discussion, stressing the need to choose a target whose kidnapping would send shock waves through the country. Since their goal was "to frighten and enlighten," as well as to free Renato Curcio, the victim had to be a man whom the government would ransom at all costs.

Lucio angrily interrupted. A kidnapping, he said, would take too much time, too many men, and there was no guarantee it would succeed. The government might refuse to negotiate.

"Not if we select the target carefully," Stephane Von Essen insisted. As for the difficulty of the operation—the time, money, manpower, and firepower—this should be regarded as an opportunity to display the Red Brigades' full range of capabilities.

Lucio claimed there was a quicker way to achieve their goals. He cited the Chinese proverb: "Kill one, frighten ten thousand."

"But we have already killed many people."

"The wrong people," according to Lucio. He claimed the country could be brought to its knees if the Red Brigades began killing tourists. "Shoot Germans, Americans, and Japanese and the whole world will notice. We could threaten to keep killing tourists, a couple every day, until Curcio was freed. Other countries will force Italy to compromise."

Stephane Von Essen objected. Everybody objected to indiscriminate violence. It was ideologically unsound and politically bankrupt. Terror had to be well targeted, murderously precise. "Nail drives out nail." That was why they had always aimed at policemen, judges, newspaper reporters, publishers, and other agents of state repression. The action Lucio proposed would alienate people, particularly the tens of thousands who depended on tourism for their livelihood.

Pierre de la Chasse suggested they kidnap Gianni Agnelli. President of Fiat International, Agnelli was a man of immense influence, and the country's most visible symbol of capitalist corruption.

Others immediately pointed out the problems. Although the Agnelli family might pay a massive ransom, Curcio's release, not money, was their goal. And the Agnellis, powerful as they were, might find it impossible to persuade the government to exchange prisoners. The Communist and Socialist parties were sure to protest any deal to save Agnelli, and the Christian Democrats would be hard put to act alone. Stephane reminded them that the German government had refused to bargain for Hanns-Martin Schleyer's life.

There was another consideration. Agnelli had the money to maintain his own security system. Some believed he was better protected than any elected official.

Because of the high risks and low probability of success, Agnelli was rejected.

"What about the pope? How many divisions does he have?" Lucio echoed Stalin's question. "Kidnap him and the government will negotiate."

While everyone granted there was a political dimension to the pope's power, there were objections to abducting him. For one thing, Paul VI was old and sick, and in his frail health he might die before the terms of his ransom could be arranged. For another thing, rather than rousing sympathy for their cause, aggression against the pope was likely to alienate Italians of every persuasion, especially members of the Red Brigades who had started off in Catholic student and worker groups.

Stephane Von Essen reemphasized that the victim had to be a political figure, a man they could subject to a people's tribunal, somebody who, in addition to serving as a bargaining chip, could provide classified information about the state's repressive apparatus.

Pierre de la Chasse mentioned Aldo Moro. President of the Christian Democratic Party, five times a prime minister, the prime mover in the proposed historic compromise between the Communists and the Christian Democrats, Moro represented everything the Red Brigades opposed. Not only did he know where all of Italy's skeletons were buried, he had gnawed the last scraps of flesh from their bones. The government would give anything to get him back and keep him from talking. Moro was a perfect symbol and, practically speaking, a perfect victim.

The vote was unanimous. They would kidnap Aldo Moro.

David glanced out the window at Massimo's stable, where the doors were flung wide and a well of orange light filled the arched opening. Sick of sitting alone at his desk, he locked the notebook in the file cabinet, grabbed a bottle of wine, and went downstairs, dodging airborne crockery and firecrackers as he crossed the street.

The horse was in its stall, head down, heedless of the racket. Equally oblivious, Massimo was sprawled in the passenger's seat of the carriage, taking long earnest pulls on a *fiasco* of wine.

"Celebrating?" David asked.

"*Ciao, professore.*" He sat up, making room beside him. "No celebrating for me. I'm just sucking on this bottle like a baby on a tit and thinking."

"Where's Osvalda?"

"Upstairs in bed."

"Thinking?"

Massimo laughed. "She sleeps as soundly as the horse. I'm the one left to do the thinking." As always, he was unshaven; his whiskers resembled the prickly, fibrous stuffing that pokes through threadbare upholstery.

"I brought a bottle to help us both think." David climbed into the carriage, and they sat staring at the cracked masonry wall and its elaborate pattern of green mold.

"We'll finish my bottle first." Massimo passed the wine. "Why aren't you out somewhere? You should be with a woman."

"I'm like you. I have a lot of thinking to do."

"When I was your age, I was always chasing some woman."

"Did you catch them?"

He laughed. "I'm ugly, but I had a lot of luck. In those days it was like I was touching my fingertips to the sky. Now . . ." He shrugged and went back to the bottle.

"Tell me what you're thinking while your neighbors are celebrating."

"I'm wondering what they have to be so happy about. Oh, I'm pleased to see this bitch of a year end. But there's another one coming. That's what the dumb bastards forget. Italians are always like that—they have to eat polenta seven times before they believe it's polenta."

"To a better year." David toasted him and returned the bottle.

"Yes, I hope so. But I think there is more chance of my horse growing tits than of my life getting better."

"What's the problem, *amico?*"

A dish shattered on the cobblestones just outside the doors. Massimo shouted an obscenity that was lost in the cacophonous night. Then he muttered, "I don't mean to sound like a fucking fascist. But these students and workers and union people, they're breaking my balls. Every time they take to the streets, it hurts my business."

"I thought you'd be on their side."

"I am, I am. I know they're poor and need jobs and have to raise hell to force the government to pay attention. But all these demonstrations, all this marching, it scares away tourists, it blocks the streets. Nobody wants to ride in a carriage when that means sitting like we are here, not moving, surrounded by hordes of *cretini* shouting political slogans."

"I'm sorry."

"No use being sorry. That's just the way it is."

"Like I said, maybe 1978 will be better."

"Yes, maybe Russia will invade." Massimo laughed. "Even Russia couldn't make order here. Italy would be their Viet Nam. We'd pull down the Big Bear like quicksand."

David opened his bottle of wine.

Massimo took a swig of it. "Thank you, *professore*. You know, we used to have a saying here. 'The right hand washes the left hand, and together they wash the face.' Now nothing makes sense. Nobody cooperates anymore. The right hand breaks the left hand and they both throw cold water in the face."

"Wish I could help."

"You have, you have," he exclaimed, clapping a huge hand on David's knee. "Your coming here has helped. Having *simpatico* company always helps."

"You mean it helps you think?"

"No. It stops the thinking and helps the digestion and the drinking."

By the time they'd finished the second bottle, the street was silent, the last dish had been dropped, the final firecrackers had exploded. As Massimo dozed off in the carriage, David fetched a horse blanket and covered his friend. Then he returned to his building, his feet rattling shards of crockery and broken glass. Massimo was right. It helped to have company. Although he had survived the holidays alone, he was relieved his solitude wouldn't last much longer.

CHAPTER II

ONE NIGHT AS ALISON LOPEZ was about to switch off the lamp, a bomb erupted, and the slats of her shutters filled with a harsh phosphorescent glare. A second explosion rocked Palazzo Vertecchi, rattling windowpanes and rusty drain pipes. Exhilarated, she threw back the covers, raced straight to the window, flung open the shutters, anxious to get her first glimpse of action in months.

A streak of flame, red as a surgical incision, arched over the city, illuminating acres of tile roofs, burnishing them the color of corrugated tin. A rocket, she thought. A ground to air—

With a deafening blast, a chrysanthemum of colors blossomed against the deep sky. Fireworks! It was after midnight, yet some fool had set off a blazing display, a Fourth of July extravaganza in January. Furious, she called down to the desk and demanded what the hell was going on. The clerk said the national soccer team had won a match. Naturally people were celebrating; naturally there was nothing he could do.

Alison returned to bed, but didn't bother switching off the lights. She was too angry to sleep. Everything about Italy defied reason; everything seemed intended to irritate her. She was sick of the country's idiosyncrasies, sick of the fattening food, sick of this hotel where the drains exuded a smell of garbage and the odd-shaped hangers in the closet left her Kamali pullovers looking like something designed for a hunchback. Although she told them not to, the maids kept unpacking her suitcases, bringing in fresh-cut flowers, feathering a tacky little nest for her.

Above all, she was sick of herself, sick of failure. For more than a month now, whenever she wasn't out of town shooting fashion layouts, she had been following up leads—every one a dead end—and following David.

It wasn't difficult tracking him on his way to work. But in the evenings, over the Christmas holidays, as she tailed him to Trastevere, the chaos had reminded her of Saigon just before the fall. Streets thronged with pedestrians; buses, cars, and motorbikes gridlocked at intersections; the air dense with excitement and smoke. Young boys lit firecrackers in the crowd and set trash barrels afire, noise and color their seasonal delights.

Once in his apartment, Rayborne seldom left except to visit a carriage driver who lived across the street. His routine varied so rarely, Alison found her suspicions growing. It seemed nobody could be such a creature of habit without considerable effort. Especially his late night visits to the stable begged for an explanation.

A few other oddities sustained her obsession long after she should have lost interest. There was no name or number on his apartment door, and in the hallway no mailbox for Rayborne. The glove compartment of his Fiat, which he left unlocked, contained no papers, nothing at all that revealed the owner's identity. The *American News* didn't list his name on the masthead and he never got a by-line. It struck her that he was going to great lengths to remain anonymous, and she meant to find out why.

.   .   .

In February, after a week of pelting rain, the weather turned mild and an overcast sky swaddled the city as if in a down quilt. On Sunday, the false spring coaxed people back into the streets, and families with groggy expressions on their pallid faces tottered along like animals that had been prematurely jolted out of hibernation. Everyone, it appeared, kept on an even keel only by carrying a furled newspaper in one hand and a beribboned box of pastry in the other.

Alison, too, felt lethargic, but made herself go out and follow David again. She knew his workday schedule; she wanted to learn his weekend routine.

He paused in a piazza to watch a teenage girl work on her forehand, walloping a tennis ball against the facade of a church. Then he shouted, "Brava!" and pushed on toward the Tiber.

Crossing Ponte Sisto, she left half the length of the bridge between them. Once, weeks ago, he had glanced back and she could have sworn he had seen her. After that, she had been more cautious. Today she wore sunglasses and had her hair tucked up under a floppy felt hat. She feigned interest in the political slogans painted on the marble embankment along the river. One motto in purple letters warned: "As long as the violence of the state is called justice, the justice of the proletariat will be called violence."

In Piazza Farnese, a crowd congregated around a man in shirt sleeves who spoke in an impassioned voice through a battery-powered microphone. Behind him several women were slapping up posters of what, at a distance, looked like mutilated corpses. More photographs of political atrocities, Alison assumed. She dared draw a little closer, thinking David might pass a message, or receive one.

Then she noticed a banner—*Anti-Vivisezione*. The posters were of chimpanzees with electrodes bolted to their exposed brains, dogs with wires plugged into their ears and noses. Still, she stayed alert. This might be his cover, the antivivisection group a front.

He walked away without speaking to anybody.

On Corso Vittorio Emmanuele a billboard seemed to mock her. An advertisement for blue jeans with the brand name of Jesus showed a woman's dimpled buttocks spilling out of denim shorts. Under the trademark, a biblical injunction: "If you love me, follow me."

In Piazza Navona, she passed from Renaissance Italy into an Arab bazaar. The East had invaded. A swarthy fellow with sensual lips glided about carrying an amplified tape recorder that broadcast chants from the Koran. European kids dressed to fit the scene in baggy Turkish trousers, embroidered cotton shirts from India, amulets from some ashram, ground-in dirt from every continent. A fire-eater was trying to attract attention, while Alison was attempting to avoid it.

Near the Fountain of the Four Rivers, she spotted something that sent a shock up her sturdy legs and brought her to a halt. David had bent down to scoop up a little boy. Then he put his arm around a woman who had straight black hair and the angular, arresting features of a Picasso portrait.

Alison stood there staring at them, her concentration so complete it widened and deepened her field of vision rather than reduced it. She became aware of a familiar face regarding her from a table outside Tre Scalini—the sociology professor, David's friend from the party, the fellow with the thin ringlets of hair and insinuating smile. She expected him to bustle over and blow her cover. But he surprised her by turning away, trying to hide.

She backtracked to the far edge of the square, waiting to see whether Bianchi would go over to David once he believed they were alone. Instead, giving her a head start, he followed Alison.

It made sense, she thought. Having caught on that she was following him, David had his friend follow her. To intimidate her? She was tempted to whirl around and confront Bianchi, but decided it was wiser to string some bait of her own.

CHAPTER III

MONDAY THE WIRE SERVICE carried a story about a riot at a rock concert in Turin. Several hundred kids had showed up late, or could not afford tickets, and so had crashed the gate. In the words of one rioter, they "liberated the concert." Then they clashed with security guards, with paying customers, and eventually with the Squadra Mobile. According to the AP, which was no doubt paraphrasing the Italian press, this was a spontaneous protest against rising prices, unemployment, and the inequities of the capitalist system.

"We can't run that," David told de la Chasse. "Not without qualification."

"Why not?"

"We just did a rock concert riot story. Remember the one in East Berlin?"

"So what?"

"So we said about that one . . ." He riffled through the files and found the clipping. " 'Western intelligence sources viewed the riot as a spontaneous protest against rising prices and the monotony and regimentation of the Communist system.' "

"So what?" With his fat, gesticulating fingers the editor managed to impart a different inflection to his repeated question.

"You can't say one week that communism causes rock concert riots, then turn around the next week and claim that capitalism does."

"Different weeks, different concerts, different countries." His fingers continued describing an arabesque in the air.

"Look . . ." He tried a new tack. "Politics has nothing to do with it. It's just kids hopped up on—"

"Run the story, David."

"What do you think causes riots at American rock concerts? The free enterprise system?"

"Lay it out on page one."

"It doesn't make sense."

"You're not paid to make sense."

As de la Chasse waddled into his office and slammed the door, David spun around, muttering furiously, and found himself face to face with Alison Lopez. His anger vanished, replaced by no small embarrassment.

Dressed in designer jeans tucked into knee-high boots and a blouse-waisted jacket of parachute silk with a green and yellow camouflage pattern, she was swatting his tennis racquet against the palm of her hand. Her crooked front teeth were poised on her lower lip—the slight asymmetry David found attractive.

"I went to turn in the BMW yesterday," she said. "I found this in the trunk."

"Show you how absentminded I am," he fumbled, "I didn't miss it for a couple of weeks. By the time I did, I figured you had left town. Nice of you to take the trouble." He tossed the racquet onto his desk. Behind him, a batch of Texans was straining to listen. Some of them must have recognized her.

She pointed to a coffeepot warming on a hot plate. "I could use a cup."

"That stuff's stronger than jet fuel. Let's go someplace where we can sit down and talk."

It wasn't just the eavesdropping Texans who made him eager to hustle her out of the office. He was ashamed of the *American News,* which looked precisely like the two-bit operation it was —about a step above a high school weekly.

In Piazza San Silvestro, the sky was bright and scoured, and a warm sun winked back from every window. It was the sort of February day when Italians start fooling themselves that winter is finished. All the outdoor cafés were full, and bees droned above the sugar bowls, as sure a sign of spring as the return of robins in the States.

It was easy to grow fed up with Rome and its blaring noise, the brutal dominion of ego, its narcissistic blindness to others. But David had only to step outside on a day like this to feel his foul mood fall away, to recognize that there was something here he loved, a spirit of place that surpassed his powers of explanation.

"Why don't we have lunch at Nino's?" Alison said.

With less than twenty dollars in his pocket, he knew no graceful escape. "Nino's is a little steep for my budget."

"My treat."

"I couldn't let you."

"Why not?"

"You'll like this other trattoria I know."

"No, I won't." She took his arm. "Loosen up. You're liberated enough to let a woman buy you a meal, aren't you?"

Between the Corso and Piazza di Spagna, the honeycomb of streets was crawling with shoppers—Japanese emblazoned with Gucci labels; Germans and Scandinavians coatless, their arms bare, believing it was suntan weather; British peering askance at a men's shop that advertised something called Harry's Tweed jackets. Italians were easily identifiable: many carried radios they had prudently removed from the dashboards of their parked cars.

The entrance to Nino's was austere, unadorned except for a

fiasco of white beans and, just inside the door, a sideboard laden with trays of salami, marinated vegetables, wheels of cheese, baskets of bread and fruit. At a nearby table, people passed around a truffle the size of a man's fist. Each one sniffed it, then shut his eyes in ecstasy as if he had snorted a rail of cocaine.

Alison called the headwaiter by name and was led to the table she wanted. But then, glancing at the menu with its predictable list of pastas, she groaned. "Let's skip the glop and get a big bloody steak and a good bottle of wine." She ordered a kilo of *bistecca alla fiorentina* for the two of them.

"Why'd you turn in the BMW?" David asked.

"Didn't make sense to keep paying rent. I've been out of town a lot."

"Where?"

"Marrakech, Gstaad, Marbella."

"I don't get it. Has war broken out between jet-set factions?"

She smiled. "I don't blame you for thinking I do nothing but look for trouble. I apologize for the way I acted when those creeps grabbed at my watch. Guess I could have gotten us both in a lot of trouble."

"Things seem to have worked out all right." The waiter brought the wine, and David filled her glass. "No cops came pounding at my door."

"I wish they had come to mine. Just for a little excitement."

"I can live without that kind of excitement."

"Oh?" She leaned closer, as if sounding him with her green eyes and finding him disappointingly shallow. Perhaps that was an overreaction on his part. Yet he thought there was something about Alison that provoked overreaction.

Pushing up the sleeves of her camouflage jacket, she exposed the tender-looking underside of her wrists. She crossed her long legs and absentmindedly scratched her thigh. "What kind of excitement do you prefer?"

"An evening at home, a comfortable chair, a good book, a glass of warm milk and a fig newton."

She laughed. "Bullshit! Are you married or something?"

"Is this a proposal?"

"It just occurred to me that's why you put up with this place. You're married and have to live here."

"You've seen my apartment. Where would I keep a wife?"

"Maybe you have a second apartment. A lot of Romans do. One for the wife, one for the mistress."

He sipped the dark, strong wine. "Don't you remember? I'm gay."

"That's right."

"What about you? Married? Ever been?"

"No. I don't like being tied down. I like to move around. The problem's deciding where to go. I may cut out for Africa. I've heard interesting reports on the rebellion in Eritrea, and that border war between Somalia and Ethiopia. Uganda's heating up too. And the Polisario's causing trouble down in the Spanish Sahara."

As she ran on with her catalog of revolt, mayhem, and insurrection, David worked on the wine, wondering where this was leading, wondering, as he had before, whether he distrusted her or himself more.

At length she paused, chewed at her lower lip, then asked, "Like to come to Africa with me?"

"What's this, Sadie Hawkins Day? I've never had so many invitations."

"I'm serious."

He looked at her. She did appear to be serious. "There's a slight complication. I have a job."

"Ask the paper to send you on assignment."

"De la Chasse wouldn't pay to send me to Frascati."

"What if I arranged for a magazine to pick up your expenses?"

"I know I'm witty and charming, and that's an asset on any expedition, but why me?"

"You speak Italian. That'd come in handy in Ethiopia. And we could play tennis."

"Oh Jesus," he said. "I see it now. If the Eritreans or Idi Amin didn't nail us first, we'd kill each other over bad line calls."

"Quit your job," she said. "We'll do a book together. I'll take the pictures. You write the text."

At her mention of a book, he thought it best to meet the subject head on. "I'd rather stay in Rome until I finish my novel."

Her gaze altered in intensity, and he assumed he had been judged and found wanting again. Then he saw what had caught her eye. The waiter had brought the *bistecca alla fiorentina*. They both fell on it like famished carnivores.

Enlivened by the wine and the bloody meat, Alison began telling him about recent assignments which all sounded like burlesques of botched connections, lost baggage, and models too blown away on pills to hold their heads straight.

"If de la Chasse thought it would cause me as much trouble as you've had," David said, "he might pay to send me to Africa after all."

"Charming guy, your editor."

"You witnessed the summit of his administrative skills this morning."

"You shouldn't be working at that rag."

He didn't care to let her leap from a general discussion of the paper to a specific critique of his non-career. "You haven't finished your meat."

"Can't. Look," she said, shoving her plate aside, "since you refuse to fly to Africa with me, will you do me a different favor?"

"I'm not going to ask Nino's for a doggie bag."

"Nothing that tacky. Remember what's-his-name? Your friend at the University of Rome?"

"Italo Bianchi?"

"Yeah. You know he asked me to stop by. He said he'd show me around and introduce me to his students. But I don't want to go there alone."

"Why not? A big girl like you, a trooper about to set off for the heart of darkness."

"I don't trust him."

"He's one of the most respected sociologists in Italy."

"Maybe so. But I'd appreciate it if you'd come with me."

"What's your interest in Bianchi?"

"None. It's the university. A lot of reporters are doing articles on it. They'll need pictures."

David was so relieved she hadn't leaned on him again about the Red Brigades, he agreed to go along. "I'll call de la Chasse and tell him I ate a bowl of bad clam sauce."

A taxi sped them up Via del Tritone, past Piazza Barberini, where the statue of Trident was boarded up because of subway construction under the square. He started to describe how the city's transportation system had been stymied for decades as workmen repeatedly ran into the midden heaps of ancient Rome. But Alison wasn't interested. "Tell me about Bianchi," she said, sitting close to David, brushing against him at the shoulder and thigh.

"Good tennis player. He'd give you fits on clay."

"What are his politics?"

"About what you'd imagine—left-wing. But he's no Party hack. He takes a pretty independent line."

"Is he married?"

"No."

"Gay?"

"Now you're confusing him with me."

As they swept by the graceful colonnades of Piazza della Repubblica, then the graceless facade of the train station, Alison lifted a Nikon from her shoulder bag and, despite the swerving and jouncing of the taxi, dextrously loaded a roll of film. The cabbie dropped them on Viale della Scienza, and they entered Città Universitaria through a set of imposing gates which funneled pedestrians through fenced-in aisles that ran past guard booths. But, as usual in Italy, the appearance of order and security came to nothing. The guard booths were empty; the fenced-in aisles spilled them onto the campus.

Unlike many European universities which consist of a warren of grimy medieval buildings crammed into some corner of urban blight, the University of Rome had palm-shaded sidewalks, grape arbors, and flower beds. Around a central fountain, students sat talking politics, their faces tilted to the sun.

"It could be UCLA," Alison said.

"Not quite." He pointed to the buildings.

Constructed in high fascist style, immense and monotonously rectangular, they aspired to grandeur, but were, at best, laughably pompous, at worst, deadening to the eye. Still, their pale pink and white walls provided blank pages for revolutionary rhetoric. Scrawled in spray paint were melodramatic calls for the people to rise and the government to fall. As she photographed these battle cries, David translated. "*La mitra è bella*, that's 'the machine gun is beautiful.' And *contropotere in tasca* means 'counterpower in the pocket.' It's slang for carrying a gun. The biggest sign says, 'Put on a ski mask, pack a gun, and take to the streets.' "

One graffito, a quote from Ignazio Silone, had a red line painted through it, but it was legible. "The Fascism of tomorrow will never say, I am Fascism. It will say, I am anti-Fascism."

At the entrance to the Sociology Department, four scruffy students in coveralls blocked the doorway and demanded that everybody who passed buy a copy of *Avanzata Proletaria*. When Alison snapped a picture of them, they covered their faces and shouted, "No photographs." She clicked off another shot and calmly kept shooting as they closed in on her. At the last second she clutched the camera to her chest and turned her back.

David stepped in and explained that they were journalists. They meant no harm. The photographer didn't understand.

"If she's in Italy, she should speak our language," one kid said. "We're not a colony."

"We're here to learn," David said.

"Buy our newspaper and you'll learn plenty."

He paid the boy for a copy.

"We don't permit photographs," they repeated.

"Fair enough." He shepherded Alison through the door. "You're just plain fearless, aren't you?"

"My motto is, if it moves, shoot it. If it keeps moving and gets mad, take more pictures and you'll get a story."

"You're also liable to get a cracked skull."

"As long as they don't break my camera." She was adjusting for indoor light.

On Bianchi's floor, the hall was almost too dark to shoot. All the electrical fixtures were disconnected; loose wires dangled from the ceiling. Students pressed close to bulletin boards, flourishing cigarette lighters to read the course schedules posted there. Others clustered around the Coke and coffee machines, bleating the city's constant cry, the country's unavailing question. *Ce l'hai spiccioli?* Do you have change?

Bianchi's office was next to the drink dispensers, and when he answered the door, David could tell he hadn't expected them. The invitation Alison mentioned must have been the one Italo issued last November. He glanced at her, then at David, then, like an actor who has remembered his cue, he flung his arms wide. "What a marvelous surprise. Come in."

He grabbed Alison's hand and kissed it. "*Sempre bella.* Are you now working for David's Nazi employer? No, I think not. You're too talented. Please sit down." He ushered them to a seminar table, pulling out a chair for her.

"I'm happy you finally decided to visit the university. Did you notice the *dantesca* architecture our late dictator bequeathed us? It's better in here, no?"

His office was furnished with a Persian carpet, an antique roll-top desk, its dark polished wood dotted with worm holes, a Savonarola chair, several Venetian masks on the wall. The shelves contained more personal memorabilia than books— tennis trophies, photographs of Bianchi climbing the Dolomites, Bianchi with Alberto Moravia, and a framed picture of fifty thousand spectators at the University of Texas Memorial Stadium, all with index and little fingers waggling the Hook 'em Horns sign. Years ago one of the Texans had clipped it from *Sports Illustrated* and awarded it to Bianchi as the Cuckold of the Year.

Sitting across from him, Alison raised the Nikon to her eye and took aim with the chilly detachment of a sniper. He froze, forcing a smile as he waited for her to shoot. Under a blue blazer, Bianchi wore a striped sport shirt unbuttoned at the collar. Just below his Adam's apple, he had etched a line with his razor and shaved everything above it. He scratched at the stubble on his throat. "Can I offer you something? Coffee?"

"I'd like to meet some of your students," Alison said from behind the camera.

"You're very lucky." He pushed back from the table. "A couple of them are preparing for an exam down the hall. I'll ask them to stop by in a minute."

After phoning from his desk, he returned to the seminar table. "They'll show you around the campus. They're much more photogenic than I am."

"You're fine," she said. "Just relax. About the university, how would you describe its mood?"

"Very unhappy."

"Is there danger of . . ."

"In the present political climate, there is constant danger." With that, he bolted from the starting blocks and delivered something like a prepared lecture. Although Italo phrased his comments with a panache that suggested spontaneity, David had brought enough reporters to this office to know that he possessed a memory bank full of quips, canned responses, and well-honed epigrams with which he avoided more questions than he answered.

But for the moment, Alison wasn't asking questions. She let him gabble on as she lowered the camera to her lap and listened with a bemused expression, her crooked front teeth nibbling at her lower lip.

In the absence of any encouragement, he charged ahead, reciting statistics that appeared in every article about the decline of Italian education. Designed during Mussolini's regime for an enrollment of 30,000, the University of Rome was now burdened with a student body of 150,000. Crowded conditions had debased the quality of instruction, caused acute shortages of equipment, undermined the value of a degree, and soured the mood of graduates, most of whom couldn't find jobs.

"It's the same everywhere in the country," Italo concluded. "Universities are preparing students for careers that don't exist. All of them are fertile grounds for frustration and violence. It isn't a coincidence that the Red Brigades were born at the University of Trento. However much one may condemn their excesses, they were the first to understand that the government regards universities as warehouses where it can park young people and keep them off the job market and, more important, off the streets."

Many newsmen, in David's experience, arrived here with knifeblades sharpened, like a convention of coroners called in to slice up a celebrated corpse. They expected resistance during the autopsy; they expected Italo to defend the country and its institutions. Instead, he expressed irreverent opinions about the body laid out before them. This confused and disarmed most journalists. But Alison's concentration was keen as a scalpel.

"What's the Communist position?"

"Do you ask because David has convinced you I am a Communist? Believe me, I have nothing except contempt for the Italian Communist Party. They have more in common with your Teamsters' Union than with true communism. They offer no solutions, no alternatives."

"Under the circumstances," she said, "what do you advise your students?"

"This is not Berkeley. I don't play the guru. I don't advise. I teach."

"But your opinions and feelings must come across in your lectures."

"I trust that ideas come across."

"What if they asked for advice? What if they asked whether you thought violence was appropriate under the circumstances?"

Italo folded his hands and held tight. David could see the white at his rough knuckles. "I don't wish to be impolite, *cara.* If you have a concrete question, I will—"

"Sure. Here's a concrete question. Are any of your students in the Red Brigades?"

Laughing, he shook his head, agitating the thin curls high on his brow. "That's not concrete. That's comic. How would I know who is in the Red Brigades when all our intelligence people, when even your CIA agents, don't know?"

Somebody knocked at the office door. Bianchi stood up, shoving back the chair with his stumpy legs. "My students. They'll enjoy meeting you and discussing their problems. Say what you will about Italians, they are seldom silent. Meanwhile, David and I will spend a few minutes together. We don't see enough of each other. For good friends, that is not as it should be."

He kissed Alison's hand and escorted her into the hall.

Shedding his blazer, Bianchi hung it over the back of a chair and plucked at the damp patches on his shirt. "Do you find it warm in here?" he asked David.

"No. But I wasn't the one on stage. Why'd you get steamed at her? I grant we should have called ahead, but you did invite her."

Although perspiration coursed down Italo's spine, he couldn't summon any moisture to his mouth. He had been seized by grave misgivings about his friend and didn't trust himself to speak yet.

From mountain climbing, he recognized this sensation of all-encompassing doubt. When you reached for a handhold that wasn't there, when you planted a foot on a ledge that crumbled, you clung tight and questioned everything—your strength, the solidity of the mountain, the physical laws of the universe. The force of your frightened breathing felt powerful enough to sweep you away. The temptation was to try some desperate leap to safety, to move quickly and compound one mistake with another. The secret was to remain motionless until you regained your grip, to act as if you had as much time as the mountain.

"*Amico mio.*" He squeezed David's shoulder and sat beside him. "Where have you been? I haven't seen you in weeks. Have you quit playing tennis?"

"I lost my racquet, then there was all that rain. Matter of fact, last time I played was with Alison Lopez."

"Oh?" Bianchi wasn't ready to talk about her. He had been trained never to move in a straight line, never to touch the sore spot until a man's attention had wandered elsewhere.

"She's not bad. Too aggressive, though. A lot of times she overplays a point."

Was David warning him? Or threatening? He studied his friend who, with his mild blue eyes and blond hair, his ruddy complexion and reddish beard, looked not much older than one of his students. "I realize I asked this before," Italo said, "but are you and *la bella bionda* lovers?"

"The answer's the same. The field's open if you're interested."

"Not at all. I'm just troubled by the company you keep. Does she always ask such questions?"

"I wouldn't know. I don't spend time around her. She told me she wanted pictures of the university. Maybe she needs background information for the captions."

"You would have thought I was on trial."

"Got on your nerves, did she? Good."

Bianchi slapped him playfully on the cheek. "Truly, David, why do American journalists all act as if they were cross-examining Richard Nixon?"

"They want to be Woodward and Bernstein. They're after a big score."

"And you?"

"Not me. Half the time I don't bother keeping score."

"But to ask if I advise my students to be violent, she must take me for a fool." He rolled his shirt sleeves. After twenty years of tennis, his right forearm was much larger than his left. "I hope you won't be insulted if I say I worry about you. To you, everything is a joke. You don't seem to believe the situation here concerns you. That could be dangerous."

"I don't follow." David regarded him closely. "What's this have to do with Alison Lopez?"

"If I were you, I'd ask myself what she's doing in Rome."

"She came for the revolution."

"But it's been more than four months and she's still here, still asking questions."

"You're paranoid, Italo. She's using Rome as her base. She's been out of town a lot on assignment. And she hasn't made any secret about what she's after. She told you the first time you met. She'd like to shoot a feature on the Red Brigades."

"You're helping her?"

"Not on your life. Not on *my* life!"

"Good. I wouldn't want to see you do something stupid."

"Look, do you know something I don't?"

"I only know in Italy it's best to be careful and not to attract attention."

"Why do you think I dress this way?" Grinning, David gestured to his work shirt and blue jeans. "It's the uniform of the proletariat. I'm blending in with the people. Comes the revolution, I'm camouflaged."

Italo smiled too. "It's obvious to everyone that you're CIA."

"Jesus, is there any American you don't suspect?"

"Only you, *amico*, only you." He tugged at David's beard. "Let's go see if Miss Lopez is finished giving my poor students the third degree."

CHAPTER IV

IN THE TAXI, on the trip back from the university, they inched down the dreary length of Via Nazionale through rush-hour traffic, past shop windows that blazed with signs of sales and discounts and total liquidations. At Piazza Venezia, David told the driver to drop him; he'd make better time walking.

Alison got out too and waited on the sidewalk, jostled to the edge of the curb by the crowd. "Going back to work?"

"It's too late. I'm going home."

"Mind if I walk with you?"

She put her arm through his as he set off past Chiesa del Gesu and the Christian Democratic headquarters. Then they crossed Via delle Botteghe Oscure, which was broad and bland and blitzed by cars. At one end of it bulked the Communist Party headquarters. For security reasons, the squat, faceless building glowed under spotlights from dusk until dawn, and remote control cameras panned the area at all hours.

They turned down Via Caetani. Alison's boot heels echoed

on the cobblestones as they entered the Jewish Ghetto. She sensed that David was uneasy and assumed it was for the same reason Bianchi had been upset; she was on to them.

"Ever occur to you," she said, "that your friend's a strange bird?"

"How's that?"

"Didn't it ever dawn on you he might be a lot more involved in things than he lets on? For a man who talks so much, he's awfully hard to pin down. What would he have to hide?"

David had been asking himself the same question. He let it hang unanswered while he pointed to the stumps of columns that erupted from the pavement on Via del Portico d'Ottavia. He said he was fascinated by those areas of Rome where some ancient buried secret burst through the surface of the modern city and reminded you that there was no end, no simple explanation to the place. Although he knew this didn't satisfy her, she asked nothing more about Italo, and he too remained silent, fearing anything he said would be seen as encouragement. He didn't care to mislead her. Or himself. Yet he did nothing to slip out of her grasp.

Once they reached the Tiber, he figured she'd head off toward Palazzo Vertecchi. But she stayed with him, letting him lead her wherever he wanted. As they passed the grey dome of the synagogue, a sudden, chill wind sluiced down the Lungotevere, the air damp near the river. At Ponte Garibaldi, he paused. "I cross here."

"I know where you live."

"There's a bus stop on the other side."

She didn't respond.

On the bridge, they caught the full brunt of the wind, and Alison's long hair waved in gold streamers. When she nuzzled close to him for warmth, he brought an arm up around her shoulder, then let it fall away, as if he had only meant to show her Isola Tiberina. The marble-faced island breasted the current like the prow of a ship; wind-driven whitecaps beat over the quais.

At Piazza Sonnino, Alison ignored the cab station and bus

stop, and glanced briefly at a newsstand which displayed pornography as though it were this week's story. Supple as mink, couples, troikas, and foursomes copulated in positions that defied gravity, but not the fevered imagination.

"Think I'll wander around for a while," she said. Then added, "It's all right. You don't have to keep me company." Still, she didn't drop her hand from his arm.

In Piazza di Santa Maria in Trastevere the wind chased plastic bags in crazy circles around the square and blew spray from the fountain onto passersby. At Sabatini's, a waiter, wearing a checkered tablecloth around his shoulders, was stacking chairs. Nobody would be eating *al fresco* tonight.

As they advanced into the complicated space of narrower and shabbier streets, David waited for some sign, some word from her. On Vicolo del Cedro, wet laundry flapped from overhead lines, cats pawed in garbage pails, the cacophony of TVs echoed off each angled wall. There was a persistent buzz and whine from metal and woodworking shops. Alison said nothing until they reached his building and he asked, "Like to come up?"

"Yes."

The hall was stone cold. Whistling up the staircase, the wind set the metal bannisters humming. They took each step in tandem. She stumbled against him, he slid his arm around her waist, the parachute silk of her jacket slippery under his palm.

He told himself, as before, that he had nothing to prove to Alison. He'd pour her a drink, chat politely, then pack her off. He thought of Stephane, he thought of Darlene, then wound up trying not to think of either.

Just inside the door, he switched on a lamp and as he swung around to lock up after them, he heard a zipper. The sound of those tiny mesh teeth unleashed a spiral of electricity along his spine. Alison was removing her jacket. Under it she wore a white T-shirt with a brand name and a pinkish tint where it stretched tight across her breasts.

She didn't move. She didn't speak. She wouldn't make up his mind for him. That irritated David. As much as anything, it was

a desire to wipe the complacency from her face that provoked
him to step forward and put his arms around her. She paused a
deliberate beat before shutting her eyes. Her chapped lips tasted
of Blistex.

He eased his hands under her T-shirt, caressing her back, her
flanks, her breasts. Following the deep groove of her backbone,
he tried to work his fingers under the waistband of her jeans;
they were too tight.

She pulled away. "You're going to have to help me with my
boots."

He led her to the bedroom. "Who helps you at Palazzo
Vertecchi? The *portiere?*"

"I don't need help unless I'm in a hurry." She sat on the
bed and extended both legs toward him, a bold inverted V.

Once her boots were off, he unzipped her jeans and helped
her pull them down too. It felt like he was peeling loose a layer
of skin. They were so snug they left the intaglio of their heavily
stitched seams on her inner thighs. When he reached for her T-
shirt, she grabbed his wrist.

"No. I don't like my breasts."

"I do." He lifted the stretched cotton, stroking her inverted
nipples. Then hooking his thumbs under the elastic band of her
panties, he drew them down the tan length of her muscled legs.
She patted the bed for him to lie beside her, but David stood
up, watching her as he took off his clothes. Then kneeling next
to her, he ran a hand along one leg, over her sparse pubic hair,
and down the other leg.

She sat up, then knelt as he was kneeling and held his cock in
her hand, moistening it between her legs, rubbing it back and
forth with slow thrusts of her pelvis. It plowed the wet furrow of
her cunt, touched her buttocks, came back. She urged him to lie
flat and straddled him, lowering herself over him with one long
smooth movement.

Suddenly he realized everything about Alison was tight—her
clothes, her skin, her sinews, her cunt, the slick tissue inside it.
Raising herself nearly free of him she straightened her legs; she

was doing the splits on top of him. With a jolt like an electric shock, he touched bone.

Sucking in her breath, she probed that spot again and again. Then she brought her legs together, cradling his head between her calves while she leaned back, bending him with her. He saw tremors flicker up and down her stomach muscles, leaping against the taut skin. She cried out once, twice, came with a drawn-out shudder, but wasn't finished.

Raising herself again, she swung around by slow degrees, using him as the spindle on which she wound the silk inside herself. When she stretched out on top of him, her back to his belly, he brought his arms up around her, one hand on her breasts, the other buried between her thighs, holding the cunt that held him. He felt her spine arch, her legs and belly tremble. When she came this time, he was with her.

CHAPTER V

ITALO SAT AT HIS DESK, staring down at his distorted reflection in the swirling grain of polished wood, his face pocked by worm holes. He knew what he had to do. Still, he needed to think; he needed to be sure he understood before he tried to make Giovanni understand. But his thoughts flew off in frightening tangents and soon he was shivering and had to roll down his shirt sleeves and put on his blazer.

Not daring to use the office telephone—it might be tapped—he crossed the campus and came out onto Viale dell'Università. Tossing in the wind, the trees were tall black flames against a darkening sky. The evening rush hour, earlier and heavier each year, had started already. In a café, Bianchi ordered a Campari and forced himself to finish it before he moved downstairs to ring his contact. Then he hurried off to another public telephone.

The wind, laced with exhaust fumes, gathered force as it

raked the streets. Dead leaves and scrolls of bark from the trees were shredded by passing cars. Leaves and bark crackled under Italo's feet as he hiked to Stazione Termini. He hated this season, the stub end of winter, and despised what he was about to do. Yet there was no chance of escaping either.

He had to tell Giovanni about David. Although he had no proof that the Lopez woman and his friend were working together, the fact was they kept popping up at improbable times and places for reasons he couldn't fathom. And when he had followed Alison, he had discovered to his bafflement that she was following David. At least she appeared to be. Seen at a distance, the three of them might have resembled a snake circling back to bite its own tail. Anxious as he was not to bring harm to David, Bianchi didn't want to be the one devoured.

The scale of the train station was vast enough to reduce most humans to the cowering insignificance of insects. But Romans were indefatigable, Italo thought, when it came to asserting themselves as the measure of all things. They had transformed this enormous, antiseptic structure into a village, with distinct neighborhoods, shopping districts, recreational areas, and slum-like clumps of alcoholics, Gypsies, and cripples. A sociologist could profitably spend a career here. But he meant to be out in three minutes.

At a bank of telephones, he stepped into a booth and stared at his watch as he dialed. The booth smelled of stale piss. How had that happened? The door had glass panels.

"*Pronto,*" the high-pitched voice responded.

"This is Scarpe. You remember the American photographer, the woman who took pictures of our friends in Milan?"

"Yes, I was about to call you."

"I've followed her in my free time, as you told me to. Well, today, she showed up at my office."

"Why?"

"She claims she's doing a feature on Italian education. She wanted pictures of the university."

"You think she's after something else?"

"I don't know. It's just . . . I've been watching her. Then suddenly she's in my office watching me through a camera."

"The reason I was going to call you, we're satisfied she's not intelligent. We got confirmation from sources in the Middle East. She's just a photographer. You can stop following her." Giovanni cut the connection before he could ask questions.

Having steeled himself to put the finger on David, Bianchi was shaken by this abrupt turnabout and felt obscurely threatened. He clung to the dead receiver, struggling to make sense of the incident in his office and the conversation with his contact. But the pieces didn't fit.

Blundering out of the phone booth, he bumped into a young man who had stationed himself next to the door. Italo murmured "*Scusi*" and started to brush past him. The fellow caught him lightly by the arm. "Are you looking for a friend?"

Confused, he couldn't say whether he had been overwhelmed by fire or ice. His guts froze, his leg muscles melted. "What?"

"Looking for a friend?"

"Are you one of our friends?"

"Of course."

"Let's move away from the phone."

He set off through the broad echoing expanse of the station, studying the man beside him. Had Giovanni sent him with a message he didn't dare deliver by telephone? Or was he a plainclothesman who had picked up a few stray code words?

He didn't look like a cop or a *brigatista*. He wore a double-breasted brown suit with baggy trousers, padded shoulders, and flapping lapels—an outfit he might have bought in a secondhand shop or costume store, the uniform of American movie gangsters of the forties, lent a contemporary touch by a pink shirt and blue silk tie. Smiling, he showed tiny yellow kernel-of-corn teeth and a glistening expanse of gum. His breath was aromatic of espresso. "I've seen you here often," he said.

"I travel a lot by train."

"Oh no." The suggestive smile again, the whiff of strong coffee. "You come to use the telephone. I've watched. I wondered when you'd notice me."

Bianchi faltered, then stopped altogether. He didn't trust himself to keep walking while juggling five different questions— how often he had made calls here, who this guy was, what he had told Giovanni, what he might have said on the phone in the past, what he would tell the police. "Well," he said, "I've noticed you now. What's on your mind?"

"I have an apartment. Let's go there."

"Safe?"

"Yes. Quiet and very clean. Friends always like it."

They set off again, jostling and elbowing their way through the crowd toward the front entrance. Italo didn't like leaving this public place. If he was to be arrested, he wanted witnesses. If the fellow was a cell operative, he wanted proof. Yet he didn't know how to get it without asking the kinds of questions which could cause him as much trouble with Giovanni as with the police. He feared giving away too much, yet felt he had no choice but to repeat the formula he had been instructed to use whenever strangers showed up at his apartment seeking a safe house. "Whose friend are you?"

The man's grin was full of dull teeth and shining gums. "Yours."

The wrong answer. Italo turned away, as if he had just remembered something. He needed a moment to find the right tone, the right face. He fought against two opposing urges—to cut and run; to grab this guy by his skinny neck and throttle him. Fear was a familiar emotion, but the ferocity of his anger caught him off guard. He was sick of dealing with disembodied voices, speaking in childish codes, cringing at shadows. He wanted to clap his callused hands on something solid and squeeze tight.

"I know another place," Italo said. "A better place. And it's close by."

"You'll like my apartment."

"My place will do."

He led him down the stairs toward the subway station, went past the ticket booths and gates, and proceeded along an empty corridor.

"Where are we going?"

"You'll see." He smiled and flung his arm around the man's shoulders. He felt frail under the padded, loose-fitting jacket.

"Not the toilet." The fellow's spine stiffened. He tried to stop, but Italo urged him on. "That's not my scene."

"What is?"

"I told you. My apartment. It's clean. We can talk."

"What if I don't like to talk?" Still smiling, Bianchi tightened his grip.

"Well, then, we'll get right down to it. I like to play rough." He smiled back.

"Is that right?" He spotted an open door. A dim bulb lit a janitor's room, a closet cluttered with mops and buckets and bottles of disinfectant. With a swift sidestep and a thrust of his hip, Italo hurled the man into the narrow space and kicked the door shut behind them. His left hand flew to the fellow's throat, fingers digging at the Adam's apple. The other hand clawed at the man's chest, his belt, his pockets, searching for a gun, a knife. There was no weapon. Pinned to the wall, he hung limp in Bianchi's huge hand, his eyes twitching in their sockets.

"What do you want?" Italo demanded.

He made a croaking, incomprehensible reply.

"What do you want?" Italo loosened his fingers to let him speak.

"Love."

"What?"

"I wanted to take you to my place and love you."

"You fucking cretin, don't lie to me." He drove a fist into his belly. The fellow tried to double over. Italo wouldn't let him. "You said you'd seen me here before."

He nodded, then, catching his breath, gasped, "I thought you were looking for friends."

"Friends?" Bianchi banged his head against the wall. "What kind of friends?"

"Like me. Look, if you're a cop, arrest me. Don't hurt me."

"You know I'm not a cop. You were listening to me on the telephone."

"I wasn't listening. I was waiting for you."

"Why? Why me?" He bounced him against the wall again.

"Every time I saw you, you looked worried. You looked lonely. I thought you wanted to be with somebody."

"With you? Are you crazy? Do I look queer?"

"You look lonely, I said."

Italo cuffed him with an open palm. "I'm not lonely, I'm not queer. If I ever see you again, I'll kill you." He knocked him sprawling among the mops and buckets of filthy water.

Then he left, slamming the door behind him, bought a ticket, dashed to the subway, and rode it as far as EUR, where he caught a cab to a bus station in the *centro storico*. Returning to the university, he transferred twice, doubling back on his traces, and once he was in his car and had sped across town to the Camilluccia district, he circled the block several times before going up to the apartment. Absorbed in these evasive tactics, driven by raw adrenaline, he avoided thinking, avoided asking whether he actually believed somebody was following him or he was just fleeing some secret aspect of himself. Ashamed of what he had done, he was even more humiliated that the man had singled him out.

His apartment, inherited from his parents, had been built during *Il Boom*, the economic explosion after the war. Full of Empire furniture, neoclassical marbles, and cloisonnerie, it had once passed for fashionable, the summit of *borghese* style. But it embarrassed Italo to live amid an expensive collection of bibelots, ormolu clocks, ivory-handled nutcrackers and letter openers, and he rejoiced whenever a Red Brigades fugitive pocketed an *objet*. He regretted that they couldn't haul away all the dark, ponderous furniture, each piece poised on claws or cloven hooves.

Since he didn't have a wife or children, he viewed this steady pilferage as a practical way to share his patrimony. Fascists dispensed largesse, creating obligations, luxuriating in a sense of superiority. But it required a different sort of man to allow himself to be robbed, one who placed little value on material possessions, even though he dressed well and drove an Alfa Romeo as part of his cover.

His bedroom was as spartan as a monk's cell—the one room that reflected what he regarded as his fundamentally austere nature. The walls were bare and bone-white. There was a chinning bar on the doorjamb, an incline bench, and a set of dumbbells. While he hadn't gone mountain climbing in more than a year, he worked out daily to maintain his upper-body strength. On either side of a single bed teetered stacks of professional journals and sociology textbooks.

Changing clothes, he spotted a black speck on the wall and, drawing nearer, was astounded to discover a scorpion. The hair on Bianchi's arms stiffened, bristling like the scorpion's barbed tail. At every turn today he had confronted some menacing shape, but this time he controlled himself. More fascinated than frightened, he fetched a toothbrush glass and trapped the scorpion alive.

Then lying in bed on his back, he gazed up at the white ceiling and walls, searching for another dark speck. He balanced the toothbrush glass on his chest; it vibrated, sending a shiver through his heart. Every few seconds, there was a mad scrabbling sound and an angry *ping! ping!* as the scorpion scuttled in a circle, snapping its stinger against a barrier it couldn't see.

He assumed the warm weather had brought it out of hiding from behind the walls or the water pipes. Wherever it came from, he figured there must be more than one. Nothing, not even a spider, could live alone.

But this thought depressed him. He lived alone; the man in the train station swore he was marked by loneliness. Maybe he was right. To his shame and exasperation, Italo felt himself sinking into a bog of self-pity, computing how long had it been since he'd had a woman. Months ago, before Christmas. The realization gave him a jolt like one he imagined he'd get from a scorpion. Perhaps it was more than loneliness that marked him.

Not that he felt any desire for a man. His worry was that he felt no desire at all. Political commitment, which he had expected to bring him closer to people, had shut him off, destroying every instinct except self-preservation. Panic had pushed him to desperation and desperation to rage. Convinced he was cornered, he might have killed that fellow. What was worse, after handing Piero over to his executioners, he had been ready to do the same to David. And for what? How could he consider sacrificing a friend for an idea? For a country that would come into being only after a revolution? For a revolution he recognized was never going to happen?

Italo blinked. He had lain there open-eyed so long, he couldn't be sure. He thought he saw on the whitewashed wall a fleck of black. Yes, a segmented tail curled and uncurled, a witch's finger beckoning.

Setting the toothbrush glass on the night table, he raised himself slowly to his knees. Then still more slowly, he stood up on the mattress. The new scorpion hadn't moved except to flex its tail. Accustomed to spiders that scurried away at the slightest threat, he admired this one for holding its ground. Did it have some dim, bug confidence in its venom?

He had read that a scorpion's sting wasn't much worse than a wasp's. He wanted to find out. Perhaps he could inoculate himself against fear the way people were said to build a tolerance for poison—dosing himself with a little at a time.

He extended a finger toward the barbed tail. Abruptly the scorpion raised its claws. Italo flinched, then furious at himself, lunged. Pain sizzled from his wrist to his elbow. He sagged down on the bed, cradling his arm. He hadn't been stung. He had hit the wall with the heel of his hand, flattening the scorpion to the whitewash. He'd have to scrape it off with a knife.

He stretched out on the bed and, switching off the lamp, heard the live scorpion scuttling at the bottom of the toothbrush glass. It sounded like the ticking of a defective clock, the timer on a terrorist's bomb. Sometimes its movement was faster than his thumping pulse, sometimes as slow and measured as his breathing. When it stopped altogether, Italo lay there listening for it to renew its futile attempt to escape an invisible cage.

CHAPTER VI

HE LAY ON HIS BACK, and she lay beside him in the crook of his arm, her cheek against his chest. He could see her head rock slightly with the systolic rhythm of his heart.

"Think you know me well enough now," David said, "to tell me about your name?"

She raised herself on an elbow and regarded him warily. "What about it?"

"Who's Alison Dove?"

"I suppose, legally, that's me."

He had his hand in her hair, rubbing a tress of it between his fingertips as a drowsy child might do with a scrap of silk. "And Lopez?"

"It's my mother's maiden name." Just as he had read in *Who's Who*. Then after her initial wariness, and without any prompting, she told him what he wanted to know, told him in a rush as if eager to set the facts straight and put them behind her, as if ever since arriving in Rome she had been waiting for this opportunity to talk about the past.

Her parents had divorced when she was a baby, and she and her mother had returned to Laredo and lived with relatives. A loud, brawling passel from both sides of the border, they spoke Spanish, were considered Mexicans by Texans, but regarded themselves as one hundred percent American. They served in the U.S. Army, rooted for the Dallas Cowboys, detested blacks, and hoped someday to have enough money to move away from the river.

Among them, Alison, who grew to be as tall as the tallest man and remained as fair as the youngest baby, looked out of place, felt out of place, and longed to set even greater distance between her and the muddy shallows of the Rio Grande. The irony was—and she had the intelligence to recognize it—by the time she was eighteen, the most effective route of escape was to embrace what she was running from and become what would make her more attractive to college admissions offices. Adopting her mother's maiden name, she won a full scholarship.

"You'd probably have gotten one anyway." He intended it both as a compliment and a signal that she needn't go on explaining.

But she weighed this carefully, candidly. "You might be right. But I wasn't taking any chances. I was looking for any edge I could get."

"Why didn't you change your name legally?"

"What if I need another edge later on? This way I can just become Alison Dove again." She paused. "Is that so terrible?"

"No. But I'm surprised you thought all this through as a kid."

"I figured I had to. I figured if I intended to do something with my life, I couldn't afford to make mistakes."

"Come on. You're bright, you work hard, you're beautiful. You were bound to do all right."

"You don't know what it's like. Those kids at the *American News*, I can understand why they keep coming to Italy. Sure, de la Chasse is screwing them around, but for some of them just getting out of Texas is the answer."

"The answer?"

"Don't say it. Don't ask what the question is."

"You remind me of a woman I . . ." He had to laugh. "A woman I never really knew. She had things all figured out. Even her name—"

She clamped a hand over his mouth. "I don't want to hear it if things didn't work out for her."

He moved her hand. "Fine. I just wouldn't want you to wind up like her." He had his fingers in her hair again, combing it. "I take it Daddy Dove is blond."

"Why assume that? There are blond Mexicans, you know."

"Is your mother blond?"

"No," she admitted. "My father is."

"Where's he?"

"West Texas. Works in the oil fields. I used to spend summers with him. Out there it's worse than Laredo."

David moved his hand down to her thighs.

"Who'd you inherit your legs from? They're wonderful."

"No. They're too heavy. I always wanted to be a dancer, a ballerina. But I'm too big. Nobody could lift me."

He squeezed the firm flesh. "I could."

"I doubt it."

"Don't ever doubt me."

"Let's see you try." She sat up.

"Not now. You wore me out."

"Sorry, but I'm beginning to doubt you." She stepped out of bed. "Prove me wrong."

He rolled onto his side. "I'd rather lie here and watch you dance."

"Not enough room." But she raised one leg and flexed it. Then she took her foot in her hand and, with a limberness that astonished David, extended the leg straight out from her hip and executed a pirouette. Through pubic hair no darker or denser than a tassel of cornsilk, he saw a swollen purse of pink flesh.

He stood up and put his hand there. "Give me the proper fulcrum and I could lift the entire planet."

"Try."

Shifting his hands to her hips, he bent his knees and hoisted her high enough for his bearded chin to nuzzle her stomach.

"That tickles." She screamed with laughter.

He laid her in bed on her back, his face still against her warm belly. The skin was smooth, moist, scented. As he slid lower, the scent was stronger. She fell quiet and strained against him, her hands linked at the nape of his neck. When he moved up on her, she raised her legs over his shoulders and let him drive deep into her, searching for that hard spot inside.

There was no talk of her returning to Palazzo Vertecchi. Braving the unheated bathroom, Alison showered, giving David time to make sure the notebook was securely locked in the file cabinet. Afterward, she crawled back into bed beside him, huddling for warmth, and soon subsided into a motionless sleep.

He remained awake, pleased by her closeness but troubled by what he had done and what he feared he would continue doing. By the time Massimo's horse came clip-clopping down Via del Panieri he was suffering the first deep stirrings of remorse and no small bafflement at the ease and abruptness with which he had cheated on Stephane.

Yet he realized this was also the first night in months when his nerves weren't jangled, and he wasn't haunted by the knowledge that he hadn't satisfied Stephane and by a fear that some failing of his would prevent him from pleasing any woman. Despite his regrets, he believed this counted for something.

CHAPTER VII

IN THE MORNING, Alison refused to get up. She said she was too tired and the apartment too cold. She didn't want breakfast or coffee. She wanted David to come back to bed and keep her warm. But he had to go to work.

"Will you be here for lunch?" she asked. "I'll sleep till then."

"Depends how busy I am. Maybe I can sneak away for half an hour."

"That's not long enough for what I have in mind."

He felt uneasy about leaving her alone in the apartment. Although the manuscript was out of her reach, he realized she might touch other secrets in his life, and he hadn't decided yet whether he wanted that. Still, there was no way to bundle her off now without an insult or a scene. "If I don't make it back by noon, leave your number and I'll call."

"That old line. I'm beginning to feel like a one-night stand getting the brush-off." She was smiling. "I may have to swipe your tennis racquet again."

He leaned down and kissed her.

At the office, proofreading the next day's edition, David tried to convince himself last night had been a lapse, a meaningless mistake. It wouldn't serve any purpose to dwell on it or to melodramatize it. But he wound up doing both.

He remembered Alison's body, the sheath of muscles in her thighs, the declivity at the small of her back lightly downed with minute gold hairs. Although it struck him as another cold-hearted act of infidelity, he couldn't help comparing her to Stephane. Alison was several years older, but hadn't had children. Her skin was taut; her limbs had a sinewy resilience. Everywhere he ran his hand, her flesh surged forward in response, unlike Stephane's, which somehow seemed to shrink at his touch.

Much as he agreed that physical attraction was mostly in the mind, for him there was always some detail of a woman's body that triggered his imagination. It might be the shape of a mouth, a birthmark, a mole. With Stephane it was her fine-boned, narrow face. Seldom was it anything specifically sexual.

But with Alison, it was her cunt—a coarse word for an organ as delicate and convoluted as an orchid. He was haunted by the smell and taste of it, the velvet texture of it against his fingers and face. When he touched her there, she appeared to accept without question that he would please her—just as she took it for granted that she could stay in his bed this morning.

Why not keep her there? At any rate keep her close to him? Not that he entertained any idea of abandoning Stephane. To the contrary, he found himself thinking this might be best for her as well. If it brought his own emotions into equilibrium, wouldn't that provide more stable ground for Stephane?

But as he reckoned the practical demands of such an arrangement, he saw it for the shabby rationalization it was. No different, no better, no more original than tens of thousands of men, he had been about to reconstruct his life according to a cliché—the basic plot of Italian farce, wherein a man kept a wife and family in one part of town while in another neighborhood he stashed his mistress, the pleasures of domesticity and sex forever divided.

He wouldn't do it. He had been an idiot and an egotist to consider it. He decided to slip away from the office during lunch on the chance that Alison might still be at the apartment. It would be easier, he realized, to avoid her and let her draw her own conclusions, but he didn't care to end things that way. He knew too well what it was like to be left without an explanation.

Long after he had gone, she lay in bed, postponing the inevitable, half hoping she had been wrong. Maybe she wouldn't find the book. Maybe it wasn't what she suspected. It might be a novel, just as he claimed. Of one thing, however, she was positive. She had to look at it. It was nothing personal, nothing against David. Regardless of what she discovered, no matter the damage it caused, she couldn't close her eyes. She had learned this about herself on battlefields, at executions, at scenes of atrocities, in Beirut when the bomb went off. It was the one unalterable principle of her life. She had to see. If she turned away, how could she force others to face the worst?

Tossing back the covers, she climbed out of bed. Under her bare feet the tile floor was a shiny mosaic of ice. Shivering, spackled with gooseflesh, she refused to rush. She pulled on her jeans and T-shirt, her boots and camouflage jacket of parachute silk. She pinned up her hair and washed her face at the kitchen sink, reluctant to go into the bathroom and be distracted while making up in the mirror. Between her legs she felt a pleasant ache. Having arrived at his place with one purpose, Alison now had a different impression of David. Whimsical and evasive in conversation, he had been direct and utterly involved when making love. He seemed to crave an intimacy that exceeded sex; he wanted to *know* her. He acted as if he already did. But she didn't allow herself to dwell on that, since his feelings and hers were liable to change after she read his book.

She checked the obvious spots and quickly discovered one file cabinet was locked. Certain he had kept the key, she considered prying open the drawers. Not yet, she decided. The apartment was so small, she could cover every inch of it in an hour. It took her half that time to locate the key on the dusty window ledge.

Carrying the spiral notebook into the living room, she sprawled on a spavined couch and began by granting David the benefit of the doubt; she tried to read it as fiction. But from the start the tone was wrong—too explanatory, too declarative— and something of fiction's shaped rhythms was missing. The dialogue, for instance, had the staccato urgency of interviews lifted from tape and only lightly edited for continuity.

After twenty pages, she recognized with a heart-clot of anger and wounded pride that it was pointless to continue the pretense. The book didn't read like a novel because it damn well wasn't one! All this winter while she had wasted time chasing them, all the while David had warned her of the impossibility of reaching the Red Brigades, he had had access to their secret documents, had visited their safe houses, recorded their tactical debates, and learned of their plan to abduct Aldo Moro.

Although she didn't question any of the facts, she did wonder when he had had time for his research. Some of it he could have accomplished before she started following him. But the last few pages dealt with recent preparations for the kidnapping, and it sounded as if David had been with the terrorists as they tailed Moro to his office each morning. When could that have been? What about his job at the *American News*?

She also had questions about the characters, his sources in the underground cell. While he claimed to have changed their names and descriptions, Pierre de la Chasse was identified. Why? The carriage driver, Massimo, resembled the seedy, disheveled man in the stable across the street. Why hadn't David made an effort to disguise him?

As for Stephane Von Essen, Alison had only once seen him with a woman. Could that dark stylish lady in Piazza Navona have been the Baader-Meinhof liaison? She had had a child with her. Part of her cover? Improbable.

One question she didn't ask was what motive the Red Brigades might have for divulging their plans. From her observations, publicity was its own reward, an advantage sought after by all. With the exception of the Khmer Rouge, every group she had known, from reactionary Phalangists in Lebanon to leftist guerrillas in Guatemala, courted attention. They needed the media to magnify their importance and their menace. She had assumed the Red Brigades must be the same. Now she was convinced of it.

It never occurred to her that she should alert the authorities or warn Moro. She believed a journalist's responsibility was to record events, not control them. After the story broke and she had her pictures, it was up to somebody else to judge who was right and who was wrong.

When David unlocked the apartment door and saw Alison on the sofa smoothing Blistex onto her lips, he couldn't at first say what he felt more—relief to find her there or doubt that he would have the willpower to break off with her. Then he noticed the notebook and his ambivalence evaporated, replaced by a single sharp emotion. He rushed across the room. "What the hell are you doing?" He ripped the book from her lap.

"It's too late. I've read it."

His face hardened. She was afraid he might hit her. She folded her arms, as if to demonstrate her resolve, but in fact to hide her shaking hands. "Where do we go from here?"

"You get the hell out of here, that's where you go."

"I don't think that's what you really want, David. You know, all I ask . . ." She reached out, touching him, "is to work with you."

"It's not what you think." He stepped back from her hand. "It's a novel. I knew you'd think it was nonfiction. That's why I didn't want you to read it."

"Don't lie. There's no point. My pictures will make it a better book."

"Lemme explain." With some reluctance, he let go of the notebook, putting it on the coffee table. Then he sat at the other end of the couch and told her how, after reading *The Day of the Jackal* and half a dozen novels like it, he had grafted the successful formula onto the Italian situation. "You just take real events and historical characters and blend them into fiction."

"Historical characters like de la Chasse?"

"No, listen to me. If you'll listen, you'll see the mistake you're making."

"Stop treating me like I'm retarded. I know what I read."

"And what you read is a plot I made up. You actually believe de la Chasse is in the Red Brigades? The son of a bitch used to work for the CIA."

"So, now he's working for the other side. With some people, it's all the same who pays them."

"That's ridiculous. I was having trouble developing characters. So I based them on people I know. Novelists do that all the time."

"You didn't *base* them. They have the same names."

"I'll change that when I rewrite. *If* I rewrite. I'm not sure it's worth revising."

"Are you asking for literary criticism?" she taunted him.

"I'm not asking anything. I'm telling you the book's fiction from start to finish."

"You haven't finished. They haven't kidnapped Moro yet. Look, David, I may not have met the Red Brigades but—"

"Neither have I."

"But I know enough to recognize facts."

"I came by those *facts* the same way you did—reading the newspaper. Then, like I said, I fleshed out the characters by basing them on real people."

"*Fleshed out!* That's a clever way to put it." She smiled a wintry smile. "Is that what I am—somebody to flesh out your book? And the woman I saw you with, is she more flesh?"

"What are you talking about?" he asked, although with a surge of dread he knew.

"Last Sunday I saw you with a woman in Piazza Navona. Who is she? Stephane Von Essen?"

"There is no Stephane Von Essen. I invented Stephane Von Essen."

"Have it your way. I'll talk to Pierre de la Chasse."

He seized her jaw and held tight, studying her face in the light let in by the window—that broad face with its jade green eyes that reminded him of an Aztec mask. Suddenly he realized how close he stood to losing his book, Stephane, his life in Rome.

"What do you want?" he asked.

"I want to work with you. You've got a valuable property. People will fuck you over if you don't protect yourself. Let me call my agent. He'll arrange it. You'll have the book rights, I'll have the photographic rights."

"You want a piece of an unpublished novel? Is that what you're saying?"

"Let go. If you won't level with me, I'm going."

"Where? To de la Chasse? What good will that do? If he was in the Red Brigades, do you think he'd admit it to you?"

"There are other ways of finding out."

"Other forms of blackmail. Other ways of ruining things for me. What we did last night, doesn't that mean anything to you?"

"What's it mean to you?" she snapped.

"It means I wouldn't hurt you."

"But you won't help me."

"I tell you, I can't."

"Fine. I'll help myself."

He squeezed her face so hard her eyes widened and blurred with tears. "Use your brain. Why the fuck would a gang of terrorists tell me they were going to kidnap Moro?"

"Why does anybody underground give an interview? Maybe it's an ego trip. Maybe to explain their point of view. Maybe to plant false leads. This plan they've told you about could be a decoy."

"You're the one who should be writing fiction. Better yet, fantasy. But get one thing straight. You kick it around that I'm in touch with the Red Brigades, you're not just putting my ass in the frying pan. You're asking for trouble yourself."

"Are you threatening me?"

"What I'm doing is warning you. The Red Brigades suspect you know something, they won't let you run around shooting off your mouth. They'll kill you. Or the police might hear the rumors first and arrest you. They'll hold you until you tell them everything you know."

"All I know is what's in your book."

"How can you prove that? Why should they believe you when you won't believe me? After a few months, I might be able to convince them it's fiction. Meanwhile we'd both be in jail. And you know who'd be in there with us? Dozens of Red Brigades. How long do you think you'd last?"

She pushed away his hand and stood up. "I don't understand you. All you had to do was let me shoot this story."

"I don't have a story. I have a novel."

She wanted to hurt him, wanted to say something wounding and final. She glanced around the apartment, at the makeshift furniture, the bookshelves of bricks and boards. "You don't have much, do you?"

"That's right." He grabbed her elbow, then loosened his grip and moved his hand up to a softer spot on her arm. "If you don't find what you're looking for, you can fly to Africa or back to the Middle East. But I've got to go on living here. Don't fuck it up for me."

"The last of the hippies," she said. "A small time loser into something much too big for him."

"Then why do you want to work with me?"

"Forget it. I don't."

After she had gone, David flung the notebook into the file drawer; his ears rang with the sound of shaking sheet metal. He punched in the locking cylinder, then worked the key onto the tight steel ring with all his others. From here on, he'd keep it in his pocket. Although he wanted to believe it wasn't too late, he didn't kid himself. There was no predicting what Alison would do. A cunt like that was capable of anything. He had to assume the worst. Yet when he realized precisely how bad that might be, he preferred to consider other possibilities.

It struck him as unlikely she would be foolish enough to call the cops or lucky enough to locate a terrorist who'd talk. She might speak to Massimo in her mangled Italian, but even if he managed to follow her line of questioning, he'd dismiss her as crazy the instant she started in about terrorists and Germans and jail breaks. To David's immense relief, no one could trace Stephane on the basis of his book. And if Alison accused de la Chasse of belonging to the Red Brigades, the fat, irascible editor would toss her out of his office on her ass.

The irony was, once the book was published, anything Alison said or did now would support his own story. After she shot off her mouth and claimed he had infiltrated a terrorist cell, she couldn't very well switch signals later and call him a fraud. Like everybody else, she would be in no position to say he had passed off fiction as fact.

CHAPTER VIII

WHEN THE RAINS RETURNED, the crowds were driven
back indoors, and if the streets are the Italians' true home, then
during those chill wet days Rome had the haunted look of a
home abandoned. Grass grew in the cracks between cobblestones, describing the intricate pattern of a net dropped over the
pavement. Metal flanges and bolts that helped hold together the
ruins bled rust like pitons left behind by mountaineers. A vast
loneliness settled over the city and nothing was more forlorn
than those empty piazzas where puddles swelled slowly into
lakes, and tables and chairs were stacked haphazardly outside
of cafés like jetsam tossed up by high tide.

At night, the loneliness insinuated itself into the apartment,
streaming in through the poorly sealed windows along with
damp currents of air that fogged the glass. From where David
sat at his desk he peered through a curtain of condensation and
found his familiar view distorted. Trastevere was breaking

into minute fragments, dissolving like powdered medicine in water.

After Alison read it, he felt his book had created its own climate, its own brooding foul weather which warped his vision of the city. Having set out with the conviction that he could fabricate a plot that would frighten and enthrall readers, he had never expected it to threaten him. But now on Sunday, when Stephane, Marc, and he walked past block after block of shop windows, he could picture what a bomb would do to all that plate glass, and what saw-toothed blades of it would do to them. He sensed unsettling presences at his back and took to glancing over his shoulder. He felt uncomfortable in crowds, but the feeling was worse in open places. To somebody on a rooftop with a rifle, he knew they were an easy target. He worried whenever Marc's school bus brought him home late, and he warned Stephane not to venture out alone after dark.

At night, the streets teemed with soldiers and police armed with automatic weapons. In the past, David had regarded them less as intimidating figures than as bumbling innocents, the embodiment of those callow good intentions with which Italy met every emergency. Now it struck him how dangerous innocence could be, how likely the best intentions were to go awry.

At the office, he clipped the usual stories and pasted them up. A bomb in Turin, another kneecapping in Milan, a kidnapping in Naples, a bank robbery in Bologna, an assassination in Rome. He still had witnessed little violence, but he had begun to believe what he read and, worse yet, what he wrote. Indulging in—drawing upon—his worst fears, he created scenes which then compounded those fears. He cursed himself for letting the book write his life. Yet he found he could not stop. For years, journalism had been no more than a job, just something he did during the day to pay for his nights. But this kind of writing was narcotizing, the free play of imagination addictive. Like the pointillist picture formed by beads of condensation on the pane of glass in front of him, a suspicion slowly took shape in David that he was no longer doing this for money. Suffering the obsession of fugitives and fiction writers, he simply wanted to know how things would turn out.

Every day some new piece of information fell into place, confirming his hunches and clarifying a design that needed only to be powerfully imagined in order to come true. Soon after he decided the central incident should be a kidnapping and that Aldo Moro was the logical victim, he discovered a remarkable article in a back issue of a right-wing magazine. "The most dangerous moment in the Honorable Moro's day," the author maintained, "is when he goes out in the morning."

He proceeded to describe Moro's penthouse apartment at 71 Via Forte Trionfale and his unvarying daily route to the Church of Santa Chiara, where he paused every morning for a few minutes of silent prayer before being driven to his offices in central Rome. Kidnappers or assassins, said the writer, could strike at any one of several points along the way and be certain of nailing him. The article puckishly concluded that one could put a poisoned tack on the correct church pew and rest assured that Moro, a man of inflexible habits, would sit on it.

In early March, David cranked his Fiat to life and, with a map on one knee and the magazine article on the other, he drove to the Camilluccia district, parked on the shoulder of Via Forte Trionfale, and stared up at Moro's building until the *portiere* trudged out and asked what he wanted. David said he was searching for Via Trionfale. Where was that in relation to Forte Trionfale? The man instructed him to swing around and take the first left. He did so, following Moro's route to Via Fani, downhill through a residential area to the intersection of Via Stresa.

Unaccountably, he was overcome by *déjà vu*. When he circled around on Via Camilluccia and returned to the intersection, he experienced the same uncanny certainty of having seen the place before. This time, however, he understood why. Although he had never been to this neighborhood, he had studied photographs of a spot just like it—the one in Germany where Hanns-Martin Schleyer had been abducted.

He left the car and crossed from corner to corner. Little traffic passed, and no pedestrians. It was a community of no charm, no personality. That was its point, its reason for being. People who lived here were tired of Italy's excess of personality, sick of Rome's charming eccentricities, and more than willing to trade the *centro storico* for cleanliness, quiet, and privacy.

The buildings were screened by walls and iron fences twined with ivy. Forsythia had bloomed—the bushes glowed with bright yellow stars—and mimosa trees were about to blossom. On the southeast corner of the intersection a flower vendor sat in his van, bathed by brilliant colors and cloying fragrance. Opposite him, an establishment called the Olivetti Bar appeared to be closed. David strolled over to it. Behind a hedge of potted plants tall enough to hide a man, or several men, for that matter, the shutters were down, the patio deserted. A sign said the bar had gone out of business.

He knew this was it, had known it the instant he coasted down the slope of Via Fani and halted at the stop sign at the corner of Via Stresa. The foliage, the patio of the Olivetti Bar, and the flower vendor's van provided all the cover a team of kidnappers would need. Other members of the gang could wait in parked cars, then jump out to block off the intersection the moment Moro's chauffeur slowed for the stop sign.

Concealed by the potted plants, David watched a white car with diplomatic plates pull in beside his Fiat. A couple climbed out—a man in a green loden coat, a woman wearing large sunglasses. They wandered around the intersection, just as he had done, as if trying to locate an address. But they didn't do the obvious; they didn't ask the flower vendor for directions.

Instead, they advanced toward the Olivetti Bar. David was uncertain whether to stay put or step out where they would see him. Not caring to call attention to himself, he thought they'd notice the place was closed and turn back. But when they kept coming, he realized he had hesitated too long.

They were on the patio, deep in the shadow of the hedge, when he said, "*Scusi. È chiuso.*"

The couple fell away from each other like the covers of a book with a broken spine. The man crouched and pulled a pistol from the pocket of his loden coat, aiming with both hands. Startled, David stumbled into the hedge. The wickerwork of limbs bowed with his weight, tearing at his clothes, clawing at his fumbling hands. He just managed to right himself.

"Don't shoot," the woman shouted.

"What are you doing?" asked the man with the pistol.

"I wanted coffee," David said. "But the bar is closed."

"Then why are you hanging around?"

"I'll go." He started edging away.

"No! Stand still. Raise your hands. Who are you?"

"*Sono straniero,*" he said in an awful accent. He could not remember the last time he had admitted being a foreigner in Rome. "A tourist. Are you the owners?"

"It's no business of yours who we are," the woman said. "Cover me," she told the man. "If he moves, kill him."

She ordered him to spread his legs wide and hold his hands high. Then she frisked him from armpits to ankles.

"You're American?" she asked.

"Yes."

"You don't belong here. Don't ever let me see you again. Now go."

And so he went, walking fast, finding it difficult to prevent his knees from buckling under him. When he was in the Fiat and had the engine running, he risked a glance back at the bar. The couple was still behind the screen of vegetation.

As he sped by their car, he noted the diplomatic tags again and thought that explained it. They were secret service agents. Somebody must have seen him snooping around and called the *carabinieri*. Since it was the most dangerous point on Moro's drive to work, the intersection was probably patrolled on a regular basis. Maybe the flower vendor was a lookout and had a short-wave radio in his van.

That had to be it. Who else but some idiot of an Italian agent would pull a gun? At least he knew now he had picked the right spot. But what a way to find out. He was damp under his arms and in the palms of his hands. His foot fluttered against the gas pedal and his breathing sounded ragged and asthmatic as the Fiat.

CHAPTER IX

ALTHOUGH HE SAW HER every evening, David felt closer
to Stephane in some ways when he was alone at his apartment,
imagining her. As if to apologize for his lapse with Alison, he
inserted Stephane in more and more scenes, he moved her to the
center of the story, he let her have the best lines. Cut off from
her in the flesh, concerned about the fragility of her moods, he
came to love her as an author loves his favorite character.

But this presented problems when he returned that night from
Via Fani and reviewed his manuscript, trying to determine how
to end it. The kidnapping couldn't succeed. As in all "faction
docudramas," something had to go drastically wrong. David felt
the internal logic of the narrative demanded that Stephane Von
Essen should die. If Aldo Moro was to live and remain free,
somebody had to be sacrificed in his place; a plot, once set in
motion, asserted its own exigencies. To his consternation, he
was learning that when you appropriated people for fiction, it

became increasingly difficult to grant them an existence apart from your purposes.

Still, he struggled to save her. He would rather ruin the plot, wrench it entirely off track, than have her die. Whatever happened to the others, her character had to survive. He was twisting the story line, trying to kill off Lucio when he was startled by a buzzer. He broke from his desk and hit the button that unlocked the street-level entrance. Then opening the door onto the hallway, he heard footsteps on the stairs, the distinctive tapping of high heels on stone. Alison! His first thought was that she had come back to hassle him about the Red Brigades.

When Stephane appeared on the landing, he was seized by a fear that the catastrophe he had labored to avert in his book had erupted in another chapter of his life. "Is anything wrong?"

"Wrong?" she said, breathing hard from the climb. "Does there have to be something wrong for me to visit you?"

"No. You surprised me, that's all. Where's Marc?"

"Home with a baby-sitter. Look, is this a bad time?"

"What do you mean?"

"Is somebody here?"

"Of course not. Who'd be here?"

"Then let me in." She laughed nervously.

"The place is a mess." Shutting the door behind them, he gathered up the plates and books and newspapers that littered every end table.

"Don't bother about that."

"At least let me clear a place for you to sit down." He took his tennis racquet off the couch.

"I didn't come here to sit." Moving up behind him, she slid her arms around his waist and hugged, leaning her head against his back. "It's been so long since we've been alone."

"You should have called. I'd have run right over."

"It's better this way. In my place, with Marc sleeping in the next room, we're like an old married couple. Here it's like an assignation." Turning him around to face her, she said, "It is all right that I came, isn't it?"

"It's great. Let me pour you something to drink while I clean up a little. I'm just not prepared for an assignation."

He splashed red wine into a glass and handed it to Stephane who had curled up on the couch. In a check suit, silver earrings and necklace, she was dressed for a rendezvous at the Hassler, not in his threadbare apartment.

Stepping into the bedroom, David thought everything was still redolent of Alison's scent. He pulled off the pillowcases and stripped the sheets. Then he stuffed his notebook into the file cabinet and locked it.

"What are you doing?" Stephane called.

"Changing the sheets."

"Tu es fou. Ce n'est pas nécessaire." She came to the bedroom door. "Let me help."

"No. Tonight, you're on vacation."

"I want to help," she insisted.

But after the two of them had tucked in the clean sheets and smoothed the blanket and spread, she suddenly seemed distracted, distant. While he undressed and crawled under the covers, she stood hesitantly in the half light that slanted in from the living room, removing her clothes with a deliberation that roused his apprehension rather than desire. He couldn't shake the suspicion that something was wrong.

Hanging her jacket on the chair, she unzipped her skirt, folded it and laid it carefully on the desk. When she was out of her slip, she paused before taking off her brassiere and pantyhose. Then she paused again, and he feared she might stop and say she was finished with him. Finally she stepped out of her underpants and climbed into bed.

"Is something wrong?" She stunned him by asking what he had been thinking.

"No. Why?"

"Don't you want me anymore?"

"Of course I do." He tried to pull her close, but she held back.

"I'm not talking about now. I'm talking about the way it's

been for weeks, months. The way it was when you opened the door. It's like you don't want to be near me anymore. You seem so far away."

"Not at all. I love being with you. The trouble is, you know, a lot of times you're tired or worried about Marc or Lucio and this custody thing. I understand what a bitch it's been. Some nights it seems better not to bother you."

"Bother me? You mean because things have never been right for us in bed? Is that why you've been staying away?"

"Baby, I stop to see you every night."

"Yes, you come to the apartment. But you're not really there. You barely touch me."

"I'm sorry. My mistake. I thought it'd be better if you didn't feel pressured, if I waited for you to say when."

"I want to feel you're with me."

"Believe me, I am." Again he tried to take her in his arms; again she held back. Reaching out a slender arm, she flicked on the lamp and rolled onto her side, staring at him. She didn't appear angry or upset, just very serious. Her hair spread in stark black threads against the pale skin of her shoulders and breasts.

"As difficult as things have been," she said, "I wouldn't be surprised . . . I mean, I'd understand if you were seeing another woman. But—"

"Jesus, why do you say that?"

"You've been patient a long time. But if this is getting to be too much, if you're sick of it and want out, tell me."

"No." He put a hand on her prominent hip bone and held tight. "You and Marc are what matter to me."

A rash of gooseflesh spilled over her arms. She was shivering, but wouldn't cling to him for warmth. "I have to know where you stand."

He moved his hand to her face, tilting it so that the hollows filled with shadow. He realized now what had always intrigued him about her features. You couldn't take them for granted. Conventional beauty was easy; it made a simple declaration.

But Stephane's face forced you to make up your mind. "I stand with you," he told her. "I love you."

"*Bon,*" was all she said.

Still, she wouldn't lie down beside him. Kneeling between his legs, she massaged his chest, the striated muscles of his stomach, the length of his standing cock. Leaning down, she wet him with her lips, and her necklace slid forward, laying its cool silver links against his balls. Then she pulled away from him, gathered a pillow in her arms, and raised up on elbows and knees, her rump canted in the air. He knelt with his thighs against her cool buttocks and felt he had met a wall. But the wall gave way an inch at a time and Stephane groaned, dropped off her elbows, buried her head in the pillow.

The sculptured contours of her back sloped in front of him, her spine a column of notched ivory. Remaining virtually motionless, he had the sensation of sustaining her on the strength of his cock as she rocked back and forth. Then abruptly she was up on her elbows again, her spine curled like a cat's. There was a cry like a cat's too. But that was David as he collapsed over her back, his face in the fragrance of her dark hair.

For a long time he lay with her shoulder muscles shuddering under his chest until finally, afraid his weight was too much for her, he slipped off to one side. Stephane stayed on her stomach, eyes shut, motionless. David pulled the covers over her and, after a while, closed his eyes too.

When he woke, the lamp was off, she was gone. He bolted to a sitting position. Hearing something in the living room, he stumbled out of bed to find her dressing in the dark.

"Oh damn," she said, "I didn't want to wake you."

"What are you doing?"

"I have to go home."

"Couldn't you call the sitter and say you won't be back tonight? I'd love to wake up with you tomorrow. I'll fix you breakfast in bed."

She touched his cheek. "That would be nice. But I can't take the chance. I don't want to give Lucio any excuses."

"Wait till I dress. I'll drive you."

"No. Don't bother. I'll phone for a taxi."

"I want to. I want to stay with you as long as I can."

"Then let's walk."

They kept to side streets where they didn't need to worry so much about onrushing cars. In Rome, David told Stephane, the view was generally better the higher you raised your eyes. This was their chance. Arms linked, they stared straight up and set off toward the river, seeing through unshuttered windows beautiful beamed ceilings, gilded scrollwork, candle-lit vaults, murals of angels and saints, and, arching just out of reach, the star-strewn spring sky.

BOOK THREE

CHAPTER I

ALISON REMAINED IN HER ROOM. In the morning, she sent down for breakfast—a rock-hard *rosetta* and a pot of powerful coffee that set her heart racing and her mind jumping around. She rarely ate lunch. She did stretching exercises, listened to the radio, paid bills, and answered letters that had lain around for months. But at the back of her mind there was always the thought of David and his book and how it might be made to serve her purposes.

Her agent called to offer an assignment in Central America. "It's been more than five months," he said. "Haven't you learned enough about Italy?"

The question caused her an uncomfortable afternoon. She didn't believe she had learned much of anything about Italy. For some people education seemed to be a welcome second prize. No matter how gruesomely things fell out in their private lives, Alison heard them claim they had had "a learning experience." They spoke of failed love affairs, broken marriages, and bankrupt businesses that had left them "street smart." But she concluded she must be dirt-road dumb because, although in lucid moments she realized how much time and energy she had already squandered, she thought the only way to prevent these months from winding up a total waste was to get the shots she wanted.

At first she considered charging into Pierre de la Chasse's office, accusing him of belonging to the Red Brigades; unless he put her in touch with them, she'd call the police. But the threat lacked bite, and he'd know it. She wanted nothing to do with carabinieri, who would be more inclined to believe de la Chasse than her. She was also half-persuaded David had told the truth about one thing—he had simply appropriated the editor's name and grotesque physique, punishing his boss for past humiliations.

Massimo she wrote off as even less likely to help. She would need an interpreter, and she knew no one she trusted. Besides, he was a minor figure, one apt to have access to nobody except his immediate superior.

Although never mentioned in the manuscript, Italo Bianchi was the man she figured David would have turned to for information, his most probable contact. Still, she didn't race off to confront him. For one thing, he had stonewalled her in the past. For another, she wanted to analyze her motives. It took an entire evening to convince herself she had no desire for revenge. As she viewed it, it wasn't a violation of journalistic practice or her own ethics to follow up a hunch with David's closest friend, someone who wouldn't want to hurt him any more than she did.

Monday morning, March 13, she telephoned Bianchi at the University of Rome and said she'd like to drop by his office.

"A personal visit," she emphasized, hoping David hadn't warned him.

"It would be a pleasure to see you," Italo said. "On a personal basis."

. . .

She wore her white dress, the one from Guatemala with the flowers embroidered on the bodice. Although the day was bright, it wasn't very warm and she shivered as she strode through pools of shade under the palms at the university. Still, Alison liked the feel of fresh air on her bare arms and legs, and she was amused by the stares she got from the students who lounged around the fountain in attitudes that had not changed in the last few weeks.

Yet when Bianchi opened his office door and gave her the same stare, when he kissed her hand and bowed for her to come in, she briskly unshouldered her bag and brought out a manila envelope. "Copies of the shots I took last time."

"How nice of you." He tossed the envelope onto his desk. In a beige linen suit and silk shirt, he resembled a weary roué just back from a summer resort. "Since this is a personal visit, why don't we go to lunch?"

"By personal, I meant I'd be alone."

"So it's personal *business*?" he said.

"Exactly." She sat down at the seminar table.

Sitting close beside her, Italo scratched at the line low on his neck where he had stopped his razor and let his luxuriant chest hair grow. "Well, *cara*, what does this 'personal business' have to do with me? If you were after an A in sociology, I would be glad to oblige."

"What I'm after is information."

"You've heard everything I have to say about the Italian situation."

"I doubt that." She tried to sound as smarmy and amiable as Italo. "Not that I'm not grateful for what you told me, and for those kids you introduced me to. But I'd like to meet a different kind of student."

"I'm around students all day. They don't interest me. You're free to roam the campus. You'll find the boys, in particular, very friendly."

"The kind I'd like to meet would be left-wing and politically active."

"And English-speaking, I presume." He was grinning. "Unless your Italian has improved."

"I thought you'd translate. I thought you'd see that it's to your advantage for me to get the right picture."

"My advantage?" His eyebrows arched. "*Cara,* it is the American habit to be blunt. But I suppose a devious Italian will have to force the issue. Are you here to ask again about the Red Brigades?"

"Exactly."

In a pantomime of helplessness, he spread his thick fingers. "As I told you, how would I know who is a terrorist when even your CIA doesn't have any idea?"

"You're one of the best informed men in Rome."

"I'm flattered."

"If you don't know how to reach the Red Brigades, I'm sure you can put me in touch with somebody who does."

"Now I'm not flattered."

"I didn't intend it as a compliment. It's a simple statement of fact."

"It's no fact. What you say could get me arrested. Or shot."

Alison remained silent, offering him an opportunity to do more than register polite displeasure. When he didn't, she proceeded. "You can trust me. If you know anything about American journalists, you know we protect our sources."

"The Red Brigades don't grant audiences. They have nothing but contempt for reporters."

"They're in the newspapers every day. They're leaking information to somebody."

"They release propaganda statements and position papers. The rest is guesswork by a few ambitious hacks with delusions of grandeur. When they guess right too often, they are kneecapped or killed. Do you imagine they would welcome a photographer?"

"The pictures I want wouldn't have to show their faces. I'd conceal their identities."

"It's absurd to discuss this. No one can reach the Red Brigades."

Unlike David, whose warnings had sounded so urgent, Bianchi didn't lean into his sentences for emphasis. Slouched in the chair, heavy eyes on her breasts, he seemed sublimely indifferent to whether she believed him. It was this smug self-possession that provoked her into the kind of bluntness Italo associated with Americans.

"I happen to know for a fact," she said, "that a reporter has been in touch with the Red Brigades. I happen to know he's been to their safe houses and sat in on meetings of the Strategic Command. He's doing a book with their cooperation."

As Bianchi languidly resumed scratching the stubble on his neck, there was the grating noise of an emery board against dry wood. "And where is this mysterious journalist?"

"Right here in Rome."

"An Italian?"

"American."

"Preposterous." Smiling, he shook his head, agitating his thin, disheveled hair.

"I happen to have read the book," she said. "Do I have to spell it out for you?"

"Please do."

"You're going to pretend you don't know who I'm talking about?"

"But I don't."

"It's David, goddamnit. He's doing the book."

He chuckled politely, as if to humor a guest who had finished a long rambling joke. "Impossible."

"Not with your help."

"You can't expect me to believe that that Nazi behemoth at the *American News* assigned him to do such an article."

"It's a book, not an article."

"And how did he meet the Red Brigades? On a tennis court?"

Studying him with ferocious concentration, ignoring his flippant questions, Alison thought she spotted a flicker of fear in his eyes. "You tell me. You're the one who arranged it."

"Am I supposed to believe he's doing this remarkable book and leaving it around for anybody to read?"

"I'm not *anybody*."

"But I've been to his apartment. I never noticed any place where it would be safe."

"What does it matter where he keeps it?" she snapped.

"Does he know you're spreading this around?"

"I'm not spreading it around. I came to you because you're his friend and you helped him . . ." Suddenly she had the sensation of sliding down a smooth slope, groping for something to grab hold of. Was it possible she had been wrong? She restrained an impulse to chew her lip.

"I *am* his friend," Bianchi said. "I want to be your friend. But I have to know what David told you."

"About you?"

"Yes."

"Not much."

"He didn't tell you I introduced him to the Red Brigades?"

"I figured that out for myself."

"Does he know you read his book?"

"Yes." After her instant of panic she was starting to feel better as, with each question, he seemed to concede that she had been right. Although he had admitted nothing specific, she had been around enough politicians and diplomats, she thought, to interpret his slippery, elliptical remarks.

"He let you read it?"

"No. He had it hidden in his file cabinet. One day while he was at the office, I found it."

Italo nodded, as if he might have guessed.

"He claimed it's a novel," she said. "He didn't spill anything, if that's what you're worried about. He protected you the whole time. I can appreciate the position you're in. I don't know how much you know about my work."

Italo gave another nod.

"I've dealt with some delicate situations. I have something

to protect too. I have my reputation. I've shot Arafat and Khaddafy. I've gone on PLO missions. Tell your people that."

"You understand," he said, "it would be disastrous if the wrong person heard about the book?"

"Of course."

"And you say David swore it was a novel?"

"Yes. But you need a better story than that. What are you going to do when it's published?"

"Let's concentrate on more immediate problems." Bianchi climbed slowly to his feet, buttoning and unbuttoning his jacket. "Where can I find you?"

"You'll help?"

"I have some difficult arrangements to make. I'll move as quickly as I can. Now, where are you living?"

She wrote down the address and phone number of the Palazzo Vertecchi.

"I'm counting on your discretion," he said. "If I hear you've spoken to anybody else, it's off."

"Of course."

He led her to the door and, for once, when he let her out, he didn't kiss her hand. Alison regarded this as a promising sign. Now that he had dropped the Latin suavity, she was sure she was getting someplace.

"Just one thing," she said before she left. "I'll keep my part of the bargain. I won't tell anybody about the book as long as you don't tell David I've been here."

"Why not? I mean, if he knows you read it."

"Mad as he is, as much as he didn't want to share his sources with me, I still hope we can patch things up and work together. But if he knows we've talked, that'll be harder."

"You'll have to tell him sometime."

"Later," she said lightly.

"When?"

"When he doesn't have any choice."

CHAPTER II

HE PUMPED HIS RIGHT ARM, testing for soreness. An
old habit, an old injury. He jabbed a finger as hard as he could
into his triceps muscle, giving sharp focus to the generalized
pain he felt. He longed to see himself as he used to be—a
professor of sociology with nothing more to worry about than a
few recalcitrant students and a mild case of tennis elbow.

He peered into his hands, which were layered with calluses.
Every ridge and bump of his palms had a hard yellow crust that
obscured his lifeline. For five minutes he refused to consider
what he had to do. Once, in a department store, he had watched
a man walk through a plate-glass window and gaze dumbly at
the jagged hole behind him, unable to comprehend what he
had done. Badly cut on the arm, the man wouldn't listen to
people who told him to lie down and let them apply a tourni-
quet. It was as if he believed he would be all right as long as he
didn't acknowledge what had happened. Finally, he had fainted.

Bianchi feared he might do the same. His labored breathing was like the ocean in a conch shell—or like the sound his lungs made in the mountains whenever he was stuck and had to cling to a cold stone sucking in the sour air he had just exhaled. To move forward one centimeter could be fatal unless you could recall your hand- and footholds in reverse order.

Searching for a pattern in events, he wondered whether Alison and David weren't working by different rules, creating an illusion of illogic to cover their tracks. Alison had been so careless and naïve, often revealing more about the book than he had asked, Bianchi suspected she might be baiting him.

There were, he remembered, three methods of flushing a mole out of hiding. Scare him. Make him feel safe. Hold out an irresistible inducement. Was that what they were doing? Trying to trick him into a mistake by offering what they regarded as an attractive inducement? Or did they mean to frighten him?

He weighed the consequences of doing nothing. There might not be a book. Or it might be fiction. Even assuming David had infiltrated a cell—and Italo doubted that—he might never be found out, might never be linked with Bianchi.

Then again, if he were caught . . . Italo didn't care to dwell on it. He knew what would happen to his friend and to him.

His one hope of saving himself was to warn Giovanni. It occurred to him that his contact, in some fashion he could not fathom, might be testing his loyalty. Perhaps they meant to see whether he had recovered from Piero's death, maybe they wanted to know whether he would protect David.

Much as this appealed to him, he couldn't sustain his belief in the possibility, for it suggested that Alison and David were working with Giovanni, and that was unimaginable. The Red Brigades might cooperate with radical cells in Germany and the Middle East, but they would never open themselves to American infiltration.

Finally, because he could not conceive that David was part of a plot to test him or to trap him, he fell back on his first reaction—Alison was lying about the book. In all likelihood,

Giovanni would dismiss her story as nonsense. The safest course was to report what he had heard and prove that he held back nothing.

He called from a café on Viale dell'Università, then hurried on to a pizzeria near the train station. Steeped in the aroma of garlic and oregano, he dialed the second number. "This is Scarpe. I had another visit from the American woman, the one who took pictures of our friends at the bank in Milan."

"I told you. We confirmed that she's not intelligent."

"I'm sure that's right. But you remember she wanted to meet our friends?"

"Yes."

"She asked again if I could arrange it. She showed up in my office and—"

"Why does she keep coming to you, Scarpe?"

"I doubt she knows many Italians. And I speak English."

"But why does she think you can help?"

"She's not a woman who operates rationally. Today she claimed to know a journalist who's writing a book about our friends. She said they welcomed him into their home and are cooperating with him. I don't believe a word of this, but I thought you should know."

"Did she name the journalist?"

Italo paused. "Yes."

"I'm waiting, Scarpe."

"David Rayborne."

"You know him?"

"A little."

"Is that why she came to you? She knows he's doing a book. She knows you know him. She assumes you helped him."

"He's an acquaintance. Nothing more. We play tennis. From time to time he introduces me to other reporters. Through them I've planted stories. It was always on your instructions."

"Go on. He's a journalist. He knows a lot of journalists. Is he intelligent?"

"I'm beginning to think that's hard to tell with an American.

All I can say is Rayborne never expressed any interest in politics. He's never fished for information. He's never done articles on our friends. He told the woman his book is a novel. I would take his word over hers. I believe they had an affair. It turned sour and they broke up. She may be trying to strike back at him."

"This Alison Lopez, what do you make of her?"

They had been on the line less than two minutes, but Bianchi was breathless, his chest constricted, his heart squeezed into a tiny space between his ribs and his pumping lungs. "I agree with our people in Beirut. She's just a photographer, an ambitious one after a story. She's bluffing about the book, lying and hoping somebody will help her."

"But she came straight to you. That's what puzzles me. What's this book about?"

"I don't know."

"Didn't you ask?"

"No. I found out all I could without rousing her suspicions."

"Call me at my red number in twenty minutes."

"What red number? I don't know any red number."

"Calm down. Do you have a pencil and paper?"

"Look, I've told you everything."

"I may have things to tell you."

"Tell me now. There's a little more time."

"Do as I say, Scarpe. Write down your home telephone number."

He scribbled the number on the white border of a 500-lira bill.

"Now," Giovanni said, "add the following digits to it—314-3115. Look at what you get. Memorize that number. Destroy the paper. Go to another phone and call me in twenty minutes."

Abandoning the pungent warmth of the pizzeria, Bianchi passed by the train station, shouldering his way through a throng of hotel touts, pickpockets, prostitutes, and hawkers of black market cigarettes, pirated cassette tapes, and patently bogus Gucci bags, Omega watches, and Fendi purses. The smells, the swarm of humanity, the swarm of chittering sparrows grated on his already jangled nerves. They reminded him of Africa, of a trip he had taken years ago to Egypt. He might have been walking the cacophonous streets of Cairo as he crossed Piazza del Cinquecento to the Baths of Diocletian, whose ruins served as stinking open-air urinals. Laborers in denim, businessmen with briefcases, schoolboys carrying books stood side by side making water against the crumbling walls.

The only sign of equality to be seen in Italy, he thought, was men from every class pissing on the bricks of their history. Who was that British author who had written disparagingly of the Turd World, distinguishing between those nations that did their dirt in public and those that had the decency not to?

He had to restrain himself from shouting insults. He knew he was only indulging his anger to divert himself from what lay ahead. A pointless exercise. He was petrified. It was one thing to recall his betrayal of Piero and vow that he'd rather die than sacrifice another friend. It was a different matter to face things squarely, to picture what Giovanni would do if he didn't cooperate.

His alternative was to warn David, flee Italy, flee Europe altogether. For David, this posed no problem. A man his age, without ambition, without a real profession, could always drift to another country or back to the States. But Italo would lose everything.

At a bar on Piazza della Repubblica, he ordered an *aperitivo*, took two sips, then went downstairs to the telephone.

"Listen to me," Giovanni said. "I want you to get that book."

"Get it how?"

"Get it any way you can."

"It's in his apartment. You have experts for this sort of operation."

"He's your friend. You do it."

"But if I'm caught, I'm no good to you anymore."

Giovanni said nothing, and in that silence he understood his utter expendability. If Italo were captured, he could reveal to the police no more than a few phone numbers which would never answer again.

"Once I have the book, what then?" he asked.

"Read it and report to me."

"Look, the only way the woman's story could be true is if our friends are using Rayborne to plant misinformation. Can't you check with them?"

"I've checked."

Bianchi's mind clicked forward a few notches. "So you know whether he's been in touch with them. If he hasn't, the book is a novel. If he has, well, our friends must have their reasons."

"You're wasting time with your guesswork. Get the book and read it. Then we'll decide if it's fiction."

"This may take a few days."

"I expect to hear from you tomorrow."

CHAPTER III

THAT MONDAY MORNING DAWNED so bright and mild—more like May than mid-March—David couldn't bear to spend the day at the office. He phoned Stephane and told her to keep Marc home from school. Then after calling the *American News* to say he was sick, the three of them left town in his Fiat, heading for the Alban Hills.

It was, at the start, a dreary drive through miles of modern apartments and the skeletons of still more buildings. Everywhere at the outskirts of the city, rusty steel girders rose in improbable places—next to farmhouses, on parking lots of restaurants, amid rubble-strewn expanses of landfill. Once the framework went up, few of these structures were completed. David had heard that businesses received substantial tax breaks while construction was under way on their property. And in Italy the definition of "under way" was simply "unfinished."

In the first broad grassy fields, they saw families who had

pulled onto the apron of the road, eager to get at their picnics. They didn't bother strolling into the meadows among the wild flowers. Unfolding portable tables and chairs, they ate with one eye on the countryside and the other on the cars roaring past, as if they couldn't quite choose between bucolic joys and the dubious pleasures of the road.

Farther on, they sped by the ruins of an aqueduct. Arches of aged brick loomed above acres of flat earth, like the remains of a railroad trestle leading nowhere. Under one arch, a farmer had built a barn. Under other arches he had corralled a few cows and stored firewood, hay, and feed.

People often said nothing in Italy was what it appeared to be. But David believed it was more accurate to observe that nothing was entirely what it appeared to be at the moment. Everything was in transition—partly what it had been in the past, partly what it might be in the future. No stage was final; the process of becoming was continuous. Palaces metamorphosed into hotels, piazzas into parking lots, churches into restaurants. It brought him inexpressible joy to think that nothing here was ever really over and lost.

As he coaxed his battered, back-firing car up the tortuous road to Tusculum, there was less and less traffic and fewer leaves on the trees. At higher elevations, the foliage had just put forth tight, shiny buds, and it looked as though a green fog, broken here and there by acid yellow splashes of forsythia, had fallen over the forest.

They ate lunch on a rocky ledge baked by the sun which drugged Marc into sleeping. Although Stephane and he were drowsy too, they stayed awake finishing a bottle of white wine and gazing at the hills that fell away in soft folds, like a baize carpet. They could see a few pastel farmhouses far below and a smudge of pink where an almond orchard had blossomed. Across the valley the tiny town of Rocca di Papa clung to a steeper range of hills like a cluster of barnacles. Stephane leaned against him; he felt her strength ebbing by degrees. Then she laid her head in his lap and dozed off, her face a pale cameo against his blue jeans. He had to restrain himself from touching her, from tracing with his fingers the fine bones, the pink shell of her ear, the faint blue, pulsing vein on her forehead.

It was strange to realize this was the woman he had written about, the woman who had taken possession of his book. Meticulously groomed even on a picnic, seemingly self-possessed even when asleep, this Stephane Von Essen resembled his fictional character in only the most superficial respects. How foolish to fear his imitation might overtake the original, or that the incidents he had fabricated could threaten her.

The woman in the book was more like Darlene and Alison— single-minded, self-absorbed, driven to the point of . . . What point? He didn't care to dwell on what had happened to Darlene. Yet he couldn't help wondering how Alison would wind up. He didn't picture her on a hillside in the sun, sleeping with her head in a man's lap, her son napping nearby, the scene framed by the paraphernalia of a family picnic. He didn't know how to see her in the end, and that saddened him and scared him too. In spite of everything, he wished her well. He wished it, but no matter how hard he tried, he couldn't imagine it.

It was easier to envision his life with Stephane and Marc. They would stay together. It was impossible to conceive of anything else. He felt he had resisted the inevitable, the altogether desirable, far too long.

Marc woke and gobbled two cups of *crème caramel*. Then supercharged with sugar, he was ready to run. When he couldn't hold the boy back any longer, David woke Stephane and they climbed down off the ledge and crossed the spongy new grass. They had Tusculum to themselves and ambled alone among the Etruscan ruins, marveling at the silence, kicking up potsherds, staring into deep, empty spaces where the earth had fallen into the foundations of the ancient city.

Then they followed a path paved with immense flat stones. Beside it bulked the gnarled trunk of a dead oak that looked older than any of the half-buried ruins. When they arrived at a small amphitheater, Stephane said, "Imagine what it'll be like by May."

"Nothing but people, wine bottles, and plastic bags."

"Let's stay here until May." Marc was eddying around them, tireless, loquacious, leaping from the lichen-covered steps. "We could live in a tent. Or buy one of those big cars that turns into a *camping*."

David supposed he meant a Volkswagen bus. "I'd rather live in a house than a *camping*." Like Marc, he pronounced it as two words, *kam-ping*. "Maybe we'll rent a place this summer."

"Houses are so expensive then," Stephane said.

"Not if we use a little imagination. When all the Romans race like lemmings to the sea, we'll head for the mountains. What about it, Marc? Where do you want to go?"

"I want to go to the movies," he answered in the breathy, strangled voice of Darth Vader. They had recently seen *Star Wars*—once in English, then again in Italian.

"It would be wonderful to get away from Rome." Stephane had her hands in the pockets of her sweater. "But won't you be working on your book?"

"I should be doing a final rewrite."

"Can I read it then?"

"Let's discuss that later."

Since the blowup with Alison, he realized he had one reason to be grateful for the complications that kept Stephane and him apart. "Pure" fiction might sound like a substance plucked from the air which everybody claimed was free. But he had learned how costly it was to weave a tapestry of lies, then try to account for the crooked warp and woof of it to someone who saw it as truth.

"You can't keep it from me forever," she insisted.

"I don't intend to. It's just . . . just that there are a few problems."

"Problems?" Preternaturally alert to trouble, her face revealed her changing moods as swiftly as a knife blade set on its edge falls to one side or the other.

"Hey, Marc." He rested a hand on the boy's head. His hair had gathered heat from the sun. "Why don't you run ahead and scout the area? Make sure no storm troopers are waiting to ambush us."

"I don't have a gun. How can I protect myself?"

"Use your hand as a ray gun. That's right."

Loping down the path, Marc aimed his finger and zapped an outcropping of rocks, a stunted cypress, the dead oak tree.

"What problems?" Stephane pressed him.

"It's not a good idea for you to read the book before it's published. And remember, it won't come out under my name."

"I still don't understand that."

"A lot of what I've discovered is bound to cause controversy. You know how de la Chasse is. He'd be furious if he found out I wrote it. I don't want to lose my job and risk getting thrown out of Italy."

"That much controversy?" As they passed a forsythia bush, she snapped off a sprig of flowers. "Have you uncovered something about the Christian Democrats?"

"No, not them." He wondered whether he dared tell her . . . not the truth, but a lie that verged on it, one that would preserve his secret, yet preclude more questions. "I've been in touch with some terrorists."

"Which ones?" she asked, excited, incredulous.

"That's the problem. I promised them absolute secrecy. If it gets around that I'm talking with them, there could be trouble."

"I see," she said with a sharp intake of breath.

"So I don't want you reading the book right now. I figure the less you know, the better off you are. I'd rather not even talk about it."

"You're worrying too much about me. I'm frightened for you."

"Don't be. Just promise me not to mention this to anybody."

"Of course not."

They walked awhile in silence. Then as she worked the sprig of forsythia into the top buttonhole of her sweater, she said,

"Even though we have to keep it a secret, I want you to know how proud I am of what you're doing."

Embarrassed, David couldn't say which he would less like Stephane to find out—that he had been unfaithful or that his book was a fraud. "By the time I finish," he said, "maybe the suit will be settled and Lucio will leave you in peace, and we'll put a lot of things behind us."

"Yes, on a day like this, it seems possible. If I got custody of Marc, there would be nothing to prevent us from going away this summer."

"Nothing at all."

"But summer's a long way off," she said wistfully. "And everything in Italy takes so much time."

"Hey, I'm glad." He hugged her. "I'm glad everything's slow here. That means our life together will last a long, long time."

"Ah, *un philosophe chronologique, comme Proust.*" She was smiling; the knife blade had fallen to the bright side.

Running up the path, his dark bangs flapping against his forehead, Marc panted, "I killed them all. Now I'm dead." He threw himself into David's arms.

As he walked on with Marc clasped to his chest, he could feel the beating of the little boy's heart. It seemed to beat everywhere on his body. His lungs were two small, strong bellows; his breath was sweet with *crème caramel.* He swung him up onto his shoulders, where Marc posted and kicked his heels impatiently, clinging to David's beard as if to a horse's mane. "Go," he cried. "*Andiamo!*" Then together they galloped down the path with Marc whooping and laughing, and Stephane laughing, too, as she hurried to catch them.

CHAPTER IV

ON TUESDAY, WHEN DAVID RETURNED to the office, his cheeks ruddy from sun and fresh air, Pierre de la Chasse rode him mercilessly for skipping work. He swallowed the insults in silence. Then when the editor stumbled back half-loaded after lunch, they fell into another argument, this one about some statistics David had stitched into a comic piece of filler. The title alone—"So I Contradict Myself"—infuriated de la Chasse.

"What the hell's that supposed to mean?"

"It's a quote from Whitman on consistency."

"Who's Whitman?" he demanded. "Whitman who?"

"Back in Austin he shot a mess of people from the Tower," one of the Texans called out.

"What are you quoting him for?"

"Have you read the article?" David asked.

"Yes. And we're not printing that piece of shit."

The article reported that according to public opinion polls Italians had had their radical political consciousness raised to dizzying heights. More than sixty percent of the population claimed to be Socialist, Communist, or far to the left of the Communist Party. Yet this revolutionary fervor had not diminished the vast numbers who each year were awarded—or who bought or arrogated to themselves—illustrious titles that lifted them above the *lumpen proletariat*. During 1977, 41,498 citizens had been added to luminous ranks of the millions who had previously been made knights and *commendatori*. Millions more —everyone who owned a suit and tie, according to the article— expected to be called *dottore* or *professore*.

David observed that this mania for titles might provide the Communist Party with just the ploy it needed to win broader support. "The PCI could easily seize power by promising to eliminate the loathsome inequities of Italian society by elevating everyone to royal status. Why settle for comrade when you can be *cavaliere?*"

De la Chassé attempted to end the argument in his usual fashion—by repeating himself at top volume. "We're not printing that piece of shit."

"I get it now," David said. "You must be up for a title."

Blood rushed to the editor's already florid face. The chair creaked as he shifted his ponderous bulk, poised to avalanche over David.

"My God, I guessed right," David cried. "How much did it cost?"

"A hell of a lot more than I'm paying you." He hauled himself to his feet. "I'm going over to the Press Club, Rayborne. By the time I get back, I want that article spiked and something better in its place."

David moved to a window with two of the Texans, Lance and Merlee, and peered down at Via del Tritone, waiting for de la Chasse to emerge from the building. When he came waddling out, Merlee did a passable imitation of a trumpet blaring a fanfare.

"Sir Fat Fart," Lance intoned in a loud voice, drawing more Texans to the window.

As if he had heard the fanfare and believed in his royal lineage, Pierre de la Chasse extended one plump arm and, with that lordly gesture, strode into the traffic. He might have been Moses commanding the water to part. It worked. He waded across the street and had set off through Piazza San Silvestro, forging a path through buses, cars, and pedestrians, when two men on a motorcycle sped up behind him.

With the streaked pane of glass and all that space between de la Chasse and them, David and the Texans watched helplessly, their horror mixed with a kind of awe at the inevitability of what was happening. Clinging to the motorcyclist, the man on back had a pistol in his free hand. He aimed low, his arm bounced twice, two tiny sparks forked from the gun barrel, and the editor's legs buckled under him.

He fell in slow motion, like a big fleshy animal going to ground, dropping first to his knees, then to his hands and knees. After struggling mightily to stand up, he flopped face down. The motorcycle circled him and the man squeezed off a few more rounds. How many shots it was impossible to tell, since David couldn't hear over the clamor of traffic and the outcry of the Texans. While de la Chasse lay twitching on the cobblestones, the man fired a coup de grace that crushed his bald head like a melon. Then the motorcycle swung around and roared up Via del Tritone.

Suddenly they were all screaming and shoving and racing to get out of the newsroom to the piazza. David, in the lead, had reached the stairs when he heard a siren. That brought him up short. "The phones, the wire," he hollered as the Texans pushed by him. "I better stay here. Go see what you can do."

The *American News* had emptied as if for a fire drill. Even the Italian typesetters and janitors had rushed out. A phone was ringing, the wire was rattling, but David ignored them and went over to the window. Down below, the crowd bristled with cops and plainclothesmen who had materialized from cafés and side streets. Then a few photographers, reporters, and cameramen from RAI-TV arrived.

As the Texans labored in their limited Italian to describe what had happened, he knew he should have gone out and taken charge. Regardless of all their battles, regardless of the man's cruel stupidity, it was hideous to see him sprawled in his blood —blood that the cobblestones broke into a honeycomb of slowly proliferating, perfectly formed red cubes.

David felt sick and ashamed. Simple respect for the dead demanded that he do something, if only carry down a coat and cover de la Chasse's shattered face. But he remained where he was. Without a residence permit, he dared not be the one to deal with the police. All he needed was for one officious cop to ask the wrong question and everything he had planned for the coming years with Stephane would be obliterated in a second.

Having watched the lethal swiftness with which his boss's life had been snuffed out, he also couldn't help worrying that his own was in danger. For the murder he had witnessed seemed to confirm the terrors he had felt building page by page in his book. Whatever his personal faults, de la Chasse had avoided public controversy and in print, at least, had never offended anybody. If this could happen to a man who took no chances, what could David expect for the risks he was running?

For ten minutes the telephone had rung without stopping. When he finally answered, a high-pitched voice, perhaps a woman's, said, "This is the Red Brigades. We have executed Pierre de la Chasse, a traitor to liberty. Others will die because he—"

"What the hell did he do?"

"We will not let the reactionary press betray the people's trust. Those who exploit their positions of power will be dealt—"

The eunuchoid voice continued reading from a prepared statement which David made no effort to record. It was the kind of flatulent propaganda de la Chasse would never have run in the *American News*. Was that his mistake? Or had he renewed his old connections with the CIA? What Darlene had done with his unwitting help, de la Chasse could have accomplished with greater ease and efficacy—sent coded messages, used the office as an information drop, a nerve center for covert operations.

But no, that was absurd. David was allowing himself to become infected by the virus of his own book. At this stage in his career, de la Chasse wanted to be a knight, not a spook.

CHAPTER V

WHEN HE OFFERED HIS CONDOLENCES by telephone to Pierre de la Chasse's sobbing widow, she entreated him to take over the *American News*. She trusted him to run it as her husband always had. Later, lest he presume he had been appointed editor-in-chief, the family lawyer rang and emphasized that this was an interim arrangement. They would discuss matters after the funeral. For reasons he didn't elaborate, David said he was content to stay far in the background, unencumbered by a title.

Stephane also called, sobbing as earnestly as Mrs. de la Chasse. She had heard the news on the radio. "You see now why I hate Rome."

"I know you're upset. It's a terrible thing. But it could have happened anywhere." He didn't believe what he said. He didn't believe there could be a murder in a public square executed with the same systematic brutality.

"I thought of you," she said. "I thought of you and your book. How can you be sure you're safe with those people?"

"I'm fine. Don't worry about me. But I have a lot to do here and I can't come by tonight. Why don't you lock up and get to bed early?"

Despite his assurances to Stephane, he felt skittish when he left the office late and, walking home, he kept close to walls and parked cars, constantly surveying the ground ahead for something to hide behind. At his building, he pressed the button in the courtyard and stood there, deeply uneasy, waiting for the time-light to flash on. A fuse had blown, the bulbs on every landing were out, and he was reluctant to climb the stairs in the dark.

He had done it dozens of times in the past, afraid of no more than tripping over a child's toy or stepping in someone's trash. Now he could imagine much worse. Ashamed of his fear, he made himself move forward, advancing by touch. He found his door, inserted a key in the first of three locks, and twisted.

It didn't budge. Jiggling the key, he discovered the lock was already untumbled. So were the two lower ones. He turned the knob, and the door swung wide, creaking like a stage prop for a haunted house. It wasn't that ghostly racket, however, which raised a rash of gooseflesh on his arms. A cold breath of air sighed from the apartment. He hadn't left the door unlocked; he was sure he had shut the windows.

Fighting an impulse to race down the stairs and out of the building, he froze, listening. When he heard nothing except the harsh, ceaseless harmonics of traffic on Via Garibaldi, he reached in and flicked on a light.

The living room pitched its whitewashed walls toward him. Empty. No one in the bedroom either. But his clothes and belongings were strewn over the floor, all the pockets of his pants ripped inside out. The bed had been flipped upside down, and his paperbacks and magazines heaped in a corner, as if for burning.

Although it looked like the shakedown the FBI had given his

apartment in New York, David's first thought was, A drug addict. He fastened on that idea, refused to consider any other.

He hurried to the kitchen, hauled the refrigerator aside, and pried up the loose tile from the floor. His passport and money—he still had more than five thousand dollars left—were where he had cached them. Dragging the refrigerator back into place, he returned to the bedroom.

He took a quick inventory of his desk top, and was curiously relieved to note that his clock and transistor radio were gone. Shivering, he shut the window. One of the panes had been broken. The front door hadn't been forced or jimmied. It had been unlocked from the inside as the thief fled. Nobody could scale the wall from the street. But if a man was desperate enough, David supposed, he could swing down from the roof and through the window.

Finally he went to the file cabinet. It was still locked, but the bottom drawer looked like it had been loosened with a crowbar. He feared he'd find a rat's nest of tattered papers and would have to spend hours sorting them out. Instead, he found nothing. Not a page, not a single stray note. He stopped shivering; he felt numb.

It made no sense, and he wouldn't accept it. Prowling around the apartment, he collected his clothes and heaved the bed right side up. He shuffled through the paperbacks and magazines. He sifted the debris of both rooms, then searched the bathroom, convinced it had to be here. No burglar, not even the most demented addict, would bother to steal a book. You would have to be able to read his wretched handwriting, what's more, read English, to realize what the manuscript might be worth.

A student, he thought. Had an English major with a fifty-dollar-a-day habit barged in here and decided somebody—the police? a newspaper?—would pay plenty for the spiral notebook?

No, he was resisting the obvious. Nobody would break into an apartment, then waste time reading. The burglar had known what he was after; he had gone directly for the bottom drawer. David sank down on the sofa, furious. Alison, she had stolen it.

Or had hired somebody to steal it for her. Then they had pulled the place apart and ripped off a few things to throw him off the track.

She knew he couldn't call the cops. At least she was betting he wouldn't. He had warned her too well what would happen if the police learned about the book. For the second time that day, he was overwhelmed by his own powerlessness.

He could guess what she might demand. Nothing he could deliver. An introduction to the Red Brigades. Photographs of all the characters in the book. She held a blank check. No, a bludgeon. Where would she strike first? She had mentioned going to de la Chasse. It was too late for that, but—

This thought, and the one that followed, hit him with the force of blows. His mind reeled. There they were—de la Chasse's death and the disappearance of his book—with jagged sparks of electricity jolting back and forth between them. Had Alison somehow made the connection she had been pursuing ever since she arrived in Italy?

He stood up too fast. The tile floor tilted drunkenly under his feet. He started running before it settled and he stumbled. At the telephone, he paused long enough to grab the receiver, then to realize there was little he could do with a call. He had to get his hands on her. Slamming the door and locking it behind him, he surged down the stairs two and three at a time, heedless of the dark, less concerned now by what might be after him than by what lay ahead.

CHAPTER VI

EARLIER THAT DAY, while David was at work, Italo had parked his Alfa on Via Garibaldi and descended the staircase to Vicolo del Cedro. Dressed in a grey jogging outfit, he meant to pass for a laborer, perhaps a plumber or telephone repairman. But he was strangely shod in EB boots, tight, rubberized climbing gear manufactured in France and famous for extra traction.

Having driven across town terrified at the idea of breaking into the apartment, he now found himself more frightened that he wouldn't be able to. When he saw that there was no chance of scaling the facade from the street, he went into the building and trudged up the steps, resigned to being arrested. He would try to convince the police he was playing a trick on a friend, just sneaking into his apartment for a joke. He was more worried how to deal with Giovanni if he failed.

On the fourth-floor landing, he tested the door; he'd need a sledge hammer to get in that way. Up a final flight of stairs, he came out onto the roof. Sheets and pillowcases flapped from a clothesline. Rattan lawn furniture and a hibachi occupied one corner where someone had improvised a patio.

Leaning over a knee-high wall, he gazed down. David's bedroom window was directly beneath him, about four feet below the roof line. He had done much more difficult descents, but not alone, not without a rope, not when he had to hurry. He figured he had a minute, maybe two, before someone spotted him and called the carabinieri.

Italo crossed to the other side of the wedge-shaped building, peering down at Via della Frusta. The Street of the Whip was quieter, less frequented. There was a window on this side too.

Easing over the retaining wall, he performed a reverse mantle, planting his right forearm and hand flat against the ledge and lowering his stumpy legs, groping for a foothold. Suddenly, he felt himself slipping. The tiles at the edge of the roof raked his belly. He grabbed a drain gutter; it dissolved into a fistful of rusty tin. Then his left toe touched the window lintel. His other toe found the shutter. The wood was splintery with age and its hinges creaked like a leather harness. Afraid to rest any weight on the right foot, he shifted it to the lintel too.

The ledge he perched on was six inches wide—room enough to do a slow half turn, then crouch, as if genuflecting, until he got his hands on the lintel. From this position, he performed the same maneuver, a simple reverse mantle, resting his weight on his right arm and dangling his feet toward the windowsill, holding tight until the last instant with his strong, callused fingers.

Once he had both feet under him, he forced the window with his elbow. It was locked. He moved his elbow to the center of one pane and pushed until the glass cracked and sprinkled into the apartment. Reaching gingerly past the spikes left in the frame, he unfastened the window and entered the bedroom, stepping down to David's desk, then to the floor.

He chose a file cabinet and pried open the lower drawer with a screwdriver, the one tool he had brought with him. He had guessed right; there was the spiral notebook. He stuffed it into a plastic bag and, after breaking in without a scratch, he wound up with dozens of bruises and scrapes as he dashed around rifling through clothes, tipping over furniture, flinging paperbacks into the corner, pocketing a few things to make this look like an ordinary robbery.

He left by the front door, short of breath, as terrified as when he had arrived. But he passed nobody on the stairs, and no one on the street appeared to notice his agitation. Holding himself to a brisk walk, he headed for his car, thinking the worst was over.

Back at his apartment, he poured himself a tumbler of brandy and settled in the den amid the distracting bric-a-brac of his parents' lives. His feet were nearly numb. The tight EB boots had cut his circulation. He unlaced them and kicked them off. Then shoving aside inkwells, ivory-handled letter openers, and antique quills, he cleared a place at the desk and examined the notebook.

Immediately he realized he had been wrong—the worst wasn't over. He started to tremble. The stigma wasn't evident. Extending his hand, he studied his fingers. They were steady. But he felt the shaking inside him and poured a second tumbler.

It was a novel, he told himself, gulping the brandy. David wasn't smart enough to penetrate the Red Brigades. Or rather, he was too smart to try. His anonymous contacts, his secret sources, they were all spurious. They had to be.

Italo desperately didn't want any of it to be true. His desire not to believe in the book became so powerful he could not distinguish it from his self-pity and mounting despair. He felt he had been victimized by a monstrous unfairness and cursed Alison and David for dragging him into this. Damn David, he thought. Damn his naïveté. How American of him to hatch such an idiotic scheme. The impulse, in his opinion, must have sprung from two basic traits of the national character—innocence and inventiveness. Americans were always making up their lives as they bumbled along. They abandoned their families and homes and settled in Rome, then felt compelled to reinvent the city, ruin it.

It was too late to consider deserting David. Nor could he bear to dwell on what would happen if he didn't discover a solution to their shared dilemma. They were linked in this now, and he continued reading the sloppily scrawled pages, anxious to find an escape for himself as well as his foolish friend.

When he came to the chapter that introduced Stephane Von Essen and Pierre de la Chasse, he thought he saw a way out. There was no chance either was in the Red Brigades. And as for the other characters, their every gesture, every phrase, revealed the influences of fiction and film, not face-to-face encounters in a terrorist *covo*. To verify this, Giovanni had only to contact the Strategic Command and confirm that these figments of David's imagination weren't in the Rome column.

When he read that the fictitious *brigatisti* intended to kidnap Aldo Moro, he had to grant that that suggested a certain primitive logic. It made perfect sense. Too perfect. That was the giveaway. For years, the Red Brigades had threatened to carry the battle to the heart of the state, striking at the most powerful men in Italy. Nobody was more powerful and deserving of punishment than Moro—which was precisely why Giovanni would see that the idea was asinine. Moro's very power and prominence made it impossible to kidnap him; he was too well protected.

While David's choice of victim was too pat, his kidnap plan struck Italo as a convoluted caper that would strain the credibility of the most devoted reader of international intrigues. And that the operation should be led by a German woman, the recycled cliché of the beautiful Nazi seductress, that it should take place at a residential intersection no more than a mile from Bianchi's apartment, revealed just how ridiculous the whole notion was. Again, with a single phone call, Giovanni could satisfy himself that the Red Brigades had no plan that was remotely like this melodrama.

Bianchi would recommend returning the manuscript before David noticed it was missing. Such books, he would tell Giovanni, should be encouraged; they muddied the water in which the Red Brigades swam.

He was pouring himself a third tumbler of Courvoisier when the door buzzer sounded. Over the intercom, a voice, not at all like the high-pitched whine he was used to hearing, said it was Giovanni. He wanted to come up.

Plunged back into turmoil, he felt as he had when he grabbed for the drainpipe and got a fistful of crumbling tin. He had never met his contact and didn't care to now. Nonetheless, he asked the question he put to everybody who showed up here seeking a safe house. "Whose friend are you?"

"I am a friend of the Italian people."

He hit the button and waited in the hall, watching him climb the stairs. A young man in his mid-twenties, tall and reedy with chestnut hair and a blond mustache, he wore a khaki raincoat with epaulets and buckles, a coat that looked vaguely military, the style this year among people who swore they despised the military.

"Your voice," he said, blocking the door, "it doesn't sound the same."

"On the phone I use a device to distort it. We have reports that the police are recording voiceprints."

"What is your red number?"

The young man moved his lips, quietly mouthing the number he had given yesterday.

Italo stepped aside. "I had to be sure."

Giovanni brushed past him.

"Is something wrong? I didn't expect—"

Giovanni signaled for silence and shrugged off his raincoat. Under it he wore a suede jacket. A shoulder holster had printed its faint outline on the nap. Prowling around the living room, he pulled the drapes shut, switched several lamps on, then off, then on again. Picking up the telephone, he unscrewed the mouthpiece and examined the wires, flipped the phone upside down and rapped it with his knuckles.

"Ever notice anything odd about your phone?"

"Sometimes it doesn't work. Just like every phone in Rome."

He twisted the mouthpiece back into place. "You have the book?"

"Yes."

"Have you read it?"

"Yes, I was about to call you. I didn't expect you here."

"We felt it was safer this way."

"You've wasted your time. It's fiction, just as Rayborne told the girl."

"How can you be sure?" He sat in an overstuffed chair that was poised on brass claws and motioned for Bianchi to sit nearby. Folding one slim leg over the other, he waggled his foot back and forth. His ankle looked the size of Italo's wrist. He had very white hands and they, along with his blond mustache and his habit of sniffing every few seconds, gave Giovanni the appearance of a hare. Not a fat comical rabbit as in the illustrations Italo remembered from *Alice in Wonderland*, but a lean, cunning *lepre* from some instructive Italian folktale.

"The book contains nothing that hasn't already appeared in the press. Every incident revolves around information easily available to a journalist. I'm convinced Rayborne never made contact with our people."

He unbuttoned the suede jacket. "He made contact with you."

Italo had expected this, although not so abruptly, so unsubtly. "If you're implying that I helped him, please remember I was the one who reported him to you. Why would I do that?"

"Conscience? A crisis of nerves? A sudden change of heart? A trap? There could be reasons."

"But how could I put him in touch with a *covo*? You're my only contact."

"So far as we know."

"Are you admitting there are things you don't know?"

"There are things nobody outside the Strategic Command knows." He spoke calmly, but the sniffing had become a constant quiver of his nostrils, as if he had caught a distasteful and dangerous scent.

"It should be simple for you to check with them about Rayborne's book."

"Not as simple as you think. We can't always keep close track of people above ground. Irregulars like you present problems."

"I've always been loyal. Even after Piero died, I was loyal."

"Did you have a choice?"

"Look, you asked me to get the book, read it, and report. In my opinion, it's fiction. Some sections may be more troubling than others, but—"

"Troubling how?"

"There's a long discussion of a plan to kidnap Aldo Moro."

Giovanni's reaction was, Italo thought, a histrionic refusal to react at all. "Tell me about that," he said quietly.

"The plan is absurd and the characters are cheap fantasy, silly counterfeits. In Rayborne's novel the *brigatisti* are plotting to kidnap Moro with the help of the editor of the *American News*. This man is well-known as a former CIA agent. There's no way he could be working with us."

He waved a soft, white hand. "On second thought, I'd rather read it myself. Did you recognize any other characters?"

He debated whether to mention Stephane. She was proof positive that the book consisted of an invented plot, populated by a few real people among many phantoms. But Italo hesitated, afraid for her and himself. There were already too many personal connections to explain. "No," he said. "My feeling is the manuscript is second-rate fiction and doesn't bear serious discussion."

"I'll decide for myself." Although still quiet, the timbre of his voice had turned assertive.

"You read English?"

"Yes."

"Well, the place is yours. I'll be back this evening."

"I'd prefer that you remain here. In the other room."

"I have a seminar to meet."

"You'll have to miss it."

"I can't change my schedule—not without making my students and colleagues wonder."

"Let them wonder."

"At least let me call and explain that I'm sick."

"No, leave the line free. I'll be getting calls. I have to make some. Now before you go into the other room, write down where we can find Alison Lopez. Do the same for your friend Rayborne and that editor you mentioned."

As dusk gathered over the domes and cupolas of the city in all its milky hues of orange and purple and ultramarine, Bianchi lay in bed, staring up at the whitewashed walls. On his chest he balanced a toothbrush glass that vibrated in his hand. Every few seconds there was a mad scrabbling sound, then the metallic *ping! ping!* that sent a cold corkscrew of fear into his heart.

At the bottom of the glass were the segmented remains of the scorpion he had caught weeks ago. It didn't appear to have died so much as broken apart like a cheap plastic toy. He had kept it out of idle curiosity, but after putting the glass in a closet he had forgotten it until today when he spotted another menacing speck above his bed. Now a live scorpion scuttled around in the desiccated fragments of the dead one.

It seemed a sign, a portent. But of what? He found it difficult to think, impossible to reason his way out of this quandary. Like the scorpion, he could only scurry in a circle, a prisoner of invisible walls. When he attempted to anticipate what Giovanni might do, he had the impression of playing three-dimensional chess—and, what's more, playing it in a mirror. With effort, he could comprehend why the man had chosen to read the manuscript here and place his calls from a clean phone. He even conceded the wisdom of holding him incommunicado until he had established the basic facts. But Italo could not understand why it was taking so long.

Already the telephone had rung a dozen times, and Giovanni had dialed as many calls himself, none longer than a minute or two, most consisting of short phrases. Among the few words he had heard distinctly were the names of David, Alison, and Pierre de la Chasse.

Given the way Giovanni was going about it, he might have been testing the airtightness of every cell in the Rome column. Why? Italo revolved the question in his mind, like a jeweler rotating a diamond under his loupe, aware that he was avoiding the facet that most immediately attracted attention. If, as Bianchi believed, David, Stephane, and de la Chasse had never come near the Red Brigades, then Giovanni must be pursuing the matter because the plan, not the people in the book, rang true.

He heard sirens in the distance, then the phone. After another fragmented conversation, Giovanni summoned him. Leaving the scorpion on the night table, he went into the living room.

The tall young man with the wily face of a hare stepped out from behind the desk. "Your friend Rayborne isn't at the address you gave."

"He must be at work."

"Where's that?"

"The *American News*."

His nostrils flared. "De la Chasse's paper? Why didn't you say they worked together?" He swung a delicate white hand that looked like it would have the impact of a Kleenex. It stung like a willow switch.

Italo lunged at him, seizing him by the shoulders. But a sudden stabbing pain knocked all the air out of his lungs. He staggered backward, gasping. Giovanni had jabbed a pistol barrel into the soft spot just beneath his sternum.

"Did you warn Rayborne?"

Italo shook his head.

"I don't believe you. You're protecting him. Do you want to die for this American?"

He shook his head again, fighting for air.

"Then prove you're with us."

"How?"

"Call him. Get him to meet you here." Giovanni prodded him with the pistol.

He dialed the *American News*, where a girl with a Texas

twang informed him David was on the other line with Mrs. de la Chasse.

"This is urgent," he said. "He'd want you to interrupt."

"No, he wouldn't. He's just now explaining how her husband was shot."

"What?"

"You haven't heard? It's been on the news all day. They killed Mr. de la Chasse."

"Who?"

"The Red Brigades."

He laid the receiver gently in its cradle. "De la Chasse is dead. I don't suppose that's a surprise to you. But this makes it hard to reach Rayborne."

"Has he guessed what's going on?"

"I doubt it. But he's in charge of the paper now. He can't come to the phone, he can't leave the office."

"We'll take care of him later. If we let him have enough line, maybe he'll lead us to his contact. Meanwhile, someone'll pick up the Lopez woman."

Bianchi remembered her as she had been the night of de la Chasse's party, then again just yesterday at his office, when she had worn the white dress with flowers embroidered on the bodice. "Why bother with her?" he said. "She knows nothing."

"She's read the book, hasn't she?"

The question didn't require an answer. It begged another question. Bianchi had read the book.

CHAPTER VII

AFTER MEETING BIANCHI on Monday, Alison returned
to Palazzo Vertecchi and instructed the desk clerk that it didn't
matter what time of day or night it was; if anyone called or
came by asking for her, she wanted to be told immediately.
Now, near midnight on Tuesday, she was sitting in bed, ignoring
the room service dinner that had cooled in a puddle of con-
gealed grease. She held a book open in her lap, but wasn't
reading. She was attempting to resist the foolish aphorisms that
floated to the surface of her mind. *Don't think about it and time
goes faster.*

Her childhood had been blighted, she thought, by the false
wisdom of peasants. Relatives in Laredo had responded to
every crisis with homespun maxims, murmuring these slogans
with the same fervor as they kissed holy cards and repeated
what the nuns, resolutely without humor, called ejaculations.
"Sweet Baby Jesus, help me in my hour of need," they might

whisper. And in the next breath, with no less unswerving faith, they would advise Alison, "The best way to get what you want is to quit wanting it," or "The quickest way to make morning come is to yield to night."

Her family professed to believe in God, but she suspected they placed greater faith in a force as capricious as a river current. Although she claimed not to share their superstitions, she refused to leave the hotel. If she did, she was convinced Bianchi would show up, and if he didn't find her here, he wouldn't come back.

She glanced at the gold face of her wristwatch. She had told David the Rolex had been a gift and had implied that it possessed great sentimental value. What she hadn't revealed was that she had given it to herself the day her first collection of photographs had been published; the sentiment it expressed was the satisfaction of having arrived. But arrived where, she wondered? Here she was nervously waiting to set out again, and the geography of her ambitions, once so easy to chart, suddenly seemed vast and unmapped.

She thought of her father and the Sunday drives she had taken with him and his second wife through the wastes of West Texas. Once beyond Odessa, there was little to see except the bleached sand dunes at Monahans, the stunted wiry plants, the road undulating ahead of them, the empty, windswept sky which the natives swore was clean but which smelled evil from oil burn-off.

On those drives they said very little, they never got anywhere. There didn't appear to be a purpose or destination. Her father let the odometer tell him when to turn back, and by the time they arrived in Odessa they could see a gas flare flickering brightly against the depthless sky. Her father broke the silence: "Better to light a single candle than curse the darkness." Then he always laughed, because his second wife was Church of God and believed in the Bible the way most people believe in the weather.

Back then, Alison had seen no reason to light a candle. She preferred darkness to Odessa. She wished the odometer would break, the gas flare would burn out, and they would keep going and going. Eventually, on her own, she had gotten her wish. For more than a decade she had been whirled about. Now she questioned where she would wind up. Although it struck her as close to heresy, she found herself thinking she should quit moving until she made up her mind where she wanted to be. Perhaps this was the source of her melancholy and indecisiveness in the last few months—the suspicion that there was no longer anywhere to go, the desire to be still, to let the past overtake her.

When she tasted blood, she dismissed it as another sign of anxiety. Then a drop splattered to the sheet and spread through the fabric, each cotton fiber a capillary. Hurrying to the bathroom, she saw in the mirror that she had chewed a sliver of skin from her chapped lower lip. Each time she licked away a bubble of blood, another welled up in its place.

She was dabbing a tissue at the cut when the telephone rang. There was a man in the lobby to see her. Alison said to send him up. Ripping the Kleenex from her lip, she dragged a brush through her hair a few times and went to unlock the door for Bianchi.

The hall was dark. "Alison Lopez?" asked an accented voice.

"Yes, is that you?"

A clean-shaven man, young enough to be a student, stepped from the shadows. "Italo Bianchi sent me. You are to come with me."

Her preoccupations disappeared. Although aware of questions she should have asked, she simply said, "Let me get my coat and a camera."

He squinted at her as she spoke so that she thought he might be lip reading. Then blood trickled down her chin and splashed to the floor and she realized what he was looking at.

"Does it hurt?" he asked.

"It's nothing." Alison advanced into the dark hall.

Minutes later, when David reached Palazzo Vertecchi, the plateglass doors to the lobby were locked, and the night clerk had nestled into a chair in a grove of potted palms and was poring through an illustrated romance. David rapped the glass. The clerk pointed to his watch and waggled his index finger.

"*È urgente,*" David shouted.

The man laid aside his magazine. "We have no rooms."

"I don't want a room. I have a message for Alison Lopez."

Sighing and grumbling, he peeled himself out of the chair and opened the door. "She just left. I'll give her the message when she returns."

"Did she leave with a man?"

The clerk reacted as if his dignity had been deeply offended. "What our guests do is no business of mine."

David tucked ten thousand lire into the breast pocket of the clerk's coat.

"She was with a man," he muttered.

"Italian?"

"He spoke English to the *signorina.*"

"And to you?"

"Italian. Look, I want no trouble. What shall I tell Miss Lopez?"

"Tell her nothing."

He crossed the street and set off toward the Corso, but once the clerk had retreated to his illustrated romance, David doubled back and stationed himself in a doorway, watching Palazzo Vertecchi. The cobblestones began to gleam in the humid hours after midnight. He felt the sweat on his shoulders cool to a clammy plaster. He realized Alison might be at his apartment, might be trying to contact him by telephone, might be calling to lay down her terms. Finally it seemed wiser to go home than to linger here, exposed, defenseless, foolishly waiting.

In Trastevere, the streets were deserted except for cats, and silent except for an occasional guard dog that hurled itself, howling, at a gate. On Vicolo del Cedro, the smell of manure was heavy in the moist air. The stable doors were wide, and Massimo sang to his wife, his sleeping neighbors, to himself as he unharnessed his horse and curried its flanks.

David was about to go in and say *Ciao* and *buona notte,* but he stopped short. From where he stood, he could see the burly, unshaven man whose bluish-purple complexion appeared to reveal the ravages of long days under a scorching sun, but in fact showed the effects of long nights under the influence of cheap wine. There must have been thousands of Massimos in Rome and hundreds of carriage drivers. Even the most rabid member of the Red Brigades was unlikely to waste time tracking down such a minor character. Still, he wanted no one to associate Massimo with him. To be his friend now was to risk ending up like de la Chasse. Although he couldn't warn him about the book without creating more dangers—it was impossible to predict how Massimo might react or whom he might tell—David decided, like the bearer of some deadly disease, to quarantine himself for the time being.

In the hallway, he again had to summon all his powers of self-control to stay calm and climb the impenetrably dark staircase, knowing that on any landing somebody might be waiting. In the apartment, he bolted the three locks behind him and, on the off chance that a set of duplicate keys had fallen into the wrong hands, he shoved a table against the door. That wouldn't stop anybody, but it would make enough noise to warn him.

Screwing a wooden press onto his tennis racquet, he fashioned a club and placed it on the floor beside the bed. Then, fully clothed, he stretched out on top of the covers.

He had known nights after Darlene's death when sleep was elusive, sweeping him to the brink of oblivion, tantalizing him for hours, then slipping away again. But tonight it never came close. Exhausted as he was, much as he longed for release from the memory of what he had watched at the office window, he held out hope that if he stayed awake a while longer Alison would call and swear she had shown the manuscript to no one; de la Chasse's death had nothing to do with his book; he needn't worry about the safety of the other characters.

When the phone didn't ring, the natural reflex of his mind was to try to recreate the day, to rewrite the last twenty-four hours. This too was something he had done after Darlene's death. He had recalled their relationship hour by hour, making a statement to the FBI and, at the same time, reimagining for himself the intangibles, the ambient air temperature of a love he didn't care to believe was one-sided. What he gave away in the deposition he regarded as the dross of their lives. What he searched for secretly was some essential, inviolate moment, the irreducible alchemist's stone which could transmute baser metals into gold. But things, he had finally been forced to admit, were immutable.

Tonight, it was the same. When he thought about his book, hauling himself through it sentence by sentence like a deep-sea diver clambering hand over hand along the slimy links of an anchor chain, he found it impossible to recast these events any more than he could change what had happened to Darlene or de la Chasse.

CHAPTER VIII

WEDNESDAY, MARCH 15, dawned with the hard-edged clarity of a winter morning. On the Janiculum, Villa Lante looked the color of dried blood and stood in stark relief against a translucent sky that had a single jet contrail across it, like the score of a diamond on a sheet of glass.

Torn between a desire to stay at the apartment, waiting for Alison to phone, and the urge to roam the streets hunting for her, David had no stomach for work. But he knew he had to go to the office and hold the Texans together. Reporters and busy-bodies would be calling about de la Chasse's death, and he had to contrive a statement that would satisfy them as well as the editor's family. This, he suspected, would require an act of sustained creativity to rival the artifice of his book.

On the way to the *American News,* he stopped at Palazzo Vertecchi, where a portly, middle-aged woman had replaced the night clerk in the forest of potted palms. She informed him

Alison wasn't there. Whether she had returned last night, the woman wouldn't reveal.

"I would like to see her room," David said.

"You want too much, *signore!*" She clasped a hand to her bosom as if she had been asked to expose herself.

"Signorina Lopez has borrowed an important book from me. I need it back."

"Are you a student?" She regarded him dubiously.

"No, a journalist." He produced ten thousand lire in lieu of a press card.

"It's against the law to let you into her room. I would lose my job."

He pushed the money across the desk. "Keep it. When Miss Lopez comes back, please call me at my office." He scribbled the number.

"Shall I tell her you were here?"

"No, don't."

"It must be very interesting, this book of yours."

At the office, he realized the woman and Alison would have trouble reaching him. The phones rang all morning and—a rare occurrence—continued to ring during the three-hour lunch break. Eating a sandwich at his desk, David fended off journalists who called to fish for more than the bland news release he had concocted. Regardless of how they phrased their questions, couching them in the most euphemistic terms, they couldn't avoid an implicit insult. Essentially, they all wanted to know why the Red Brigades had bothered to kill the editor of such an inconsequential newspaper.

"Maybe it was a case of mistaken identity," David told one wire service bureau chief.

"Who the hell ever looked like de la Chasse?"

"Maybe it wasn't the Red Brigades."

"Are you suggesting somebody with a grudge had him shot?"

"I'm not suggesting anything. We're waiting for the police to finish their investigation."

"You're aware of his background. Is there a chance he was doing intelligence work again?"

"I'd be the last to know."

"There've been rumors."

"I'll bet."

When Bianchi got through to him late that afternoon and declared that they had to meet at once, David dreaded hearing another of his friend's paranoid theories about plots, cabals, and the CIA. It was all he could do to cope with the horrific possibilities his own agonized conscience had produced.

"I can't make it, Italo. It's chaos here. We're two hours from deadline."

"Then we must meet right after work."

"I really can't tonight."

"You have to." A pause. "It's about your book."

Once, when David was in the bathtub rinsing himself with a detachable shower nozzle which Italians call a telephone, the hot-water heater had short-circuited and he had received a shock that crackled along the hose and into his hand. He had been startled more than hurt—baffled that fire had somehow combined with water. He felt the same shock now and was slow to comprehend the connection between Bianchi and his book.

"Did you hear me?" Italo asked.

"I heard you. Do you have it?"

"I know where it is."

"Alison? Does she have it?"

"I don't want to talk on the phone."

"Have you read it?"

"Yes."

"It's a novel."

"I'd rather not talk on the telephone."

"Not a damn thing in it is true. You know that. Or do you imagine Stephane is off every day hatching kidnap plans?" After a night of icy terror, he was coming to a quick boil. "I don't know what Alison told you. I don't know what you and she have going, and I don't give a shit. But I don't appreciate having my apartment broken into. I never thought you'd fuck over a friend like that."

"Listen to me, David. It is because I am your friend that I'm calling. You want the manuscript back?"

"You're goddamn right."

"You don't expect me to mail it, do you?"

"I expect you to lay it right in my hands. Today!"

"Then meet me."

"Where?"

Bianchi cupped a palm over the receiver and whispered to someone. Alison? "Meet me at seven o'clock. At Carpano's on Via Veneto."

"I want Alison there with you. I want a few words with her too."

"Just you be there, David. And come alone."

It made perfect sense, he realized as soon as he hung up. Who else would Alison have to turn to? Who else except a skilled mountain climber could have swung down from the roof and into his bedroom?

Fortunately, Bianchi, more than anybody, would know better than to believe a word of the book. Much as David didn't like to think Italo had jeopardized their friendship just to get Alison into bed, he was relieved to learn the manuscript was safe and had had nothing to do with de la Chasse's death.

Shortly after nightfall, he left the office, hiking up Via Francesco Crispi past shop after expensive shop. The display windows had been lit as if for the diversion of motorists stalled in their cars along the traffic-clogged street, and from where they sat, swathed in exhaust fumes, assaulted by horns, it may have been soothing for drivers to gaze out at that all but unbroken tapestry of silk ties and designer scarves, costly leather coats, purses, and shoes. But it was an area of Rome he had never liked, an area where David, bearded, dressed in blue jeans and a poplin windbreaker, felt out of place, equally estranged from the elegantly dressed Italians and the jaunty American tourists ambling toward the Excelsior and the Eden for cocktails.

Tonight, that didn't diminish his exhilaration. He believed his life in the city had been restored and as he reached a level stretch of Via Ludovisi, he had to restrain himself from running to Via Veneto.

For all his high spirits, however, he didn't intend to let Italo off easily. He meant to give him and Alison hell. He would listen—up to a point—to the lecture Bianchi was bound to have prepared on his trivialization of current events and his bourgeois depiction of terrorism. But he wouldn't admit to having written anything except fiction. Again, he counted on Italo to confirm that.

As friends had described it to David, Via Veneto in the late fifties had been a surrealistic sideshow, a slice of bizarre high life whose glossy patina Fellini had done no more than scratch in *La Dolce Vita*. Now it had the low-life look of a home movie—"Mom and Dad's Trip to the Eternal City." All the sidewalk tables were occupied by businessmen in polyester, employees of the American Embassy, hookers of various sexes, and tourists with name tags proclaiming, "Hi! I'm Corky!" "Hi! I'm Lavinia!"

A gruff, familiar voice called, *"Ciao, professore."* Massimo was in his carriage at the curb beside Café de Paris. With his three-day growth of beard, bulbous nose, blue-veined cheeks, and patchwork clothes, he looked so extraordinarily shabby he might have been stationed there by a temperance society as a living, wheezing warning of the dangers of drink.

"How goes it?" David asked.

"Slowly, slowly. These tourists all want to sit and stare."

"Tell you what. I have to meet somebody. But if you're here when I get back, I'll take a ride." He thought he'd return the book to his apartment, then cross the river and pick up Stephane. He was in a mood to celebrate.

"I'll be here. I haven't moved in hours. My ass is rooted to this spot."

"Shall I have the waiter to bring you a *cappuccino?*"

Massimo laughed.

"That's how we do it in America," David said. "It's called curb service."

Massimo laughed again. "I'll wait for you, *professore.*"

Up the street at Carpano's, across from Wimpy's hamburger bar, Bianchi was sipping a cup of espresso. He looked profoundly fatigued, his eyes dark-circled, his thin, wavy hair disheveled. Under the café's green canopy, his complexion seemed jaundiced. Even a blazer with gleaming brass buttons didn't brighten his haggard appearance. When he saw David, he didn't bother to smile or offer his hand. He signaled the waiter for the check.

"Where is it?" David asked.

"You didn't expect me to bring it here. What if it fell into the wrong hands?"

"It already has."

"We'll go where we can talk."

"I don't care about talking. I just want it back."

"*Pazienza.* Let me pay the bill."

"Where's Alison?"

"I don't know."

"Don't bullshit me. She's in on this. How else would you have heard about the book?"

"Please, hold your voice down. Don't blame her. She told me about it. But I'm the one who took it."

"Why? I know what she's after. You're supposed to be a friend. Is this what you have to do these days for a piece of ass?"

Bianchi tossed a few thousand lire on the table and left. David followed him past Harry's Bar to Porta Pinciana, wondering whether there was an angle he hadn't considered. If Italo wasn't sleeping with Alison, what was his interest in the book? "Where are we headed?"

"My car's in the Borghese Gardens."

They went through the city wall and, dodging traffic on

Piazzale Brazile, walked up a path into the dimly lit park which smelled of damp earth and hedges and freshly mown grass. Although they could still see the lights of hotels and offices along Via Pinciana, they might have been deep in the country, under a colonnade of pines. Their feet crunched the gravel path. A chorus of insects fell silent as the two men approached, then piped back to life once they had passed.

"Where the hell did you park? Parioli?"

"My friend, you have done a very stupid thing." Bianchi's voice broke, as if he might begin sobbing. "I wish I could express how sad I—"

"I'd say you've done the stupid thing. What if I had called the police?"

"We both know you couldn't do that."

At a fork in the path near a street lamp, there was a white marble statue of Lord Byron. Atop his tall pedestal Byron held a book, one finger marking his place among the stone pages. His left foot was propped on a skull.

A man in a tan trenchcoat stepped out from behind the statue, hands in his coat pockets. "We'll stop here and talk," the man said.

"He speaks Italian. He can understand you," Bianchi said.

"Who is this?" David was instantly on guard.

"Let's speak English then." The man had a British accent. "I want a few words with him before we meet our friends."

"Who the hell is this?" David backed off, ready to run.

"Don't move." Giovanni pulled a pistol from his coat. The polished barrel was extended by a silencer.

"Do what he says." Italo sounded more frightened than David. "He has some questions about the book. Just tell him what you know."

"You told him about it?" He turned to face his friend. "Are you fucking crazy?"

"In fact, I've read your book," Giovanni said. "A very intriguing report."

"It's a novel."

Motioning with the pistol, Giovanni said, "Make sure he isn't armed."

As Italo patted him down, David started trembling. He could feel Bianchi trembling too.

"Come here," Giovanni said.

When David was close enough to see the wispy mustache and twitching nostrils, Giovanni grabbed him by the collar of his windbreaker and jammed the gun barrel into his ribs. "I'm going to do you a favor. I'm going to give you a chance to answer my questions before we meet my friends. I promise you, it will be much better if you talk to me."

"Please," Bianchi said, "your only chance is to tell him the truth."

"Listen to your friend," Giovanni said. "He doesn't want to see you hurt."

"Who are you?" David repeated. "Are you cops?" He was speaking now to both men.

Giovanni jerked him by the collar, dragging him next to the statue of Byron, and forced him to bend over until his face was a foot from the pedestal. Chiseled in stone, a line from *Childe Harold* read: "Oh Rome! My country! City of the Soul!"

There was a muted noise not much louder than a slap. Shattered glass sprinkled the gravel path. Giovanni had shot out the street light; the line from Byron blurred. He jammed the gun barrel back into David's ribs.

"Who told you about Operation Moro?"

"Never heard of it."

Giovanni slammed him head first into the block of marble. Orange light flashed in front of his eyes; pain exploded in his skull, then sizzled through every vertebra of his spine, popping in sequence like a long string of firecrackers. He dropped to his knees, stunned.

"Get up." Giovanni yanked him by the collar. "If you don't tell me about your book, you'll tell my friends. Why not spare me the trouble and yourself a lot of suffering?"

"He means it, David." Bianchi squatted beside him, begging. "Do what he says."

"For Chrissake, Italo, you know it's fiction. How would I find out about the Red Brigades?"

"Through a contact," Giovanni insisted. "Who was it?"

"You don't understand." Shaking his head clear, he staggered to his feet. "I never even tried to reach the Red Brigades. I just read their propaganda and articles in the newspaper and—"

The crown of his head crunched into the marble. His mouth slapped shut, grinding his teeth together. The night crumbled around him in great chunks of glittering white and black.

He came to in the grass, curled up, cradled in pain. He tried to talk, but his mouth was clogged with blood and jagged bits of enamel. As Giovanni and Bianchi hauled him to his feet, his head reeled, his eyes wouldn't focus. He felt himself being hurtled off into darkness, then rushed back to this spot where a bright furnace of pain poured over him.

"Listen, listen," he gasped. "Tell him, Italo. Tell him I made it up."

"Don't ask your friend to lie for you." Giovanni punched him in the kidney with the pistol butt, and David collapsed again, clawing the ground. "No more talk about novels now. You're not dealing with *cretini*. Who is your source? Where is this safe house?

His belly had cramped. He began to heave; nothing came up. Above him, Giovanni's face and Italo's dangled like stylized masks, one signifying anger, the other anguish. Their voices reached him from a great distance.

"I believe him," Bianchi said. "Long passages read exactly like our position papers and propaganda statements. He invented the characters."

Foggy from pain, David couldn't understand why Bianchi didn't admit he knew Stephane and swear she wasn't a terrorist. Then as his head cleared, he realized what Italo was doing—protecting her.

"And the plan?" Giovanni demanded of Italo. "How do you explain that? Help me lift him."

They leaned him against the statue, and when he opened his eyes, the lights on Via Pinciana tugged at his pupils. They lunged elastically from their sockets, then snapped back to a near point. He saw that his blood had streaked the marble slab, filling the chiseled inscription from *Childe Harold*, black against white.

"This woman from the Red Army Fraction, this Stephane Von Essen, is she your contact?"

"Look, let me explain about her." He fought to make sense, to form words into sentences.

"Who is she?"

"I made her up."

"You mean you made up the name?"

"Yes, it's not a real name."

"What's her real name?"

"I made up everything."

Giovanni bounced his head lightly, almost playfully, against the pedestal. "The truth now."

"That's what I'm telling you. I made up Stephane Von Essen, I made up the story, I made up the Red Brigades. I made up everything except Rome and a few—"

Giovanni released him with a shove; his skull thudded against marble. David's legs dissolved and he slumped like a puppet cut from its strings.

"Your friend is very stupid," Giovanni told Italo.

"But if he doesn't know anything—"

"He knows."

"But if he doesn't, all this is for nothing."

"What's it matter? We can't let him go now anyway. Think of yourself. He knows you're with us."

"I'll handle him. He'll get out of Italy. You're safe. He doesn't know anything."

"Why are you protecting him?"

"Why are you torturing him?" Bianchi was shouting. "He's my friend."

"I'm not going to take the blame for a leak in my section. You have some questions to answer too." He turned the pistol on Italo.

"Don't point that at me, you bastard."

From where David lay, eyes swimming with blood, he saw Italo surge forward, acting on angry impulse, grabbing the gun barrel in one hand and Giovanni's wrist in the other. The two men staggered, awkward dancers out of rhythm, each struggling to lead, their feet skidding on the gravel. Giovanni's strength was no match for Bianchi's, but he had enough to pull the trigger.

The pistol coughed once, then again, and Italo sighed, sounding more disappointed than hurt. A third shot knocked him sprawling. As Bianchi let go, Giovanni stumbled backward, tripping over David's outstretched legs, dropping the pistol into his lap. The man scrambled to his feet, but didn't know where the gun had gone. His hands fluttered about searching for it, pale as moths trapped on a screen.

David closed his fingers on the pistol and fired without aiming. A bullet plowed the gravel at Giovanni's feet. The man went rigid as a plank. When David fired again, the shot ricocheted, grazing Giovanni. He screamed, wheeled around, plunged through a hedge, and sprinted into the park.

David crawled over to Bianchi. His friend's feet were twitching; above the waist there was no movement. He had caught the first two shots in the chest. The third had hit his face. His right cheek had a small hole in it; most of his left cheek was missing.

David struggled to stand. The earth spun under him and pitched him to his knees. He got up again and stumbled toward Piazzale Brazile, across the sweet-smelling swale of grass, lurching from pine trunk to pine trunk, shoving off from the rough bark of one tree, catching hold of the next one before he fell. When he reached the edge of the Borghese Gardens, he collapsed at the curb, still clutching the pistol.

Over the thunder of the traffic and the delirium of his pain, he heard someone shout his name. He raised his head and couldn't keep it from flopping backward. His eyes flooded with stars, his mouth fell open. He thought he felt wind rush with terrific velocity over his cracked teeth, but that was the crescendo of his own screaming.

Massimo was beside him. "What happened? Have you been shot?"

"No." He shoved the pistol under his belt.

"Where's the other man?"

"Get me out of here."

Massimo lugged him to his feet, half-dragging, half-carrying him through the traffic across the piazza. "When I saw you meet that man and go into the gardens, I decided to wait at the gate until you returned." His carriage was outside the wall at Porta Pinciana. Massimo hoisted him onto the hard leather seat in back. "Did he do this to you? Should I call the police?"

"No police."

"Of course. First we'll go to the hospital."

David had enough self-possession to insist, "No hospital."

"You need stitches."

"Please, Massimo, just move me away from here."

Nodding uncertainly, he climbed into the driver's seat, released the brake, and whistling to the horse, rolled toward Piazza del Popolo, following the tortuous curves of Viale del Muro Torto. David tried to brace himself, but his head lolled on the weak stem of his neck and a whirlpool of nausea churned his insides.

"To your apartment?" Massimo asked.

"No, not there. I think they know where I live."

"Who knows? Who the hell did this?"

David didn't answer. He dabbed at his forehead, trying to staunch the bleeding, and flicked his tongue over his teeth. He counted a dozen that had been chipped.

"Why won't you tell me?" Massimo asked. "Did you kill someone?"

"It would take all night to explain."

"It's just that I'd like to help."

"The best way to help is do what I say, then forget you saw me. Can I count on you to do that?"

"*Certo.*"

.   .   .

When, after an agonizing ride over the rough cobblestones of the *centro storico*, they reached Piazza Sant'Eustachio, he asked Massimo to pull to the darkest corner, near the rear entrance of Palazzo della Sapienza. His friend lifted him down from the carriage and propped him against a parked car.

"Look," said Massimo, "I know a doctor. A veterinarian. A good man. He'll sew you up and ask no questions."

"I'm okay. You go back to work."

"Are you sure, *professore*?" He kept a hand on David.

"Yes. I'll see you tomorrow. Thanks a million."

He waited until Massimo was out of sight and Via Teatro Valle was empty. Then he pushed away from the car, floundered as far as Stephane's building, and pressed the buzzer. When she hit the button that unlocked the street entrance, he kept his finger on the buzzer until she answered the intercom.

"Is Marc in bed?" he asked.

"Yes."

"Asleep?"

"Yes. What's the matter?"

"I've had an accident. It looks a lot worse than it is. Don't be upset."

"Shall I come down?"

"No, don't."

In the *belle époque* elevator, he propped himself upright in a corner to prevent blood from dripping onto the plush banquette. The quivering cables of the lift felt as though they were being dragged from the soles of his feet straight up through his spine and out the crown of his skull. When the elevator jerked to a halt, his head seemed to float up and bounce off the ceiling.

At the door, Stephane took one look and let out a strangled shout. In her horrified eyes he saw how bad it must be.

"Was it Lucio?" she said.

"No." He staggered through the hall, tracking blood over the tessellated floors. "I'll explain. First I have to use the telephone."

"No, first you have to take care of those cuts."

Shaking, she led him to the bathroom, removed his wind-breaker, and sat him down on the toilet lid. She was surer of herself now and moved with the same solicitude she might show Marc. Crooning, "It's all right, it's going to be all right," she wet a towel at the sink and swabbed away most of the blood.

"You'll ruin the towel," he said.

"Shh. It doesn't matter." Tilting his jaw in her firm hand, she said, "Hold tight. This is going to hurt." Then she doused the cuts with Mercurochrome. His forehead felt swathed in flame, as if she were cauterizing his wounds, searing them shut with a flat iron.

"This one at the hairline," she said, "it looks like it needs stitches."

"Just bandage it."

She folded down the flaps of skin, taping them together with vertical strips of adhesive. Then she applied a broad swatch of tape, like a sweatband, across his forehead. "Oh David, it's going to be awful when you tear that off. You should let me call a doctor."

"No doctor." Steadying himself at the sink, he stood up. His head was a helium-filled balloon sailing into space, nearly lifting him off his feet. As his vision swam into focus, he stared at himself in the mirror.

Both his eyes had been blackened and his face appeared to have been knocked off center. Even his wild, curly hair couldn't hide the lumps and contusions on his head. As Stephane gingerly scrubbed at the blood that matted his beard, his skull throbbed and his legs threatened to fold under him. He feared he had a concussion, but there were things he had to do before he worried more about himself.

With Stephane's help, he hobbled into the living room, dialed 113, the emergency number for Rome, and reported that a man had been shot in the Borghese Gardens. When the operator, who sounded like someone working at an airline information desk, asked for his name, address, and phone number, he described the location of the body and hung up while she went on wearily repeating her request for his name.

He called Palazzo Vertecchi, where the desk clerk informed him Alison Lopez was out. He refused to say whether she had been back during the day. David considered leaving a message, but didn't care to disclose his whereabouts or Stephane's phone number.

"You'd better lie down," she said.

"I've got more calls to make."

"Later."

He let himself be steered to the couch, where she eased his head back until it rested on a pillow like a hot, glittering jewel. She noticed the pistol in his belt. "What are you doing with that?"

"I got it from the fucker who did this to me."

"The man you said was shot in the Borghese Gardens?"

"That was somebody else." He couldn't bring himself to talk about Bianchi. He couldn't accept that his friend was dead; he didn't know how to account for all the contradictory things Italo had done today. He only knew that Italo had saved his life.

"You have to tell me what happened," she pleaded.

"It's hard to say. I'm not sure I understand everything."

"Is it your book?"

He nodded, then regretted that he had as the room quaked. "Somebody found out about it. Somebody broke into my apartment and stole it."

"Who?" Stephane sat on the coffee table in front of the couch, one hand skinning her hair back from her face.

He saw no reason to mention Alison's part in his troubles. "The Red Brigades."

"But you told me you were in touch with them. Why would they steal it? Didn't they know you were writing about them?"

He felt disoriented by this reversal of roles. For months, he had listened to her problems, soothing her with reassurances, evading her questions, convinced he should protect her from the truth. Now he realized he had to tell her what he had done. She had a right to know. But he couldn't bear to watch her face as he confessed he was a fraud.

Stretched out on the sofa, arms straight at his sides, he shut his eyes and imagined himself a stone figure on a sarcophagus, as far from anything living as Bianchi and de la Chasse were now. He slowly spilled his guts, piling one fact atop another, pausing to figure out which piece fit where, which cause had produced which effect. When he saw the shape that events and people had assumed, the plane geometry of his life seemed to turn solid and the full weight of what he had done pressed down on him. He didn't have the strength to duck the consequences. He could just sense with dread the unraveling of the plot.

"Wait," Stephane cut in. "You say you made up everything in the book. The Red Brigades should have realized that when they read it. They'd know your characters weren't from their group."

"It wasn't that simple. Like I told you, I used real names. I used your maiden name. Then I claimed I had changed everybody's identity and description to protect my sources. It wouldn't have been easy to sort things out."

"Still," she insisted, "they would have known the plot to kidnap Moro didn't add up."

His head began to hammer so hard he feared it would crack. He saw where this was leading and didn't care to go on.

"If they took your book seriously," she said, "it must be true."

"No, I invented it all."

"Yes, but what you invented turns out to be the truth. Or close to it. That's why they tortured you. They thought somebody had leaked the plan to you."

"Bianchi," he mumbled, opening his eyes.

"What?"

"Italo, he's the one who stole the book. He brought me to the Borghese Gardens. There was a man waiting there."

"Are you saying Italo's in the Red Brigades?"

"Yes. He tried to convince the guy my book was fiction. The

bastard didn't buy it. He must have assumed Italo was my contact. They fought, and he shot Italo."

Stephane stood up. "We've got to do something."

"It's too late. He's dead."

"I'll call the police." She burst into tears.

"No, don't!" He repeated what he had warned Alison. The carabinieri would never believe he hadn't been in touch with a terrorist cell. They would question him for weeks, months, holding him in prison where they couldn't protect him against reprisals any better than if he went on living in Trastevere and waited for the Red Brigades to run him down.

"But if there *is* a plan to kidnap Moro, we have to tell somebody," Stephane said.

"Who? Nobody'll believe us. The police get dozens of crank calls every day. Besides, whatever plan those people had, it's bound to be off now. They won't move again until they're sure it's safe. Meanwhile, I've got to get out of Italy." He pushed himself to a sitting position. "They'll be looking for me."

"You can't go anywhere." She urged him back onto the pillow.

"But I've got to pick up my passport and the car and some money."

"Not tonight."

Reluctantly, he agreed. He couldn't do much in his condition and he didn't care to stumble through the dark alleys of Trastevere, then up the unlit staircase to his apartment.

"We'll leave first thing in the morning," he said. "I want you and Marc to come with me."

"You know I can't take him out of Italy. If I try, I could lose custody to Lucio."

"You're not going to leave the country. I'll drop you in Como or Domodossola. I'll cross into Switzerland. That way I'll be close enough to drive back and see you every day. It's temporary. Just until I figure things out."

"Are you doing this because you're afraid the Red Brigades will be hunting for me too?"

"No. They'd never find you from what I wrote. I just don't want to go away without you."

She looked down at him, her dark eyes disappointed, her face wet with tears. She nodded. "I'll pack."

His hope was that in a couple of days his cuts would heal, his head would clear. Although at the moment he felt lost in some nightmarish labyrinth, he believed the maze was one of his own making. He had created it; he could, given a chance, discover a way out of it.

But then, while Stephane was in the bedroom packing, he pulled the pistol from under his belt and wasn't sure of anything. With its glinting barrel, its silencer, and its etched inscription—.32 Skorpion—it looked cunningly designed and murderously efficient. Yet having lived so long in a country where the telephone, electricity, and plumbing inevitably broke down, he had never placed much faith in mechanical devices.

He knew he couldn't depend on people either. It wasn't only the killer in the Borghese Gardens who seemed to him unknown and unknowable, a lethal virus loose in the city. He thought of Alison and Bianchi, how little they had revealed of themselves, how scant his comprehension had been. And he wondered about himself, recalling that moment when he gazed into the mirror at his rearranged features and hadn't recognized the man who squinted back in pained amazement. But there he was. Much as he'd like to lay it off on Alison and her ambition, or Bianchi and his duplicity, or that psychopath in the park, David realized he was the one to blame.

CHAPTER IX

THEY HAD PLANNED to set off early, soon after sunrise.
But David slept poorly and Stephane, spending a night in the
same bed with him for the first time in months, slept even
worse. She thrashed and groaned and cried out as if she, not he,
had been battered and bloodied. Was she dreaming of her past,
of the torment she had suffered from Lucio? Or had her uncon-
scious mind conjured up some monstrous image of the future
with David? These questions kept him awake until the slats of
light at the shutters had turned a deep shade of mother-of-pearl.

Next morning, two facts registered the instant he opened his
eyes to the fierce light of day; Stephane was missing and some
dwarfed, dark-haired stranger was staring at him. David let out
a muffled cry. Startled, the stranger shouted too.

Marc stood beside the bed, straight as a stick, eyes wild
with fear.

"Jesus, buddy, you scared me," David said.

"*You* scared me." The boy puffed his lower lip as though he might start sobbing.

"I'm sorry."

"I thought you were dead. You looked like dead people on TV. What's wrong with your face?"

"I had an accident."

"In a car?"

"Yeah, that's it."

"Weren't you wearing your seat belt?"

"No. That was dumb of me, wasn't it?"

"You should have buckled your seat belt."

"Remind me next time. Where's your mother?"

"In the kitchen."

With difficulty, he climbed off the bed. Although his head still teetered painfully on the wobbling stalk of his neck, he didn't feel too unsteady once he was on his feet. He advanced through the apartment slowly, shuffling toward the aroma of brewing coffee. As he came into the kitchen, Stephane sent him a sidelong glance.

"I'm okay," he said. "A lot better than last night."

She chose an unmarked spot on his cheek and kissed him.

"Is that a real gun?" Marc asked.

"We're all going on a trip today," Stephane told him. "Go to your room and choose a few toys to take along."

"What about the gun in David's belt?"

"We'll talk about it later."

When Marc left, she poured coffee for David, who had lowered himself into a chair. On the table in front of him lay a copy of *Il Messaggero*. Just below the crease on page one, a box in bold print reported that a body had been discovered in the Borghese Gardens. Police had identified it as Italo Bianchi, a sociology professor at the University of Rome. Since he hadn't been robbed, authorities could only speculate about the killer's motive. One unidentified officer said it reminded him of the Pasolini case. As the article explained, Pier Paolo Pasolini, a prominent novelist, political commentator, and film director, had been murdered two years ago by a male prostitute he had picked up at the train station.

David shoved the paper aside and sipped his coffee. Scalding hot, it had the same effect on his chipped teeth as a dentist's drill. In his stomach, he felt a watery weakness, a fear almost indistinguishable from sorrow or pain.

"I've been thinking," said Stephane, sitting next to him, holding his hand. She wore slacks and a navy pullover. Even without makeup her features were sharp, distinct, her eyes no less alert for the difficult night she had passed. "Why don't I go to the apartment and pack your things?"

"I know where the stuff is. You get Marc ready. I'll get the car and come back for you."

"But if somebody's there, they'll be looking for you. They won't recognize me."

"Nobody'll be there."

"At least let me come with you."

"No."

He told her to bring a bath towel, and they rolled it tight and taped it around his neck as a brace. Cumbersome as that was, it relieved much of the pain. Then Stephane helped him into one of Lucio's old suit coats, which he wore instead of his blood-stained windbreaker.

"Shall I call a cab?" she asked.

"No, I'll catch one on the street."

"Are you taking the pistol?"

"Yes."

"Isn't that dangerous? What if the police stop you?"

He tucked his shirt tail over the pistol butt. "I'll ditch it on the way back."

He considered phoning the *American News* and telling the Texans to take over. But he didn't care to explain why he wasn't at work. He did try the Palazzo Vertecchi. Alison was still out and the desk clerk still refused to say whether she had ever returned.

Before he left, he took Stephane in his arms. "I don't want to scare you. But there are a few things you have to remember."

"I'm fine," she insisted.

"Good, then listen to me. If anybody calls or comes by here asking about me, say you don't know me. You never heard of me. Whatever you do, don't admit your name was Von Essen. You're Mrs. Novelli. While I'm gone, look through your things. You find anything with Von Essen on it, burn it. Understand?"

"Yes." She kissed him on the cheek.

"I want a real kiss," he said.

"It'll hurt."

"No, it won't."

She pressed herself to him and lifted her lips to his. She was right. It hurt, and he had to pull away.

When he hailed a taxi near Piazza Navona, the cabbie took one look at his face and was as full of questions as Marc. David pretended his Italian wasn't adequate to explain. As they nudged through the crowds on Campo dei Fiori, then sped past Palazzo Farnese, every bump, every cobblestone, closed a talon of pain on his spine. The pain had one advantage. It prevented him from thinking clearly about what he was doing, where he was going, what lay ahead.

Caught by a traffic light at Piazza Trilussa, they sat in a warm pool of morning sun. David closed his eyes against the glare; his stomach swirled, and he felt faint. He opened his eyes as they accelerated across the square, scattering pigeons.

The streets of Trastevere were empty and many of the shops were closing. Storekeepers yanked down their shutters, the iron grates rumbling, then striking the pavement like melodramatic thunder. He glanced at his watch. It wasn't quite nine thirty.

"Something's wrong," he said.

"Wrong how?" the cabbie asked.

"The shops shouldn't be closing."

He shrugged.

"Turn on the radio," David said.

The man switched it on and instantly his indifference vanished. He spun the dial as if expecting better news on a different frequency, but he had caught it right the first time. Slapping the steering wheel, he unleashed a splenetic outburst of obscenity expressing equal measures of anger, bafflement, and fear.

A breathless, adenoidal announcer kept repeating the bulletin.

"Aldo Moro has been kidnapped by a group of terrorist commandos. The incident took place near the Parliament member's home in the Camilluccia district, at the intersection of Via Fani and Via Stresa. The terrorists, assumed to be members of the Red Brigades, attacked the escort that accompanied the president of the Christian Democratic Party. They forced Moro into another car and fled the scene. It is not known whether he was wounded. All five of Moro's bodyguards were killed. According to reports, the kidnappers were led by a woman who shouted orders in German. Police are looking for a white Ford van with . . ."

At first David, like the driver, ranted out loud. "They did it. They fucking went ahead and did it." But a moment later, he fell quiet, wondering, Why? Was it possible the man in the park was too badly wounded to make it back to warn them? Or did they decide David wouldn't have time to find anybody who would believe him?

Slumped in the seat, head braced against the door, he recalled the day he had driven to the Camilluccia district, drawn to the intersection of Via Fani and Via Stresa—a corner waiting for a crime to happen. When that couple came upon him on the patio of the Olivetti Bar and the man pulled a gun, he had assumed they were secret service agents. Now he knew better. They must have been Red Brigades casing the neighborhood just like him.

There was nothing uncanny or extraordinary about it. It couldn't even be called a coincidence. If you meant to kidnap Moro, it had to be there. Yet he was seized by the conviction that his lies had somehow led to this deadly truth. He didn't need to regard his book as a prophecy mysteriously fulfilled to wonder whether it had helped the Red Brigades with their plan, or had at least rushed it into effect.

Where Via Garibaldi began to mount the Janiculum Hill in a series of steep, twisting curves, the cabbie, still cursing steadily, pulled over to the staircase that led down to Vicolo del Cedro. From this vantage point, David could see his building, tapered like the bow of a ship. He paid his fare and waited at the top step until the taxi drove off. He couldn't decide whether the news improved his chances. The Red Brigades might be too busy now to waste time on him. Then again, they might want to wipe the slate clean. Either way, he had to get his passport and money.

He descended the crumbling stairs, between the scorched brick walls, through the litter of glassine bags and syringes. Ahead of him, Vicolo del Cedro was deserted. At the bottom step he paused, checked the action on the Skorpion, switched it from his belt to his jacket pocket, and kept a hand on it there. Breathing hard, he glanced down a side street, Via della Frusta. It was empty all the way to the corner, where at this hour a carpenter's shop generally gave off a shower of sawdust and the whine of power tools. Now the shop was shuttered and silent.

He crossed to the apartment building in three quick strides and paused again. He heard the tinny babble of radios and TVs all tuned to the news of Moro's kidnapping. Much nearer, there was the frantic thump of his heart.

At the door to the building, he drew the Skorpion and ducked into the hallway. The time-light was still broken, but the sun's bright reflection in the courtyard lit the steps up to the second landing. It looked abandoned, but somebody could easily have hidden in an apartment, or in the shadows on higher landings.

Climbing the stairs, he kept close to the wall, his shoulder scraping the whitewash. Chalky powder flaked off. David could smell it, could taste the dry bitter dust on his tongue. The Skorpion sweated in his palm. He had had no trouble pulling the trigger last night. He feared it would be different in daylight if he had to face the man he was firing at.

At his apartment door, he stood off to the side, reached over and untumbled one noisy lock, then another and another. If anybody was inside, they had to have heard him. He shoved hard and slapped the door back on its hinges, setting off an explosion of lime dust as the knob hit the wall.

The living room was empty. He rushed to the bedroom. There was no one there.

In the kitchen, he dragged aside the refrigerator and, squatting slowly, careful to keep his spine straight, collected his passport and the fat sheaf of bills. He packed a duffel bag with his shaving kit, several changes of underwear, some shirts and blue jeans. Shedding Lucio's suit coat, he pulled on a Fila warm-up jacket, Stephane's Christmas gift.

Then, head roaring with pain, pulse thrumming with tension, he took stock of what he was leaving—a few paperbacks, stacks of magazines and old newspapers, miscellaneous tennis equipment in the closet. He didn't have room for anything except his racquet. After stuffing it into the canvas bag—the handle jutted out at an angle—he combed through the apartment again, each movement awkward, agonized. He wanted to be sure he left nothing with his name on it. No letters, no papers, no personal effects, as a police report would put it. He wanted to turn his back on this place and have nobody know he had lived here.

Pausing at a window, he looked out at the red tile roofs all aslant, the terraces banked with flowers and shrubs, the thicket of TV antennas. He couldn't accept that he was seeing this view for the last time.

He locked the door behind him and descended the stairs as hurriedly as his pounding head would permit. With the duffel bag in one hand and the Skorpion in the other, he peered out onto the street. When he noticed nothing unusual, he stuck the pistol back under his belt.

He was making his way toward the Fiat, just outside Massimo's stable, when he heard the throaty rumble of an engine. To look behind him, he had to swivel his shoulders, his entire upper torso. In the noose of the towel, his neck was twisted tight as a candlewick.

He saw a motorcycle skid around the corner. Both the driver and the rider on back wore ski masks. David broke and ran. He didn't hear the gun go off. The shot was lost in the high torque of acceleration. But a bullet hit the duffel bag, ripping it from his hand, knocking him off stride. He fell, head colliding with cobblestones, and lay dazed in front of the stable doors as the motorcycle hurtled by and the man on back fired a wild second shot.

Sputtering and backfiring, they braked at the end of the block, where the two of them put out their feet, paddling at the street, maneuvering to turn around. Fists on the handlegrips, the driver flexed his wrists for speed while the man on back aimed a .38, waiting for a point-blank shot. Before he could fire, David flipped over once, twice, a third time, and rolled under the stable doors. He struggled upright and floundered past the horse, the water trough, the carriage. A splinter of wood the size of a pencil floated past his ear. The man was shooting through the doors.

He ran up the tunnel toward the second set of doors, the ones that led to the next block. They were wide open. Confused, David stopped. This time of day, they should have been locked. Then he heard the revving engine and realized the men were coming around. They knew about this entrance too. He stood no chance on the street.

He hid behind the right-hand door, fighting to quiet his hoarse, erratic breathing. The engine was idling; the men had put down their feet again. As they hesitated at the dim mouth of the stable, David's hand went to the pistol at his waist and he considered firing a warning shot, hoping to scare them off. But the driver gave it some gas and glided forward.

Too late, he tried to slam the door. The thick planks of wood caught them broadside. The motorcyle swerved, and the man on back flung out his arms like an aerialist flapping for balance. They sideswiped one wall of the tunnel. The man on back fell off, but held onto his gun and bounced up at once. David fired. Because of its silencer, the Skorpion made no more noise than the solid *thwack* of metal on meat. The man threw out his hands again and his revolver sailed away, ringing against the stone floor. David shot him a second time, and he went down.

The horse reared up in its stall, strident with panic, trumpeting long streamers of foamy saliva as the motorcycle careened out of control. It struck a corner of the water trough and toppled over, trapping the driver beneath the heavy chromium cylinder heads. As he wriggled to free himself, David shot him. He stopped moving. David fired again to make sure.

Then he closed the doors, lowering the iron bar that locked them. In the abrupt silence, he became aware of a strangled sound. One of the men was panting through his ski mask. David peeled away the wool, and blood spurted from a neck wound, pumping fast, then slow, with the beat of his failing heart. The man's eyes rolled back and a pack of muscles in his chest jerked in spasms as he choked on something he couldn't spit out.

The horse was still straining at its tether. It shouldn't have been here at this hour. David rushed to the carriage. Massimo was sprawled on the back seat, shot in the chest, a stone stuffed in his mouth. Because he had talked? Or because he refused to? Strangely, his eyes were still in focus. He didn't look frightened or in pain. He looked furious, like a dead snapping turtle with its jaws clenched on a last bite.

He found Osvalda at the bottom of the trough. When he thrust his hand into the water, her face appeared to fall to pieces. He thought it was some illusion of light on rippling liquid. Then he saw that she had been shot in the head; flaps of her skull waved loose.

David started shuddering and couldn't stop. What began like a death rattle deep in his chest ended in a fit of vomiting. The Skorpion slithered from his fingers into the water trough. Sinking to his knees, he longed to keep going, to lie on the cool stones and never rise, never have to face what he had done. But when his convulsions passed, he knew he had to hurry back to Stephane and Marc.

Ducking under the doors onto Vicolo del Cedro, he fetched

his duffel bag and went to the Fiat, his tennis racquet banging his knee. The plastic sign on the dashboard invited thieves to have a look at his worthless, unlocked car. As he swung the door wide, he recoiled from the stench of rotten meat, the snarl of a hornet's nest. They were flies, not hornets—thousands of flies crawling over a corpse that had been dumped under the dashboard.

He recognized the blond hair and long bare legs. He never would have known the face. Alison's lips were swollen and split, her cheeks pockmarked by cigarette burns. Some had blistered; others had gouged out deep blue craters. Just below the right kneecap, her shin bone, slick and yellow-white, jutted through the skin.

He slammed the door. The adhesive tape on his forehead felt like a metal band tightened by a screw. He made himself move, fleeing Massimo, Osvalda, and Alison as much as the police and the Red Brigades.

He clutched the duffel bag and tennis racquet as his disguise, imagining they marked him as a tourist. Unsure whom he had to fear more, he debated whether to walk on back streets or broad boulevards. Reaching the Tiber, he decided to take his chances with the police. He had seen what the Red Brigades would do.

At Ponte Garibaldi, carabinieri patrolled both ends of the bridge, stopping cars, checking IDs. But they barely glanced at David as he proceeded up Via Arenula, past the heavily guarded Ministry of Justice. The city wailed with sirens. A helicopter clattered overhead, dipping low, then darting back and whirring up to the Janiculum, a giant noisy dragonfly.

Several cars from the Squadra Mobile careened around a corner, their tires shrieking nearly as loud as their sirens. He was tempted to run. Even after they swept past like blips on a radar screen, he wanted to bolt. But he kept to a slow walk, pacing himself, trying not to overtax his strength. Trembling, he sucked air into his lungs in long ragged gulps.

He marshaled his thoughts as strictly as his movements. To

dwell on the wrong things now, to entertain any doubt, threatened paralysis. Escape was all he would allow himself to consider. He figured he had a few hours head start. The police would need at least that long, maybe much longer because of Moro's kidnapping, to sort out the mess on Vicolo del Cedro. If he was lucky, if there had been no witnesses, the Red Brigades alone would realize he had slipped away.

Even if someone had seen what happened, nobody in the neighborhood would willingly cooperate with the carabinieri in a case involving foreigners and the Red Brigades. Although a few people might recall that the car was his, he doubted they'd talk. And if they did, he would soon be out of the country, and his ties to a job that was off the books, to an apartment that didn't exist, and to an unregistered automobile with '68 Maine license plates would be too tenuous to drag him back.

David knew better than to catch a plane. The airport was the obvious place to watch, the easiest spot to nail him. What's more, an airline would record his name on a manifest. For the same reason, he didn't rent a car; an agency would demand his name and passport number. There were no documents indicating he had lived in Italy; he wanted no written evidence of his departure. 'f he didn't panic, if he kept up this pace, shoving one foot methodically in front of the other, he would make it. He'd pick up Stephane and Marc and catch a train and cross the Swiss border before nightfall.

But as he plodded the length of Largo Argentina like an old man laboriously pausing before each step, he felt his mind slip a cog. He sensed the error in his reasoning, saw it take form and rear up in front of him as hideously as the oblivion he had left strewn behind. He had to stop and lean against a storefront. The taste of vomit soured his breath, so strong he suspected any passerby could smell it. It was as sick making as the stench in the Fiat—the stink of death, the contagious infection he carried with him wherever he went. He didn't dare go near Stephane and Marc. Everybody he came into contact with died. It was imbecilic to assume he would solve anything by dropping them in some tiny border town while he crossed into Switzerland. He would recontaminate them every time he returned to visit. If anybody were after him—now or later, the Red Brigades or the law—he would lead them straight to the two people he loved most.

On their own, the Red Brigades would never discover who Stephane Von Essen was. They would search among their secret operatives, in their safe houses, not in an apartment on Via Teatro Valle. They would hunt for a German terrorist, a member of the Red Army Fraction, not a French housewife known by her Italian husband's last name.

He pushed away from the storefront and retraced his steps around Largo Argentina, skirting the fenced-in ruins where hundreds of sleeping cats lay timeless and immobile as hunks of worked marble. The city had suddenly fallen quiet, and except for police cars, the streets were almost empty. He passed a few pedestrians with transistors at their ears. He thought he heard the Tiber purling between its banks. But that was the sibilant murmur of the radios all repeating the same word, *Moro, Moro.*

He decided to walk to the train station. That would give him time to think, time to reconsider. But he couldn't control his thoughts. They rioted through the buzzing hive of his skull. He fantasized losing himself in the city. People disappeared here every day. He'd shave his beard, change his name, find a new apartment, a different job. Invent another life. But then he remembered he had to disappear not just from the police and the Red Brigades, but from Stephane as well, and that defeated the purpose of staying.

Already, the streets he advanced through had changed. This wasn't the Rome he had lived in. It was the Rome he had written about and ruined for himself. Going by the glowing white confection of the Vittorio Emmanuele monument, he felt like a man walking on melting snow; his footprints would dissolve seconds after he passed.

He gazed about wildly, anxious to recall what he was losing. But nothing he saw had the same vividness as his pain, the same searing immediacy as his guilt, the same driving force as his fear. He wouldn't need snapshots to remind him of this place. For the rest of his life, its signature would be scrawled on his face.

From Via dei Fori Imperiali he cut off onto Via Cavour and followed it to the train station. Although less raucous than normal, Termini was noisier and more crowded than the streets. Soldiers armed with automatic weapons patrolled the waiting areas, the ticket booths, the entrance to the quais. A few glanced curiously at David's lopsided face and bandaged forehead. One laughed and asked if he had won the fight. But nobody seemed suspicious, and for once he was grateful to have his blond hair and accent give him away as a foreigner.

After buying a ticket, he waited next to the wall, watching for anybody who might be watching him. Everyone was preoccupied by conversations—they were as vociferous as family arguments—about the kidnapping, the Red Brigades, the impotence of the government and the police. Chimes rang: a garbled voice, slurred with static, announced the arrival and departure of trains. David strained to hear it. He wouldn't let himself reflect on the past or speculate about the future. He was here now and he had to concentrate on getting somewhere else.

He'd been through all this before. The first step toward starting over was to blank out and submit to a self-induced lobotomy. Whenever he found his mind drifting toward forbidden subjects, he pressed against the wall and sent shocks of pain up his spine. Better to enter that pain, he thought. Inhabit it. Better to have it overwhelm him than weaken in his resolve to save the people he loved by leaving them.

Yet he refused to do what Darlene had done. He wouldn't simply vanish. Ten minutes before he had to board the train, he found a telephone booth and dialed Stephane.

"Where are you?" Her voice cracked. "We've been waiting."

"I couldn't call until now."

"When I heard about Moro, I was afraid you—"

"Listen to me," he cut in. "I won't be coming. I can't take you with me."

"But I packed. Marc's here with me and . . ." She started crying.

"I'm sorry. You can meet me later."

"How? Where? When?"

It sounded as if she were reciting some journalistic formula, stressing the essential questions every news story should answer. But David couldn't answer them. He couldn't bear to hear them. He stared, unseeing, at the wall and tried to remember her face—that narrow, complicated face. It occurred to him he didn't have a photograph of her, just as he didn't have one of Rome.

"I'll call once I'm out of the country. I'll always keep in touch."

"Why are you doing this to me?" she wailed.

"When we're together I'll explain."

"Together? You know I can't leave Italy."

"After the divorce."

"That'll be years."

"Please don't cry. You've got to remember what I told you this morning. If anybody asks about me, you don't know me. You never knew me."

"What do I tell Marc?"

"Tell him I love him. You two may hear things about me. You may read them. Don't believe anything."

"What do you mean?"

"I can't talk about it now."

"Oh God," she said. "Please, rest."

Please rest—it had the ring of some heartfelt prayer that he might find peace. But then she repeated herself, adding, "Please rest on the line," and he realized she was confusing French and English and meant, Stay. Don't hang up. Don't leave me.

"I have to go," he said. "I love you." He cut the connection.

At the gate to the quais, the carabinieri demanded his ticket and identification. But when he showed an American passport, they waved him through.

He climbed into a second-class car and walked the length of it and two others before he located an empty seat in a compartment crowded with seven swarthy, solemn-faced men who were passing around a gallon jug of wine. Above them, the luggage racks were piled to the ceiling with cardboard boxes, string bags, and imitation leather suitcases fastened by plastic belts.

David sat with his duffel bag on his lap, the handle of the tennis racquet jutting out at a jaunty angle. But he didn't look much like a sportsman on holiday. He looked as battered and forlorn as these men, who, he supposed, were on their way to Milan or Munich to find work.

As the train rocked away from the station, pitching and swaying, the man next to him offered the wine. David thanked him, took a swig, and handed it along. Then they all stared out the window, watching the tracks slice through the underside of the city, exposing the backs of soot-stained apartment buildings where clothes hung drying in the grimy air, blighted neighborhoods where windows had been bricked up, uglier and more pathetic areas where women and children poked among the weeds for empty bottles, pine nuts, and edible greens.

There were no famous monuments here, no familiar landmarks, none of the gauzy pastels he always associated with the city. Heartsick, he struggled to recapture Rome, his Rome. But it seemed too immense to survive in the mind. A perplexing warren of alleyways, dozens of scattered restaurants and churches, the view from his terrace, the Tiber observed from different bridges, his apartment building the color and shape of a wedge of cheddar cheese—fast, then faster, they fell away.

His eyes stung. He ducked his head to hide his tears. The muscular little man beside him jostled his elbow and offered the wine again.

David reached for the jug. It may have been the effect of blinking back his own tears, but it seemed that all seven men had moist eyes as they craned their necks, watching the city disappear.

Born in Washington, D.C., in 1943, M I C H A E L
M E W S H A W *graduated from the University of
Maryland with a B.A. in 1965 and earned a Ph.D.
in Literature from the University of Virginia in
1970. The author of five critically acclaimed novels
and two books of nonfiction, he has received a
Fulbright Fellowship, a grant from the National
Endowment for the Arts, and a Guggenheim Fellowship. He has written articles and reviews for
the* New York Times, The Nation, The New
Statesman, *and other publications in the United
States and Europe. He lives in Rome with his wife
and two sons.*